DARK CARGO

A ROGUE WARRIOR THRILLER

IAN LOOME

INKUBATOR
BOOKS

Published by Inkubator Books
www.inkubatorbooks.com

ISBN (eBook): 978-1-83756-547-4
ISBN (Paperback): 978-1-83756-548-1
ISBN (Hardback): 978-1-83756-549-8

1

SAN DIEGO, CALIFORNIA

After four months, the city was still unfamiliar, a hilly, sun-drenched grid of whitewashed low-rise buildings and pale concrete. Bob Singleton looked down at the slip of paper and the address, then across the road.

The apartment buildings along Forty-Eighth Street were two stories, with flat roofs. They'd been built in the 1940s and '50s, the dry local air helping preserve stucco and adobe exteriors for decades.

Each building was set back from the street and behind wrought-iron fencing. They were L-shaped, separated narrowly at the back by a rear gate and path. Each had exterior stairs up to the second-floor front doors, an upper concourse around the perimeter facing a U-shaped courtyard. They reminded him of an old detective movie, Elliott Gould playing Philip Marlowe as a seventies tough guy.

Even just after noon, there was enough shadow laid down by the blazing sun to make the buildings seem slightly ominous. The street ran for blocks, and there was movement along it, albeit far enough away for him to remain unnoticed.

But the apartment blocks seemed almost devoid of life. All but one of the front parking spaces, ahead of the seven-foot fence, were empty; a molded-plastic children's playset and slide sat in the middle of the courtyard, unappreciated, its colors fading in the sun.

He scratched his short, neatly cropped beard, cultivated over the four months since arriving from Maine. *No time like the present.* He crossed the street and tried the front gate.

Locked. Bob scanned the doors on the building to the right, looking for number six. He watched the windows to either side of its door, looking for any signs of movement, curtains or shades being moved, any sign the exterior was being watched.

Then he checked the street in both directions. It was quiet, just a cube truck pulling away from the curb four or five blocks away. But there were enough windows facing the street to provide plenty of potential witnesses. His gaze flitted to the back of each building, where paths ran to the rear alley.

Climbing over the front fence might prompt phone calls, he knew.

He followed the right-side path to the back and the other side of the rear gate, a set of steps and a handrail leading to it.

Bingo. Bob checked the alley both ways, then ran towards the three-foot rail, leaping up to push off it with his left leg, the extra boost helping him vault the seven-foot fence. He dropped to the concrete on the other side, then straightened up quickly, checking his surroundings to ensure he was undetected.

He jogged over to the steps and followed them up to unit six. There was a window beside the door, and he leaned in, craning an ear against the glass. The muffled vibrations suggested people were home.

He flexed his left hand. The knuckles were slightly swollen already, from punching the young gangster at the bodega on Thorn Street. But it had been a quick and effective route to obtaining Pascal Brown's home address.

Still... it also meant they'd be expecting him. The young man in question had been a hard kid, a gang lifer, the type who figured threats were just angry insincerity. He was the type to call ahead and warn his friends, not pretend he'd never met Bob in the first place.

Here's hoping the badge works. It had occurred en route that, like most of the old apartment buildings in City Heights, there wouldn't be a back-door option. That meant the only way to get in was through the front door. It wasn't the kind of neighborhood where forcing the issue was a good idea, a kid had just been killed in a gang shooting a few blocks away, and though most of the neighborhood was just hard-working, working-class folks, the lower rents attracted a bad element.

He'd stopped at a discount toy and joke store and bought a San Diego police detective badge, as well as a dark-blue marker to fill in the lettering so that it matched the real thing. Clipped into his billfold-style wallet, it looked reasonably convincing.

He took it out of his pocket and held it open with his right hand. Then he pounded on the door three times with his left.

The door opened on the chain. The man on the other side looked more cautious than surly, Bob figured.

"What you want?"

Bob held up the badge for a second, tilting his head the other way at the exact same moment, an old CIA trick taught as part of sleight of hand, the secondary motion drawing the man's eye just enough to deter serious study.

"Pascal Brown," Bob said. He pocketed the badge.

"He ain't here."

"Where can I find him?"

The young man just shrugged. "I ain't his secretary."

"But this is his apartment. It's a safe assumption you'd know." Bob put his left hand on the door and applied gentle pressure. "You mind if I come in?"

The man leaned on the door, ending the debate. "You got a warrant?"

"Warrant? To have a polite conversation?"

The young man nodded again. "Uh-huh."

From somewhere behind him, a woman shrieked, the sound shrill and muffled. The man's eyes widened.

Bob leaned back and booted the door, slamming it into the door guard before he could close it. The man staggered backwards, going over before he could retrieve the pistol from his waistband, the gun flying loose.

The guard tried to rise, but Bob crouched as he threw a right cross, knuckles slamming into his chin, the man's eyes rolling back as he slumped unconscious.

Bob kept low as he picked up the pistol, a Ruger American Duty, chambered in 9mm Luger. He hugged the near wall to his right. There was a corridor running towards the back of the apartment, a doorway a few feet along the wall from his position. To his left, the living room sat empty, the TV blaring an old Bugs Bunny cartoon.

He followed the wall down the corridor, checking the

kitchen entrance halfway and seeing it empty, keeping his step slight and quiet.

A man's head and shoulders popped out from behind the stairwell at the other end of the hall, pistol extended. Bob flattened to the carpet as the man took two shots, rolling left to force the man to lean further out, firing back with the Ruger, but deliberately off line, just enough threat to force the man back into cover.

Can't kill anyone. Don't want a war with a street gang.

He got up and began to sprint, his feet light, the polished concrete floor keeping his steps quiet, reaching the end of the hall just as the man's head popped out of cover again. Bob stepped into the kick, catching the man full force in the side of the chin, his head rocketing sideways and caroming off the banister post.

Bob checked the man's pockets, keeping an eye on the stairs. The man had a stun gun in a small belt pouch. Bob withdrew it. He thought about restraining the man, who would doubtless be awake in under a minute. But that scream suggested he didn't have the time to spare.

He sprinted up the stairs. At the top landing, a figure leaned out the second door on the left wall. Bob ducked behind the corner, grateful the old building wasn't made of modern drywall, bullets flattening, then cascading to the ground.

Glock 17, based on the racket. That meant at least seventeen rounds, and only four down. *Shit.*

He took another quick look, ducking back into cover immediately, another four shots sounding, plaster and plywood chunks filling the air ahead of him.

He's firing in a pattern. Bob leaned around the corner for a brief moment, just enough to draw more fire. On the fourth shot, he took his chance, crossing the hall to the other side of the upper landing just as the other man found cover once more.

It cut off his attacker's angle of attack so that he'd have to step out of the room and aim down the adjacent wall, had he realized his target had moved. Bob rounded the corner slowly, flattening himself against the left wall. He had just a few feet, he realized, before he'd come into the man's line of sight again. The gun protruded from the doorway, held steady for a few moments. Then the barrel dipped slightly, the gunman doubtless wondering where he'd gone.

Bob sprinted forward, covering the last few feet. The gunman, hearing his approach, stepped out of the room just as Bob swung a right hook, gauging the height of the man's gun hand from his prior actions, his fist slamming into small wrist bones, the crack audible as they fractured.

The gunman bellowed, dropping the piece, his expression shocked as Bob stepped into the kick, his foot catching the man square in the groin. His target collapsed into a fetal position, groaning. Bob kicked the pistol to the end of the hall but kept moving, stepping to the other side of the door, expecting more gunfire.

"HELP!" The woman's cry was fervent, desperate.

"Shhh! Shut the fuck up, bitch!" a voice hissed, trying to keep the volume down. The man's nervous tone suggested he was the last standing.

Bob held the badge around the corner. "POLICE!" he yelled. To his left, he saw the man who'd come out shooting stagger to his feet, cupping his groin. He looked back once, then began to limp as quickly as he could towards the stairs.

With any luck, the guy downstairs is already running, Bob

figured. Neither would be stupid enough to want more than escape with police in the picture.

"Don't come in here!" His voice was young, shaky. "I'll cap this bitch, I swear!"

"WE JUST WANT THE WOMAN, SAFE," Bob bellowed. He snuck a peak around the corner. The gunman was just a teenager, one arm around the woman's throat, half-dragging her, using her as a shield as he tried to clamber out the window.

Jasmine. She hadn't been at the building site all week, prompting worry.

"We're two stories up," Bob called out. "HEY!"

He chanced another glance. The kid was half out the window but was trying to drag Jasmine Williams with him. Bob raised the Ruger and put a bullet through the glass, the hole fracturing the pane in a web pattern.

The kid let her go and rolled through the opening.

Bob sprinted into the room. He heard a distant grunt and yelp from somewhere behind the building.

"Oh God! Oh my God..." Jasmine managed as she met him halfway, throwing a hug around his shoulders.

"You're okay. It's okay." Bob gave her a couple of reassuring pats on the back, then broke loose from the hug. He looked out the window. The kid was limping away, dragging his right leg as if he'd broken an ankle.

"How did you know where I was?" Jasmine asked. She leaned forward and doubled over, hands on her knees. She began sucking in air, her anxiety so overwhelming she felt winded. "Oh God, I think they were going to... I mean, they were talking about..." She let the brutal notion tail off.

Bob nodded towards the door. "They'll have called their boss by now, or reinforcements. We need to get out of here."

They left the apartment and jogged back to the car, Bob's head on a swivel again as they crossed the courtyard and headed out the front gate. Down the street, Bob could see the man who'd opened the front door getting into an older model sedan. It backed into the street, then turned in the opposite direction, the driver motivated.

"Get in," Bob said.

He backed the car into Forty-Eighth Street, then turned south, Jasmine silent in her shock for a full minute.

Eventually, she said, "You came looking for me." To Jasmine, he was Bob Davis, an itinerant day laborer and generally quiet guy.

"Everyone's worried about you. We're building a house for a needy family, but the person who designed it has missed nearly a week straight, with no explanation."

She hung her head. "I should've talked to everyone, but... it's embarrassing. There. I said it."

"I'm not the most judgmental dude in the world," Bob said. "Give me a try."

She sighed, half fatigue, half exasperation. "It's my little brother, Eric. He's in trouble, like, serious trouble. And if I can't help him, I'm afraid his life is over."

2

Bob sat patiently as Jasmine took a sip of coffee from an oversized mug, her hands gripping both sides. He'd insisted she explain the entire situation, and she'd countered that it could take a while.

So instead of dropping her at home, they'd stopped a few blocks away at a café, a chance to decompress.

Bob had his usual green tea, keeping caffeine to a minimum. Seeing the young architect and community organizer so tense was new and out of place. In the handful of months he'd been living in San Diego, she'd been his project manager on the "sweat equity" project, which gifted a house to an underprivileged family in return for their efforts to help build it.

It didn't pay, but he had money in the bank already, and it was still the best job he'd had since Chicago. Jasmine had taken him on without questions, without a background check, taking his desire to work on something meaningful at face value. She'd also agreed to be a reference, had his landlord asked for them. Despite no local history, she'd treated him respectfully, inviting Bob to the group's weekly nights out, which he politely declined.

She closed her eyes blissfully for a few moments and inhaled the drink's aroma. "I never thought a simple coffee would taste so good," she eventually said.

"Uh-huh. You know, when I offered to teach you and your lady friends from the project self-defense, the general idea was to use it to escape. I'm guessing that wasn't an option."

She shrugged. "If the guys who kidnapped me had been a single mugger trying to grab me from behind, they'd have broken noses and I'd be home nursing the bump on the back of my head. But they just grabbed me right off the street at gunpoint, and there were three of them. So... yeah, fighting back wasn't really on the table."

"I'm sorry I wasn't there to help. It must have been terrifying."

"Not at first. Like you told us, the adrenaline kicked in. For the first hour or so, I was pretty cocky. Then one of them started leering at me, and... I don't know, I'm just glad you showed when you did."

"So explain Pascal Brown to me. What on earth would possess you to go looking for a local gangster?"

She set the coffee down and leaned back against the booth cushion, closing her eyes for a moment and letting out a deep breath, allowing the tension to eke out of her.

She opened her eyes, her expression momentarily distant, as if caught in a memory. "He's always been a great kid, my brother. I should say that right off the get-go. He's only nineteen, but he's big-brain smart, a math whiz. He could accomplish anything, if he got a chance."

"But he's in trouble."

Jasmine nodded gently. "That... would be an understatement, yeah. He was picked up at San Diego International last weekend with a suitcase full of cocaine."

"Ouch." Bob felt instantly uncomfortable. Despite the odd case out of Asia, the average smuggler carrying that much product usually wasn't tricked into it somehow. "And... he's working for this Brown fella?"

"No!" She clearly didn't like the assumption. "I mean... no. I can see why you'd make the leap. But... just let me explain."

The explanation didn't seem a whole lot more solid. Eric had been volunteering for a church-affiliated relief group, Voice of Our Redeemer, supplying clothing to charities for kids in Colombia. He'd gone down once a month for a year, she'd explained, before a spot check on his suitcase in the airport baggage area had uncovered the drugs.

"How much are we talking about?"

"Seven kilos of powder cocaine in brick form, worth about a hundred grand. He's already been denied bail. He has an arrest from when he was younger, but nothing major, shoplifting candy with his little friends. I think they see a kid from a bad neighborhood, they put two and two together. They've torn my parents' home apart, looking for more drugs, crashing through the door on a pair of seniors with no idea just what in the heck is going on. But I get it."

Bob figured he did, too. But if he'd learned anything from his time in the CIA, it was that a lack of intel and context could mislead. "Okay. So... how does Pascal Brown figure into this? Because he's the jerkwad I figure will come looking for yours truly, in short order. I just beat up three of his guys." He didn't want to upset her, but he needed more, an explanation of how the pieces fit.

"He's the biggest coke dealer in City Heights. We've lived there our whole lives. I figure if someone's going to use a local kid against his knowledge—"

"You figure someone just snuck fourteen bricks of cocaine into his bag." Then he realized how sarcastic it sounded. "Sorry. I don't mean to presume, but—"

"Oh... I get it." She sighed again, as if weighed down by others' doubts. She took another sip of coffee, then studied the cup's logo at arm's length. "Don't worry, be happy," she read. "Yeah, sure."

"You understand it sounds far-fetched?"

"I mean, what else am I supposed to believe, Bob? That this sweet kid who avoided trouble his entire life suddenly decided to not only become a major drug dealer but also hide any sign of it – in lifestyle, finance, behavior, you name it. Not just hide it, but from his family? From me, a person who sees him almost every day? I mean... come on."

"How did the charity react?"

"They're mortified, of course. They're a national organization, so they're accustomed to having the odd staff member in trouble, but nothing like this. All the local volunteers are in our church community. I think we're all as embarrassed as one another. Scratch that, I'm more embarrassed than any of them, even though it can't be true. It's the stares, the judgment."

"Do they believe he was acting alone?" Bob knew he had to tread carefully. His best friend, Dawn Ellis, was a churchgoer. She was fiercely logical most of the time but could be just as fierce about protecting her beliefs and congregation. "Did they check out or arrest any other volunteers?"

"Heck no!" Jasmine looked shocked at the notion. "They're one of the biggest charities in the country, Bob.

Their founder, Anderson Rowe, has the Presidential Medal of Freedom. He's unbelievably rich and unbelievably generous. I can't even imagine what he must think of this."

Bob sensed a palpable swell of humiliation, as if she couldn't abide being judged negatively by someone so successful.

The day finally made sense. To Jasmine, Eric was an angel being used by a vicious criminal and discarded when caught.

It seemed a convenient narrative. But they'd been working together on the charity housing project for nearly three months, and Jasmine had been a rock her co-workers could cling to whenever troubled. She'd helped a battered wife get shelter, a senior who'd lost his apartment find a new home. She'd accepted Bob despite him walking into the project's main office off the street, unknown. She deserved support.

Even tried to get you out socially, settling in, like you belong. Increasingly, Bob figured he'd never fit anywhere, never settle anywhere. Not without attracting attention from the Agency and the ghosts of Team Seven, his former CIA black ops squad.

But he knew he could still do good. It was the only thing he still controlled.

"Okay. So what you need, really, is for Pascal Brown to confirm or deny whether your brother worked for him. Do I have that right?"

"I think that would help. I could at least take whatever you find to the San Diego Police. There's a detective there who knows Eric a little."

"But not enough to prevent the charges?"

"They weren't involved. The Port of San Diego Harbor

Police handle international investigations and are their own outfit, technically. Once they arrested him, it was up to the district attorney's office whether to charge, and given the evidence..." She let the thought trail.

"So... what you really need," Bob said, "is evidence he was duped, somehow."

"That would be ideal, but I am not certain that's even possible."

The sense of futility came off her in waves, Bob figured. He looked up and gave the waitress a small wave to get her attention, letting the conversation pause while she came over and took his order for another pot. Jasmine needed to relax, and slowing things down would help.

"So tell me about him. What's Eric like?"

She thought about it for a few moments. "Tough. I mean, he doesn't come across as that. But he has dyslexia – he has trouble reading because the words show backwards for him, sometimes – and he got teased pretty badly for it in school. I'm fifteen years older than him, so I wasn't there to protect him. He handled those bullies on his own, graduated school a year late but with good marks."

"But nothing criminal."

"Lordie, no! I mean... he was arrested when he was fourteen for shoplifting candy, to impress some other boys. But other than that, nothing bad at all. If anything, he's the boy who'd reach out to troubled kids, try to get them on the straight and narrow."

He downed the dregs of his first cup and put it back on the saucer. "No connections with this Brown guy?"

"Not really. There was an incident about a year ago where a couple of corner operators were harassing him, trying to get him to sling dope on his block. But he told them to get lost. I think he said they were Brown's men. But that's it, and there was no follow-up."

Bob knew he needed a lot more information. "Okay, here's what we do: you handle your brother's legal issues for now. I'll tell Mike at the building site that we both need a week. Then I'll track down Mr. Brown and have a chat."

"Oh! No… Bob, you don't understand! Pascal Brown is an OG in City Heights, a fearsome individual. He has a reputation. You… well… you lay and tape drywall for us." She said it sympathetically, like a parent gently chiding a misguided child. She leaned across the table and grabbed one of his hands in hers. "What you did today was very brave, but this is a matter for police or, at worst, family or trained professionals—"

"I've done other things besides hanging drywall and laying roof shingles," Bob said. "Some of them involved training. The concern is appreciated but not necessary."

She sat back slightly in the booth seat and eyed him curiously. "Other things?"

"Military. Nothing you'd find too interesting. But… I've found a few people, too, solved a few problems like this. Just… give me a couple of days, okay?"

"You think you can track him down that easily?"

"I found his apartment in two hours. Finding the dude himself isn't going to be difficult. Trust me."

3

But Pascal Brown clearly did not want to be found. The apartment was a front, a place used to sell drugs, but not in Brown's name. And after a day of watching it, there was no indication he ever visited.

After four more days of hunting City Heights, filled with small-scale bribes and lots of backing away slowly, Bob had avoided beating anyone else up. But he was no closer to finding the man and had heard the phrase "I wouldn't know nothing about that" at least a dozen times.

He'd stopped at bodegas, other alleged trap houses, at dive bars and flops.

Eventually, he'd assumed, Brown would come looking for payback for rescuing Jasmine, if only to shore up his fearsome rep. But there had been no sign of revenge either.

So he'd put on his only suit and gone to see the only man Jasmine figured knew Pascal Brown really well and had the stomach to cross him.

Assistant District Attorney Jim Sheinbein stared across his desk at the man who'd walked past his secretary, claiming to be a friend of Jasmine Williams, and slowly shook his head. "Jasmine called just before you got here," he said. "Officially, we're not having this conversation." Then he gestured for Bob to close the office door.

"Okay," Bob said before doing as requested and sitting down.

Sheinbein leaned back a little in his chair. "Sorry, the walls have ears in this place. Can't have parts of this discussion with the rest of the office listening."

"So what CAN you tell me, if you can't give me another address?"

Sheinbein's office landline buzzed. "Yes, Nicole."

"Sir, should I call someone?" his secretary asked.

"No, it's okay. Mr. Davis and I are just having a little chat." He released the intercom button and turned his attention back to Bob. "Typically, when someone bursts into my office on five minutes' notice, the protocol is to be polite, then remove them as judiciously as possible while I contemplate whether I should buy some self-protection."

Sheinbein had a fearsome rep and, from Bob's quick newspaper database research, a high closure rate. But he was a measured man, not prone to ranting or ideology, and he clearly had a sense of humor. "Yeah, sorry about that. But you know the chances of me getting an appointment anytime soon on my own were slim to none."

"True enough. And you got straight to the point. Mr. Davis, may I ask why you want to find this guy?"

Bob explained Jasmine's story. By the end, Sheinbein was wincing. "Mr. Davis... you're basically telling me that you're trying to undermine a case my office is prosecuting."

"Uh... yeah, that's pretty much it," Bob said. "But if Eric's guilty, that won't happen, right? I mean, worst-case scenario for me is that I find Brown and he decides to have an epiphany, admits he set the whole thing up, and wants the rehabilitative benefits of time in a federal pen. We know that's not going to happen, but if it did, it still wouldn't exonerate Eric of working for him, right?"

"True enough."

"So really, the only risk is that the original story is full of holes and you've got the wrong guy. You should WANT me to test the strength of your case."

"But... I don't *know* you," Sheinbein stressed. "For all I know, you're some guy who hates Brown and wants to kill him, or you're working for some rival. The only reason I'm even talking to you is that Jasmine Williams is a noted architect who has an excellent reputation for helping the city's underprivileged community, and you claim to be working with her. I like her, so you get five minutes of my time. But... again, she's the sister of the accused."

"I'm a forty-four-year-old construction worker from the UP in Michigan," Bob said. "Do I look like I work in the local drug trade? And does Jasmine seem like the kind of person who's going to interfere with the law? She's sure Eric is innocent. That's all this is."

Sheinbein hung his head a little and sighed wearily. "I've been doing this a long time, Mr. Davis..."

"Please. It's just Bob."

"Okay. I've been doing this a long time. I would like to be able to say we always get it right, we always send the right person to prison, nobody plays favorites, politics are never involved. And... any grown adult would know that's bullshit. But what I can tell you is that we play the game as straight as I can make it. And in twenty-seven years with this office, I've never seen a drug trafficker of that scale who had somehow been duped."

"But there's always a first," Bob offered. "And if it was someone from City Heights..." He let the thought trail.

"It would be someone either working with or against Pascal Brown. Sure." Sheinbein wore a troubled expression, as if he was conflicted by his options. "They rule the world, his type. The self-interested and selfish. We just try to get in the way. And usually, we barely even slow them down."

"I just need a few words with him."

"There's every chance he will kill or seriously injure you. I can't—"

"It's less likely than you think," Bob interrupted.

That gave the man a moment of pause, and he peered through Bob like a math professor lost in an equation, weighing the angles. "I suppose there's one scenario that might mitigate my concern. Every time one of Pascal's men goes down and has a first appearance, Pascal shows up at the courthouse to support him. And everyone in the trade and in law enforcement here knows that. So I'm not telling you anything that isn't common knowledge."

It was actually useful and didn't expose anyone. The man was clever, Bob had to admit. But... "How do I know when one of his guys is making an appearance or has been arrested?"

Sheinbein shrugged. "That, I cannot help you with, Mr. Davis. But if you can meet him there, he's unlikely to act unilaterally, not with so many officers of the court nearby. Now, if you would give Ms. Williams my best, it would perhaps be sensible for you to go now. I think your decision to breeze in here made some of my people nervous."

Bob rose. "Thank you. I know you're just doing your job."

Sheinbein frowned, a thought occurring. "How did you get by the downstairs security? Usually they call up."

"I came by yesterday and took a look at who just walks by and who doesn't. They tend to let the guys in suits approach the elevators without challenging them, so I wore a suit."

"I'll have to tell them to do better," Sheinbein said. "A little more notice next time, please. Nicole will find a spot in my schedule if need be."

Jasmine had a watering can in one hand when she opened the apartment door.

"So?" she said as he walked in. They wandered over to the kitchen, Jasmine setting the watering can down near a potted plant before joining him at the table.

"Sheinbein was surprised, but you called it right. He seems like an honest sort of guy. For a lawyer."

"And?"

"He gave me a lead. He told me Pascal Brown always shows for his guys at court."

She looked puzzled. "But… how are we supposed to know when one of his guys is going to make an appearance?"

Bob allowed himself a slightly smug smile. "I had an idea about that."

"Okay."

"I'll have to see if it works, first."

"BEFORE you fill me in? Uh-uh."

Bob held up both palms. "I'll be safe, don't worry."

"Sure." But she didn't look sure.

4

Bob sat behind the wheel of the beaten-up Hyundai and watched the fourplex down the block. A group of men milled around outside. Every so often, a kid of twelve or thirteen would pop around the corner and run into the building. Then they'd go back around the corner.

Like most of San Diego, Marlborough Avenue was sunny, with whitewashed walls and facias giving some of the apartment blocks a certain glow. But it flattered to deceive; the buildings were all walk-ups. Every other one would have a boarded-up or busted window. Windows were covered up by security bars, and the street was devoid of the expensive sports cars seen in so many other neighborhoods. Cracks in the sidewalk let weeds through; graffiti and tags covered the odd formerly bare wall. Years earlier, the street had been lined with public phone booths, to accommodate poor people who couldn't get a landline. But they'd all been removed to discourage "dial-a-dopers," with an acceptance that pay-as-you-go cell phones were an adequate replacement.

Jasmine said the drug houses themselves weren't hard to find. The key was identifying a "runner," one of the underage delivery boys Brown used to get drugs from a property to a customer. The runners were the only carriers. The drugs would be kept in one apartment, either derelict or with no one living in it and officially responsible. They'd be passed to the runner, who would then take them around the block to the customer's car window.

It's like an old-fashioned drive-in restaurant, minus the roller skates, window trays and good intentions.

He put the car into drive and cruised down the block, circling around so he could watch the cross street from the north side of the road. A handful of kids were lolling around a fence, sitting on the edge of its concrete lower wall, a young man seated on a plain molded-plastic chair a few feet away.

A car pulled up. The older boy got up and walked over, leaned up to the partially open passenger window. He reached into the car for a second and took something from the driver, which he shoved into his pocket. Then he walked back and said something to one of the younger boys, who sprinted down the block and around the corner, towards the drug house.

Everyone is isolated. Clever. The guy who takes the money never touches the drugs. The guy who gives the drugs to the kid never touches the money. It wouldn't mitigate possession with intent to traffic charges if the drug house was busted, Bob figured, but the entire setup would make proving ultimate responsibility very difficult.

The weak link for his purposes was the money man, not because he was the most exposed but because Brown would care most about being hurt financially. It was late in the afternoon. If Jasmine was correct, they'd probably sold several thousand dollars' worth of crack already.

The older boy had a pistol tucked in the back of his waistband that showed slightly whenever he leaned towards a car window.

Bingo.

Getting a dealer to turn himself in, so that Bob himself didn't have to be involved, had been unlikely at best. He'd thought about scaring the older kid so badly that he ran to the police, but inner-city gangsters didn't scare easily.

Instead, he'd come up with an idea that required both audacity and patience. He kept his eyes on the seated young man for another two hours before a second guy, in maybe his early twenties, showed up to spot the money man off.

The money guy headed down the street and around the corner. Bob reversed course, taking the Hyundai back around the block. As he pulled up to the curb, the car idling, the money man was getting out of a black Mercedes SUV parked half a block down the street from the house.

And the money goes to someone more trusted, who takes it back... to Brown? *No, too easy. He wouldn't be that direct.* It would be a lieutenant of some sort who would make bank drops or cryptocurrency buys.

And that guy would, without a doubt, be even tougher to shake down for information.

Instead, he followed the young man for a couple of blocks before traffic forced Bob to pull over and continue on foot. Five blocks south of the drug house, the young man walked up the steps to an apartment building, Bob hanging back until he had his keys out of his pocket and had checked his surroundings.

He slotted the key into the building's front door.

Bob broke into a sprint, the young man turning in surprise at the sound of him rushing up the steps. His hand went to his waistband, but before he could pull the piece, Bob drove a punch into his solar plexus; wind lost instantly, the young dealer doubled over. Bob grabbed him by the collar with one hand and retrieved his pistol with the other.

Then he turned him towards the door, the gun shoved into the small of the man's back. "If you want to be able to walk tomorrow, open it."

"Uhhhh..." The dealer was trying to regain his breath. "Uhhh... Can't..."

"I'd give you more time to recover, but we don't have it, and if you can't help me, I'll have to kill you," Bob offered.

He gasped once more, then said, "Unnhh... Hey! Just... chill, okay?" He opened the door.

Bob pushed him inside. Traffic had been passing, and it was possible someone would call in an assault or robbery, but the neighborhood suggested otherwise. He used his foot to close the door behind them.

The kid had his hands up but turned anyway at the waist to try to get a look at Bob. "Man... you don't know what the fuck you're doing right now! Y'all know who I work for, motherfucker?"

"Yep. What's your name?"

"Motherfucker..."

Bob clubbed him lightly with the pistol, the clunk of metal on skull enough to dissuade him from being difficult. "If you're no use to me, I might as well shoot you now. If I don't know your name, I figure you don't want to communicate, which means you're no use to me."

"Man... who the fuck—"

Bob used his open left hand the second time, cuffing the young man with an audible slap. "Now you're starting to piss me off. I asked for your name. You don't get mine."

"It's... it's Turner."

"Okay, Turner, which apartment are we going to?"

5

Turner lived on the second floor in a one-bedroom. It was disgusting; the tiny living room was strewn with boxes of half-eaten pizza, paper plates with days' old food on them. The carpet crunched every few steps from old detritus, bits of potato chips never swept up. In the corner of the kitchen, an oversized garbage bag had been left open, and the room was full of fruit flies.

"Sit down," Bob said, pushing him towards the chaise-lounge-style sofa. "Couldn't you at least hire a cleaner or something?"

"Yo, fuck you, man," the young gangster muttered. "I come to your crib and start bad-mouthing it?"

Bob directed him to sit down. "I'm not going to keep you long. Let's say I get you to call Pascal Brown and ask to meet him."

Turner let the hypothetical hang there between them for a second, then laughed off the notion. "Yeah, sure, he just takes my calls."

"That's what I thought. Stand up for a second and turn around."

The young man did as demanded. "Yo… I'm telling you, man, you don't wanna do this. I got a family. I'm just working is all, just hustling like anyone else."

"Relax," Bob said. "You're no use to me dead."

Turner was flexing his fists, certain he was about to be executed. Bob didn't want to prolong his discomfort despite his lousy profession.

"I'm telling you, man," the dealer spluttered, "I've got kids need support. My old lady—"

Bob used the pistol butt as a cosh, clubbing the lower back of his skull, consciousness lost instantly, Turner slumping onto the sofa. He stripped off the dealer's shoes and bundled his socks. Then he removed a set of plastic wrist restraints from his jacket pocket and bound the dealer's hands behind him before shoving the balled-up socks into his mouth. He took Turner's belt off and used it to tie his ankles together.

After about a minute, the kid's head began to twitch forcefully. He woke seconds later, immediately realizing his predicament.

"Hmmm!" he protested. "Hmmm!"

"Relax, and you'll be okay," Bob said. "I don't really need you. I just need your gun."

THE DRIVE back to the drug house took less than five minutes. Bob lingered across the street and down the block for a while until traffic seemed light.

The same three men were seated on the drug house

stoop. Bob got out of the car. He walked across the street, hands in his jacket pockets, his right holding the pistol.

He was twenty feet away and angling towards them when the biggest of the three stood up. "Yo... you got a problem, my man?" he asked loudly. "What you looking at us for?"

Bob removed his left hand from the jacket pocket and held up one palm. "Not meaning to be any trouble, gents," he said. "I was wondering if you could help with some directions."

"Yo, get the fuck out of here," one of the other gangsters suggested. "You crazy or something?"

Never really been a "shoot first" sort of guy. But for this to work, somebody has to get arrested. He looked back towards the other corner, where the preteen child had just been busy slinging dope.

Bob pulled the pistol and shot the standing man through the left femur, aiming for a point just above the knee to take the femoral artery out of play. The big man let out a yelp. Before the other two could react and fully rise, they'd each taken a gunshot to the upper chest, Bob aiming high, catching them both right below the collarbone.

The two seated men went right back down on their backsides, clutching their wounds. Their bigger friend went for the pistol in his waistband, limping towards Bob. Bob sprinted towards him before he could level the gun, the leaping side kick catching him in the chest, the big man's balance thrown off by his leg injury. He crashed to the ground, the pistol clattering on the sidewalk.

Bob kicked it out of the way and turned quickly, leveling his pistol at the other two to ward off any notion of going for a gun. "Ah!" he warned. "I wouldn't. Toss them! Pieces on the ground, now!"

He kept his eyes on them as they complied. He needed only a quick glance before he pulled the trigger again, pumping another bullet into the big man's other thigh.

"HNNNNH!" the big man bellowed.

"Oh shit!" one of the others declared. They began to back away, crawling backwards up the stairs despite their wounds.

"Stay still," Bob ordered. "Or I might hit something important."

"You might... oh, goddamn!" the same man declared, trying to rise and turn.

Bob shot them each once, through the thigh, being careful again to avoid the femoral artery. The three men lay bleeding and moaning. Then he checked traffic both ways and, seeing no cars, crossed the street back to the beaten-up Hyundai.

"I'm... dying," one of the men sputtered.

"No, you're not. Didn't nick any arteries, based on the amount of blood, and there are no vital organs in the leg, so you won't bleed out. You'll be okay."

"Man... fuck you, man."

He took out his burner phone as he drove back to Turner's apartment.

"911 emergency, go ahead, please," the operator said.

"Yeah, I'm at the corner of Marlborough and Landis. Three guys were just shot outside a trap house there. They're lying on the sidewalk, bleeding."

"Sir, are you injured?"

"Nope."

"Okay, I'm going to dispatch an ambulance and police. What I need you to do is stay on the—"

"The guy who shot them is named Turner. I know him." He gave the woman the other gangster's address as he pulled the car up outside the apartment block. "He has a gun. I seen him hide it in the toilet, in the tank thing."

"Okay, sir, but—"

Bob ended the call. The tip was outlandishly specific, and that would raise police suspicions, potentially. But it didn't matter; he just needed the man arrested, not convicted. He got out of the car. There was a sewage drain a few feet ahead of the car. He took the burner out of his pocket, stepped on it, then tossed the broken remains down the drain.

Shame. That one lasted a long time, comparatively.

He walked to the building's front door, kept open with a piece of tape covering the automatic lock's hasp, and pulled it open. At Turner's apartment door, he checked the hall both ways for security cameras before going inside.

The young man had wriggled off the sofa but lay face-down on the carpet, trapped by his immobility.

"There, see, that wasn't too bad now, was it?" Bob said. "I've got to take a leak, and then I'm out of your hair."

"Hmmmm! Hnnmmh," the young man bleated incomprehensibly.

Bob headed into the bathroom. He removed the Ziploc bread bag he'd brought for the occasion and placed the young man's Smith & Wesson nine-millimeter in it.

An upside to having his fingerprints removed by the CIA was that he didn't have to wipe things down. Any of the young man's prints would be badly smudged, looking at best like an attempt to wipe them down. But they'd be intact on the magazine, which Bob hadn't touched.

He placed the baggie inside the toilet tank, waited a ten count, then flushed the toilet for effect.

He went back out to the living room and removed the

man's makeshift ball gag, then his wrist restraints, leaving his feet tied. "I'm keeping the piece, by the way," Bob said.

"Man… I don't know what the fuck this proves to anyone, beating up on me," Turner muttered. "I don't mean shit to nobody, but they're still gonna smoke your ass when they find you."

"Uh-huh," Bob said. He checked his battered Seiko wristwatch. It had been nine minutes since he'd called the police. Typical response time in City Heights was seventeen minutes, but that would be to the crime scene. They'd send someone right from there, though, he figured.

He sat down in the armchair a few feet away, keeping one hand in his pocket, index finger pressing against the fabric to mimic holding the gun the young man already knew he had.

"What? You're just going to sit there?" Turner asked.

"For another…" Bob checked his watch. "Four minutes."

The dealer squinted, a pained expression as he tried to figure out what was going on. "You're just going to… sit there? You ain't banging?"

"Nope."

Turner went silent, confused.

The time passed. Bob rose and walked over to the door. "On the other hand, try to follow me and I will kill you," he said.

He closed the door behind him and headed down the opposite flight of stairs, to the back door and out. He rounded the building and walked two blocks to the Hyundai. He was another half block away when the squad cars passed him and pulled up, lights flashing, outside the building.

6

"You did what?!" Jasmine demanded. She'd insisted on updates, so Bob had driven over to the family home in neighboring North Park, where she was visiting her elderly parents.

He sat down at the kitchen table and took her mother's proffered cup of coffee. He usually avoided caffeine, but it only seemed polite.

The elderly woman had leaned in, given him a peck on the top of his head. "You're a good man, helping my son. We had him when we were too old, but he's the best thing that ever happened to us since Jasmine, and I know he didn't do nothing wrong. It ain't in him."

"Thank you, ma'am," he said as she wandered into the next room.

"Bob..." Jasmine said to draw his attention back. "You did what?"

"I needed one of his guys arrested. So... that has now happened," he said.

She sat down across from him. Her expression suggested cynicism. "Uh-huh. Just like that."

"Well... more or less."

"And how, exactly, did you manage—"

"Oh, that, you don't want to know about," Bob said. "That would make you a party to several felonies."

Jasmine took a deep, cleansing breath as she tried to get a handle on the situation. "Bob, when I agreed to let you help, I didn't expect—"

"Look... it's no secret to you that this part of town can be dangerous, Jasmine. It's your home, not mine. If it wasn't that way, I wouldn't have been teaching you self-defense."

"But hurting a potential rapist who is standing behind me by headbutting him in the nose isn't 'being a party to several felonies,' it's self-defense!"

"These aren't saints or innocent victims like Eric. And we know Brown goes to the courthouse when one of his guys is arrested. That's according to Sheinbein. Always does."

"Okay, but how do you know when—"

"Because the State has to arraign someone the police have arrested within forty-eight hours, tell them the charges they're facing. It's" – he checked his watch – "seven o'clock on Tuesday. So he has to be on the docket and in court by six-ish Wednesday."

"That's..." She didn't finish the thought aloud, instead hanging her head as if worried.

"It's okay," Bob said. "Yeah, some people got hurt, but they were—"

"I didn't ASK for that," she replied curtly. "I DON'T believe in violence! Again, what did you do, exactly?"

"Well... let's just say that as far as the SDP are concerned, one drug dealer wounded a couple of other drug dealers, then hid the evidence where police could easily find it."

"Oh. Oh my God." She rose. "This... I can't allow this..." She turned towards him. "What were you *thinking*?"

"That your brother doesn't deserve to go to jail. Even Sheinbein must have his doubts, or he wouldn't have helped me. We both clearly trust your judgment."

She crossed her arms over her tiny torso defensively. "Well... I'm not sure I trust yours." The look in her eyes bordered on betrayal, Bob figured. "Who ARE you, exactly? I thought I knew."

"Nobody's going to die," he said. "We had a problem tracking down the guy who might be ruining your brother's life. Now... we no longer have that problem."

"So he shows up at the courthouse and... what, you just follow him back to wherever he's hiding out? Something like that?"

Bob downed the last of the coffee and got up. "Exactly like that. And nobody's going to die when I talk to Mr. Brown, either."

"I mean... except maybe you! Or him! I thought getting you involved was crazy because you're a construction worker, not a cop. Now I'm worried about both of you. I mean... congratulations, Bob, you've done the impossible. You've managed to get me worried on behalf of Pascal Brown."

Bob held up both hands. "I apologize. But... don't worry about me. Or him. I'm not going to hurt him."

Not seriously, anyway, Bob thought to himself. *Just enough.*

. . .

Turner Abbott showed up on the docket court schedule the next morning. Bob was at the courthouse to check it right after opening at eight thirty. The young dealer had a hearing set for two thirty that afternoon.

He'd phoned Jasmine and told her where to meet him, then gone for breakfast and a workout. He'd used some downtime to check whether Adam Renton, his freelance mission handler, had contacted him, or his friend Dawn.

But with nothing new, he'd gone back to the courthouse a little early and perched on the bumper of the Hyundai parked in the public lot along Union and W B Streets, where he could see people leaving the parking lot and walking over to the twenty-five-story tower.

Pascal Brown had avoided felony arrests his entire adult life, and he was in his early thirties. It had taken Jasmine the entire day to find a picture of him, from a charity associate's backyard barbecue when Brown was in high school.

She handed it to him as she sat down next to Bob. "It's not much," she said.

Bob frowned. It was blurry, and he looked young. "That's it?"

"He's careful, clearly. More careful than you."

He pocketed the picture and looked around, but there were no new arrivals. "Did they take all the benches off the streets downtown or something?"

"Yes, well... God forbid someone indigent or a runaway sleeps there for a few minutes," Jasmine said. "Hey, here's an idea. Instead of rousting the homeless from downtown, why don't we just hire you out to the city to shoot them?"

"Very funny. Are you going to be resentful about how we came to be here for the entirety of this? Would it help if I apologized for worrying you again?"

She couldn't hide her obvious doubt. But Jasmine shook her head anyway. "No, it's fine. It is what it is, at this point. If I freaked out and reported you or tried to turn you in, the police would probably charge you with attempted murder even though that's clearly not true."

"But you thought about it."

She turned and stared at him. "I had to. I'm a decent person. Decent people do not solve their problems by assaulting—"

"Innocent bystanders?" Bob interrupted dryly.

"I was going to say other people. What he did or does for a living doesn't change that. You... do realize that, right, Bob?"

Maybe she had a point. But Bob was having trouble seeing past the actual problem, that Pascal Brown controlled the cocaine trade in City Heights and either had framed Eric or probably knew which of the other dealers did. Gangsters running business-level enterprises didn't generally miss the small details and remain breathing.

"Well... while I generally agree, I'd also say whatever your brother's tied up in could cost him his life," Bob reasoned. "Prison is hard time, anywhere, even California. Maybe especially, in a few cases. And if Brown is responsible, he stands to greatly benefit if the 'guilty party' were taken care of in prison, and no loose ends were left. On the other hand, I could defer to your gentility towards Mr. Turner Abbott and his ilk, who when I first observed them were using eleven- and twelve-year-olds as drug mules."

She pursed her lips. "That's not good either."

"Nope. And that's a dangerous corner he's working; three guys got shot there just yesterday."

She threw him a sour look. "Also not funny."

I mean... it was a little funny. "Duly noted." Bob frowned, noticing the dark circles under her eyes for the first time. They hadn't been there a week earlier, when she had been perched over the blueprints at the worksite. "You're... otherwise okay, right?"

She exhaled deeply. "Just... exhausted, is all. I do what I do for the community out of choice. The city, in return, shows its appreciation by awarding me plaques and certificates instead of just spending money to help the poor, which is what would be actually appreciated. They don't really care; they're just too damn busy to let emotions factor, it seems. And the people we help? They feel condemned by the generosity of others, as if it's revealing terrible things about them."

To their left, nearer the road, car doors slammed in unison. Bob shot a quick look. *Four men getting out of a black Lexus SUV, annnd... there's Mr. Brown, right on cue.* Jasmine began to turn her head, and he pulled on her other arm to divert her attention. "Don't look," he whispered. "These guys clock unwanted interest for a living, and we're sitting on a car bumper."

The group strolled past them, one man ahead of the dealer, the other two behind, each making occasional perimeter checks. Brown was well built, wearing a dress shirt and tie, tan slacks. He'd shaved his head and had a gold stud earring in his left lobe. The first man opened the door, and the group went inside.

"Okay, this is where you head off," Bob said.

She sighed again as she rose. "Please don't do anything I wouldn't do. He is my brother, not yours."

"Duly noted."

7

An hour later, the black SUV was taking the downslope to an apartment block's underground parking along Third Avenue.

Bob found a spot on the street and double-parked despite the ticket risk in late afternoon. It was important to get to the building's front door quickly.

It was unlocked, the building mixed-use, a security desk near the elevators manned by an older guard keeping an eye out for trouble.

The lobby was empty, but the elevator car was climbing, from the parking garage. Bob watched it as it climbed to the fourteenth-story penthouse.

"Excuse me, sir!" the man at the security station called out. "Can I help you?" He pointed over the top edge of the desk to the general vicinity of a plastic sign that read "All Visitors Must Check In With Security."

Bob smiled and gave him a little wave. "Oh! Hi... yeah, sorry about that. They had a vacancy notice in the *Union-*

Trib classifieds last week." The building had to have hundreds of units; he figured the chances were reasonable.

"Already gone," the guard said. "In fact, I think it took three days. In this economy you have to move fast, my young friend."

"Ahhh... Shame," Bob said. "Good part of town. Do you know what they were asking?"

"I think, like, twenty-two hundred a month, something like that."

"Ouch! That come with a pool or anything?"

"There is a pool in the basement, and a full fitness room. We have a brochure and some sales documents in a package..." The security guard shuffled through a drawer and found the package, then passed it over.

"And – no offense, but are you the only security? What if someone slips past you? I wouldn't want a place where salesmen could, like, door-knock me and such."

The man scowled a little at that. "Never had one slip by in twenty years of doing this; not going to happen. Not Mike, the night guy, either. Besides, it wouldn't help them. There's an elevator key lockout for the upper-floor residences. They only go up if I let them up."

"Good to know," Bob said. "And I'm glad they don't make you sit here twenty-four-seven. A man has to eat." He gave the guy a knowing finger point. "Thank you" – he stared at the name tag – "Emre." He made a show of looking around the vast lobby again. "It's nice. It's a nice place."

Bob beat a retreat to the door. He knew he'd have to move the car to a spot as close to the front of the building as possible if he was going to spot the security guy leaving.

. . .

The replacement guard showed up four hours later, at eight o'clock. Bob supposed it was a twelve-hour shift, or there was an overnight gap for a few hours when the desk was unmanned. The elevator lockout probably gave them an unwarranted sense of security.

He waited until the man had been in the building for a few minutes, his colleague, Emre, getting on a bus just down the street. It figured that neither man got a parking space. The building was dripping in money, but as usual, he figured, not enough dripped down to the guys actually working there.

He checked his watch. The twenty-four-hour convenience store down the block was a two-minute walk away. He bought a package of brown manila envelopes and, for good measure, lifted the clerk's empty clipboard as he turned back to the register.

Back in the car, he clipped the sales package to the clipboard, the eight-by-eleven sales documents facing backwards so it seemed like they were just white pages. He wrote down the numbers one to ten, then filled in some generic addresses next to them.

Then he reached down into the passenger footwell and retrieved the brown bag and empty sandwich wrapper from the supper he'd bought, stuffing them into the manila envelope and sealing it, puffed up. Then he realized he should've scrawled Brown's name on it before filling it, but he'd already sealed it. He improvised.

Hmmm. Actually looks better illegible. Doctor or lawyer handwriting.

He got out of the car and headed for the doors, clipboard in one hand, improvised package in the other.

Inside, a guard in an olive-green cap and zip-up jacket

was sipping a coffee, slurping it over his bushy brown mustache, watching a tiny TV hidden behind the security desk countertop. Bob approached it. As the guard looked up, Bob quickly tipped his baseball cap slightly in greeting.

"Evening. Got a delivery for a P. Brown, floor 14, this address." He held up the clipboard quickly to show the list of addresses. "I'm told you've got to buzz me up or something."

The guard shook his head. "Can't do it, sir. Apologies."

Ah, hell. "I can't leave it here. I need a signature," Bob said. "I do that, I'm breaking company regulations. They won't accept that, no, sir."

The guard sighed and shuffled in his chair impatiently. "Like I said..."

Bob took a calculated gamble that Brown's anonymity extended to his building. "You know who this is for, right? You've seen the guy's bodyguards?"

"Sure."

"They're there because he's a major new recording artist. This package is some last-minute contract stuff, legal. It has to be delivered today, it has to be signed today, or heads will roll, mine included. Yours, too, if he doesn't get it."

The guard studied him cautiously. "I'll call up," he said.

Well, this is going well, Bob thought dryly. *The only way this could get worse would be if he asked—*

"Hey," the guard said, a landline in hand. "You got any ID or a card or something?"

Think of something, Bobby. Quickly. "Just tell him it's from Turner Abbott."

The guard spoke into the phone for a moment, then hung up. "He's sending someone down."

Bob gave him a thumbs-up. "You're a gentleman and a

scholar..." He made a show of looking at the name tag. "Michael."

The guard just nodded once and went back to his TV show, glad to be rid of him.

Bob strolled over to the elevators. One of the two cars was already on its way down.

Have to time this right. He watched as the orange light flitted downward from number to number, three... two... one...

The doors pinged and began to open. The car's lone occupant, a bald, muscular guy, was staring straight at Bob.

He stepped into the car before the new arrival could react, leaning into the left cross, his target making the mistake of going for the gun in his waistband with his right hand, leaving that side of his chin open. Bob's knuckles crushed the mental nerve, the man's eyes briefly rolling back as his eyelids fluttered shut, his legs lost all strength, and he collapsed, unconscious.

Bob turned and hit the "door closed" button, then floor 14. He crouched and tossed the clipboard and package aside, then took the steel-reinforced wrist restraints out of his pocket. He rolled the unconscious man over and cuffed his hands behind him. Then he relieved him of his Stoeger 9mm, checked to make sure a round was chambered, then stashed it in a jacket side pocket.

The car continued to rise. On the floor, the unconscious man's phone was buzzing. Bob crouched again and withdrew it. A text bubble had popped up.

What up?

Bob tapped the bubble. An answer box popped up beneath it.

Dunno. Some papers from Turner.

He watched the screen, but no further response came. He had a sinking suspicion it hadn't worked.

On the elevator floor, the guard began to stir. Bob crouched on one knee. The man's eyes opened. Bob hit him with a right cross, knocking him out again.

The elevator doors pinged.

He looked down at the phone again.

No response.

The doors slid open.

Bob leaned cautiously out into the hall; a bullet shattered the window at the near end of the corridor, the crack of the pistol sounding a moment later. He caught a glimpse of a guard at the far end of the hall, by the only door.

Just try not to kill anybody. He crouched low, then fell sideways out the door, the Stoeger braced in his right hand. He fired three shots, aiming for the man's legs twenty-five feet away, all three bullets striking home.

8

Bob sprinted out of the car and down the hall as the guard collapsed, clutching his wounds, moaning, a sound Bob knew usually meant a bullet had hit bone. An arm swung free of the apartment door, and Bob raised the nine mil, firing two wild shots to push the shooter back into cover.

On the third shot, the pistol jammed.

Shit. The doorway was just a few feet away. The second guard leaned clear of it, taking a bead on Bob. He tossed the jammed pistol hard, the overhand throw of a frantic shortstop trying to nail the man at second.

It smacked off the bridge of the man's nose, and he stumbled backwards, cracking his skull off the doorjamb as he fell to his backside.

Bob ran straight into the kick, a soccer goalie boot that caught the prone guard under the chin and made sure he wouldn't retaliate. From the corner of his eye, through the doorway, he saw the third guard crouched on one knee for balance. Bob threw himself backwards, into the cover of the wall, putting a few feet of extra space between himself and the doorjamb, bullets perforating the drywall.

On the floor a few feet away, the second guard's pistol lay two inches from his hand. Bob stretched one leg out, past the opening, his toe almost able to reach… and then snatched it back, the remaining guard firing three more shots into the plaster and drywall behind him.

Shit. Have to get that piece. And he had to do it quickly. Its owner had been out cold for at least thirty seconds, which meant he was liable to wake any moment.

The third guard hadn't put two and two together yet to take advantage of Bob not having a gun and the ability to shoot him through the wall. *But he's bound to.*

Stretching for it hadn't worked. Bob took a couple of steps backwards and leaped forward, flying past the door opening, the gunshots too late. He crouched and picked up the Sig Sauer P220. The second guard began to wake, eyes swimming in their sockets as he leaned his head forward. Bob threw a hard backhand left at his chin, using the pistol to knock him out again.

He peeked around the edge of the doorjamb in time to see the third guard slam a fresh mag home. Above him, on the ceiling, a modern art chandelier in tiers of smoked glass pyramids lit the huge open-plan penthouse brightly. Bob lined up the Sig's sights and fired twice, the chandelier cord severed, the massive objet d'art crashing down on his opponent.

The man tried to move, twice, then lay still, pinned down.

Bob checked the room one more time, then reached into his pocket and took out a second set of wrist restraints. He bound the second guard's hands.

Then he rose and moved to the doorway, leaning quickly in and around, checking both sides.

The living room to the right and kitchen to the left were both empty. There was a short corridor at the back, along with two doors on the back wall to other rooms.

Now where has he gotten himself to? Brown had a fearsome rep, according to Jasmine, which suggested he'd bunker in, maybe in a master bedroom.

But... that guy, the guy who takes control. He'd have been out here from the start, trying to take me out. So maybe...

He let the thought hang, bracing the pistol with his left hand as he entered the living room. In the near corner, a door led to a wide balcony, barely perceptible through the interior reflections on the wraparound windows. Bob moved cautiously, creeping towards the door, alert to any movement he might glimpse through the glass.

He opened the door slowly.

Then he lowered his pistol.

At the far end of the balcony, the fearsome Pascal Brown had climbed over the edge of the wall and was trying to negotiate a narrow ledge that led to the balcony on the other side of the building. It was about the width of his sneakered foot.

Bob strolled over to the end of the balcony, about four feet from the man. "That looks perilous." He resisted the urge to warn the man not to look down, which would probably have caused just that and, possibly, cost him his chance to ask any questions. "I'm guessing you ran out there as the nearest exit, then realized you had nowhere to go."

"I've got money," Brown said, his demeanor verging on terrified.

Bob smiled wryly.

Sometimes, a reputation was just that, nothing more.

Five minutes later, Pascal Brown was seated at the far end of the massive sectional sofa. He had the physique of a middleweight boxer, but his nerves had obviously been shaken by the incident.

Bob couldn't remember the last time he'd been that shaken by anything. He felt a pang of sympathy for the little dude.

At the back of the room, his three guards were seated on dining chairs from the breakfast nook, the man from the elevator binding the first guard's leg wounds. Two of the three shots had struck him, passing through cleanly.

The four men looked disconsolate, like naughty schoolchildren. Bob had left the wrist ties on two of them to both make the point of who was in charge, and to be careful. One of them had a black eye, swollen shut after being hit by the heavy chandelier.

The penthouse was thoroughly soundproofed, Brown had insisted, so that his friends could party unimpeded by annoyed neighbors.

"Also convenient if you ever need to shoot someone," Bob had mentioned as they sat down, ten feet apart. Bob put his pistol on the glass-and-steel coffee table. Brown was shaken; the best approach was to let him think Bob knew what he was up to.

"Man... do you know how much that light fixture cost?"

"Nope. Don't care, either," Bob said.

"More than my mama' s house. And... I don't ever need to shoot no one," Brown said with mild incredulity. "Who do you think I am?"

"The biggest coke dealer in City Heights."

"Well... I mean, that's what some people say. But I don't need to shoot people. Guys in my crew, guys in other crews, sometimes they trade blows, you know? I don't demand that. I don't sanction that."

"Good to know. You're a gentle gangster."

"No, I'm a wise businessman," Brown said. "You have an easy time tracking me down?"

"No."

"That's my point. Don't believe the hype, man. You think I'm some movie gangster who wants to rule the 'hood or some shit."

"Well? Don't you?"

"Man..." Brown sounded genuinely frustrated. "Have you ever even seen me in City Heights? Look at where I live. When I look out at the water from my balcony, do you think I'm really thinking about the 'hood? I moved to this address to get away from that life."

"It's not that far away."

"It's not far enough," Brown said. "Just as far as I can go and still make the money I make. You going to kill me?"

"Nope." Bob had to admit, he was considerably less loathsome than he'd expected. *Probably ruthless as shit when it's not scared out of him, though.* "Eric Williams. Why? He's a good kid."

Brown nodded. "Jasmine's brother. What? You think I had something to do with that?"

"That's the general consensus."

"Yeah, well... the same people probably told you I'm the reincarnation of Freeway Rick, right?"

Bob nodded. "So explain. Who else, in City Heights...?"

Brown was already shaking his head. “Man… I do not know.”

“Come on, Pascal, you can do better than that. Give me a reason, a rationale that will help me keep my temper.”

He said it flatly, devoid of emotion. In Bob’s experience, it unsettled people.

The dealer was no different. “Look… just… be cool, okay? Just chill. All I know is that about a year ago, there was new competition. I mean, real cheap product, being fronted by some outfit from out east somewhere.”

“Because?”

“Associates who supply me were seeing the same stuff in Chicago, Detroit and San Francisco. But there was no sign of how the stuff was coming into the city, and nobody – but *nobody* – was talking.”

If the guy was lying, he was damn good at it. It was entirely possible, Bob knew. But his intuition was that Brown was telling it straight. “So, who in this town has connections in those cities and Colombia?” Bob wondered.

Brown raised both palms and shook his head gently. “You’ve got me, man. You’ve got me.” He licked his lower lip quickly, and Bob braced for an emboldened question. “You… working for his sister? You five-oh?”

The badge. The men at his other apartment. “About that,” Bob said, ducking the question. “Why’d you grab her? She thought they were going to assault her.”

Brown looked down at his shoes, mortified. “Man… I just said to hold her for a few hours. I wanted to talk to her, tell her I asked Eric to work for me but that I wasn’t going to hassle him or nothing. We, like… we need the inner-city folk to get along, to not worry about us, not make too much noise to the powers that be. You feel me? They weren’t supposed to scare her even a little. Look… the entire God's honest truth is that I don't know who set Eric up. But the answer's probably wherever he was in Colombia, not in City Heights."

"Yeah? You figure if Eric was available, he'd see it that way? He as fond of you as you are of him?"

He tilted his head and gave Bob a withering look. "Man… I know who I am, okay? And who Eric is. I shot my shot, and he wasn't interested. He ain't no fan of mine."

Bob rose. "I'm going to leave. If I encounter any resistance or you send someone gunning for me, I'll be less charitable than I was tonight."

"That's… it?" Brown's doubt was writ large. "You ain't gonna…"

"No, man. Despite a few people's belief to the contrary, I don't really like shooting people, either."

Bob headed for the door, keeping a wary eye over his shoulder on Brown and his men. "If we're both lucky, we won't run into each other again, Mr. Brown," he said.

"No argument here," Brown said. "But you'd better expect trouble downstairs. My apartment is soundproof; I highly doubt the same is true of the elevators. So those first few shots you took at my guys…"

"They fired first."

"Still and all… won't satisfy any cops downstairs. Without a warrant or probable cause in the moment, I can tell them to fuck off when they knock on my door. Dude wandering through the lobby won't be so lucky."

"Point taken," Bob said before disappearing down the hall.

9

Bob took the elevator down but hit buttons for both the second floor and the lobby. That way, anyone waiting for the car would presume someone else got on before its arrival.

Instead, when the doors pinged and opened, he got out and followed the second-floor hallway to the rear emergency stairs. He trotted down them briskly, taking them one at a time to avoid additional noise, pausing occasionally to look down the center well, between banisters, to see if anyone was obviously waiting below.

At the building's back door, he pocketed the pistol. He paused for a few beats to make sure no one had heard him on the stairs and was waiting to ambush him. When no one else pushed the back door open, he did so slowly, making sure to take a peek outside as soon as the gap was wide enough for his head.

A pistol brushed his temple. "Out, now!" The police officer yanked the door open and backed away before he could snatch the piece.

"Hands behind your head. Up against the wall!"

Bob did as commanded. They'd probably split up, his patrol partner checking out the fourteenth floor. He knew what came next, and was ready. As he leaned forward and placed his hands against the wall, the officer leaned in with one foot to kick his feet shoulder-width apart. Bob reacted before first contact, throwing his right foot up and back, his heel hammering the officer in the groin.

He felt testicles compress and winced, even as the officer collapsed to his knees, dropped his gun and vomited. "Geez... really sorry about this," Bob said. He leaned in, smacking the officer in the chin with his right hand, knocking him out. He remained leaning and caught the man before he fell over, lowering him to the ground gently.

Ah, hell. Don't feel good about that, he thought as he headed down the alley and away from the building.

JASMINE LIKED to get to work early. Bob had barely been asleep for six hours when the sun came up, and her phone call came shortly thereafter.

"So tell me straight: was Pascal Brown's apartment in a building along Third Street?"

Bob rubbed his scalp and squinted through one open eye, sunlight peeking through the apartment's bedroom window. "Annnnd... good day to you, too," he said.

"Answer the question."

Ah, hell. She's heard something. No point lying; no good will come from it. "I believe it was, yes."

"ARE YOU KIDDING ME?!"

Bob pulled the receiver away from his ear to avoid losing an eardrum. When she'd stopped yelling, he cautiously repositioned it. "Is that really necessary at six thirty in the morning?"

"You promised nobody would be hurt!"

"I promised nobody would be killed. I also tried to make sure no one was hurt."

"And yet there's a news story on KOGO this morning that a police officer was assaulted after a gun call last night. 'Residents were uncooperative,' it said. So what happened?"

"Well... for one, Pascal Brown was not exactly as advertised. He's... built up a bit of a legend. The actual guy is more measured, less street. We had a chat."

"You had a CHAT?! And then... what, five-oh knocked on his door, and he hit the guy? What? What happened?"

"Brown didn't do anything to anyone except have his men try to dissuade my visit. Shots were traded, but nobody was seriously hurt."

"Except the officer."

"What!?" Bob was genuinely surprised. "What happened? What did they say?"

"Oh, NOW you're worried. I mean, they said he'd been released after a hospital check. But the fact that they even had to take him..." She let the thought trail, sounding horrified.

"Oh, for crying out loud!" Bob paused, then exhaled hard, the tension ratcheting up. "Look, getting a concussion check does not fit into what I'd term a 'serious injury,' Jasmine. In fact, it's standard procedure any time someone in law enforcement takes a blow to the head."

"A BLOW TO THE HEAD?!"

Oh, for pity's sake, woman... Bob held his tongue. She wasn't wrong, really. Hurting a cop wasn't ever his ideal goal. Instead, he said, "Look, I get what you're saying, but he's not hurt, and it was necessary to avoid being arrested. In the meantime, I notice you haven't asked me yet about Eric's situation."

"Because I'm worried about another human being other than my brother, who is locked up," she said. "Has it occurred to you that maybe – just maybe – your pursuit of this is verging into 'relentless' territory? I mean... I love that you're trying to help, but this has clearly spiraled out of control," she said.

"He said he had nothing to do with your brother."

"Shocker."

"But he also said he believes someone framed him, the same person who's been flooding City Heights with cheap dope for months."

That gave her pause. As worried as she was about others and appearances, Jasmine knew her neighborhood better than most. "Really? He told you that?"

"He did. He thinks they're bringing the stuff in from Colombia, and it's showing up in other cities as well. That suggests a large, coordinated effort, not one local kid smuggling a few keys."

"Wow."

"Yeah, you got that right. Anyway, what I really need is more information about the charity he was working with, other people who'd have access to his suitcase, maybe to other volunteers as well."

"Well, then it's a good thing I've arranged a meeting with its founder, Father McKay, with the Catholic archdiocese."

"That's good."

"Assuming you don't punch him out."

"Hey... be nice."

"I'm trying, Bob, really. It's advice you could probably heed as well."

"When's the meeting?"

"This afternoon. You... said you wanted to speak with Eric as well?"

"Yep."

"He's still in pretrial lockup. No access except his lawyer, at his request. I can get him a list of questions, though, potentially."

That wasn't ideal, Bob knew. There was probably some detail, something he'd seen that he wouldn't have already told Jasmine. But there didn't seem to be any way around it.

"Okay. So we'll see what Father McKay has to say first," Bob said. "Maybe once we've dug around a bit, I'll have something to ask his lawyer."

10

It took Bob another half hour to get dressed and downtown. The offices of the diocese were in a vast former convent, formerly run by the Benedictine Sisters of Perpetual Adoration, the buildings in the style of a whitewashed old Spanish mission complete with bell tower.

The entire complex was impressive, Bob figured as he parked the Hyundai beater. A few spaces away, Jasmine got out of her ten-year-old Chevy sedan and waited for him to join her. She looked less enamored as they strolled under the palm trees, towards the offices of Father Jensen McKay. It was typically warm, the sky brilliantly clear and blue, the temperatures drifting towards 90 F. The place seemed appropriately pastoral and quiet, with just the call of seagulls for background noise.

"What's up?" Bob asked. "You look like something's eating at you."

"It's nothing."

"I mean, I know you're from here, so you've probably seen all this a thousand times but—"

"It's not that." She stopped walking and crossed her arms nervously. "I… just feel a little like we're accusing the man of something."

"That's not my intention," Bob said. "Really. We just need to know as much about the Colombia end of things as possible, and he goes down there on the regular."

She nodded, but didn't look up at him. Instead, she said softly, "You're sure about Pascal Brown?"

"I think so, yeah."

She composed herself. "Okay. Okay then, let's go talk to Father McKay."

Father McKay answered his own office door. "Come in, come in! Very nice to see you again, Ms. Williams."

His office was formal, with deep-piled carpet, teak bookshelves on both walls, a grand, carved walnut desk by the arched, wood-framed windows. Near the entrance was a small seating area with a pair of undersized antique Louis XVI-style cabriole-leg sofas and a wingback chair. "Please…" He gestured to the sofas as he planted himself in the wingback.

Bob sat on one, Jasmine on the other.

"Now, Jasmine, you mentioned Mr. Davis had some questions about Hope Street?" He turned Bob's way. "And who are you with, Mr. Davis?"

"I'm a friend of Eric's," Bob said. "I'm volunteering right now, working on a home project for Jasmine."

"Your group does fine work," Father McKay said. He clasped his hands together on his knee and leaned forward slightly as he spoke. He had a creased face and bulbous nose, his half-sized glasses slipping down it slightly. Bob figured it gave him an aura of Big Grandpa energy. "But I must admit, I don't really know much about what happened. I'd only met Eric on a handful of occasions."

"In Colombia, they must work with locals, I assume," Bob said. "Is it possible someone slipped something by your people?"

"Oh! I see where you're going with this, Mr. Davis, but I'm afraid I'm not the person to help. You see, all of our operations there, in terms of actually distributing the clothing, are fully secured and audited by SatMast International, our main benefactor."

Bob shrugged. "Apologies. I'm guessing I should be familiar?"

"SatMast is one of San Diego's biggest telecom firms," Jasmine said. "It's owned by Anderson Rowe. It has a charitable branch called Love and Light that funds many ventures for the poor."

That name was more familiar. "Silicon Valley doucheb… businessman?" Bob suggested, catching himself, but not in time to prevent a sour look from the priest.

"Mr. Rowe is one of the most generous of the original Silicon Valley tech giants," Father McKay said, his tone more patient than condemnatory. "His charities donate millions of dollars to help the poor across this country every year, Mr. Davis, and I'd thank you to please be more respectful. Clearly my office is not a house of God, but he dwells within each of us."

That was one way of looking at it. The article Bob had read about Rowe on a long cross-country bus ride had suggested he was also a creative destructionist: he believed that forcing social mechanisms to break down and fail is the best way to rebuild and improve them quickly. He'd given millions of dollars to crypto companies, to anti-government agencies, to politicians who'd de-regulate businesses of things like environmental and employee protections.

There was no indication in the piece that he worried much about the people affected by those "creative" failures.

"He's an interesting man," Bob said tactfully. "He funds Hope Street in San Diego?"

"For the most part, he funds it across the country, doing God's work to minister to those most in need. His subsidiary company, Love and Light, takes clothing and household good donations to our southern neighbors and funds trips for optometrist care to the poorest rural regions of Colombia, Bolivia, and Guatemala. They then bring back arts and crafts created by artist collectives and sell them to the market here, returning the money to the collective."

"It's incredibly important work," Jasmine echoed. "The income isn't a lot, but it helps to both raise the artisans out of poverty and preserve traditional culture."

Clever. She can sense I make the priest edgy, so she doubles down on Hope Street's value. "Did the police visit?" Bob asked. "I'd assume they'd want more information on Eric's behavior."

Father McKay nodded. "A detective from the airport outfit. They were most polite and seemed genuinely surprised that Eric didn't have gang affiliations."

"Did they say anything about the arrest?"

"The detective seemed to think it was a matter of opportunity," Father McKay said. "The inserts Eric used—" He caught himself and looked over at Jasmine sheepishly. "My apologies. The inserts that they found in Eric's case were clever, a mix of lead and ceramic material. They sat just inside each side of the case and presented the interior as legitimate if scanned. But they think he was banking on the bag not being opened."

"Why's that?" Bob asked.

"The charity has volunteers bringing back dozens of cases of charity materials per week and has a customs waiver, based on its longstanding social value and Love and Light's standing with the federal government. Like all waiver recipients, they have to endure the odd spot check, but for the most part, their imports aren't inspected."

"Ideal for someone wanting to get something into the country undetected," Bob said. He glanced quickly at Jasmine; she was looking increasingly uncomfortable.

"We do criminal background checks on all of our volunteers. Of course, in Eric's case his only arrest – which he told us about personally – was as a juvenile. So there was nothing to indicate—"

"Because he hasn't done anything wrong," Jasmine interjected, uncrossing her legs to lean in forcefully as she said it, her voice strong. "Let's please keep that in mind, Father."

Bob could sense her building irritation. He needed to get the subject off Eric. "And does Mr. Rowe know about all this? How has he reacted?"

"I am told he is quite perturbed," Father McKay said. "We have not talked in person yet about it, as such, but his team passed along some helpful media advice in case reporters call. I'm quite sure he's very busy."

"But he'll make time for someone trying to work this all out, right?" Bob asked, gently putting the priest on the spot. "I'm sure you could make a call and smooth the way, for all the good work Jasmine's done in your parish."

If the request irritated the priest, he hid it well, Bob

thought. “Of course, Mr. Davis. I’m sure he can find a few minutes.”

11

A few minutes turned out to be a "ten-minute window" the next afternoon at SatMast's headquarters, according to Rowe's personal assistant.

The building was less modest than the description. Sitting in prime real estate on the waterfront's North Harbor Drive, the three-story brick complex featured a massive office complex on one side, including a charitable outreach at street level. On the other side, a nightclub, the Surf, occupied the entire top level. Below it, there were two floors of boutiques, including a pair of marijuana dispensaries, all three levels connected by traditional mall escalators.

It seemed busy enough, people crossing the lobby, dress shoes clopping on polished marble. There was a reception desk towards the back of the area and, past it, glass doors to the business's first-floor office.

An elevator adjacent to the charity's interior entrance led up to the second-floor reception, which was spartan in ecru marble and smoked glass. Bob waited for five minutes, turning down a coffee from the receptionist. Eventually, a man trotted down the stairs from the third floor.

He was broad shouldered, squat, built like a rugby player. He looked vaguely familiar, Bob thought immediately, but he couldn't place him.

"Mr. Davis?" He held out a meaty hand to shake. "I'm Sebastian, Mr. Rowe's personal assistant. Would you like to follow me?"

"Sure."

They headed towards the stairs and began to climb them. "Did they offer you a coffee or water?" Sebastian asked.

"Yeah. I'm good," Bob said. The man's demeanor was perfectly normal, but for some reason, Bob's hackles were up. He looked around as they entered the third-floor lobby, where a single receptionist sat at a desk closer to the stairs. Behind her, there were two doors on the left wall, one to the rear.

"These are our executive offices," Sebastian explained. "Mr. Rowe designed the building to be the most energy-efficient mixed office/retail space in the entire Greater San Diego area."

"Sounds sensible."

"Mr. Rowe is an eminently sensible man, a champion of the environment and a great gift to humanity. His philosophies are what make SatMast the global powerhouse it is today." There was a certain reverence to his tone, like a college student describing a professor they worship.

They approached the desk.

"He'll see you now," the receptionist said, barely looking up.

They walked past her to the single door on the wall.

They were still five feet away when it swung open, a slight, fiftyish man with tight gray-white curls leaning out, shirt-sleeves pushed up, tie knot down. "Ah, yes! Come in, you two, come in!" he enthused, beckoning for them to move quickly. He had beady blue eyes and exuded energy.

They entered after him. The office was enormous, taking up a third of the floor's square footage, ceilings fifteen feet above, a modern industrial feel to it, the walls featuring exposed brick and artworks. The entire back wall from top to bottom had been converted into a gigantic aquarium running the width of the building, more than sixty feet. Fish ranging from fitting in a palm to the size of a small dog flitted past each other in hues of purple, red and gray, some mottled, others striped, some rounded, others diamond shaped or elongated. At the west end, it seemed to have a sharp corner, as if emptying into a large space behind the wall.

"Mr. Rowe, sir," Sebastian said, "this is Bob Davis, Jasmine Williams's friend."

"Yeeesss..." The businessman looked him up and down. He clapped his hands together as if acknowledging how nice it was to have visitors. "Coffee, Bob? Tea?" He gave off a Willy-Wonka-meets-your-grandfather vibe, Bob figured.

Not what I was expecting. "I'm good."

"As long as we asked!" Rowe enthused. He turned his head quickly to follow Bob's line of sight. "Ah! I see you're admiring the tank. Yes... my pride and joy, really."

At the bottom of the tank, a three-foot-tall gray-blue octopus slithered across the sand and disappeared into the murky backdrop. Schools of smaller tropical fish flitted past, to the far right end of the tank, where they seemed to vanish.

"Where does it go? They seem to disappear around the corner, some of them." Bob gestured with a flick of his head.

"Ah, yes! You may have noticed the back wall of the third floor appears to make the room much smaller than it appears outside. That's hiding their storage tank, where they have much more space to move around and a more ideal ecosystem that we've created for them."

Bob watched as an aquiline, flat nose appeared around the corner, the figure getting larger as a giant fish entered the visible portion of the tank, a jet-black eye set high in the left side of its head. Its mouth gaped wide enough to accommodate a microwave, the barest outline of its jagged teeth visible. It was perhaps six feet long, its tail thicker than Bob's thigh.

"That's Roger, our blue shark," Rowe said, shoving his hands casually into his trouser pockets, his body language relaxed as he studied his prize. "He was going to be put down because of a chondroma – that's sort of what we'd call a cancer of the cartilage. We put a fair amount of resources behind helping him instead, took him away from the water park that was showing him off. Now he's got twice the tank size and a chance to maybe enjoy life a little longer."

"How do you keep him from—" Before Bob could finish the sentence, Roger suddenly accelerated, swishing his tail to drive him forward, his mouth opening wider as it enveloped a stingray, the flat fish fairly sucked into his maw, as if it had its own undertow. The teeth slammed shut.

Bob peered past him, the water bending light, warping the glass on the other side of the tank. "Is that... What is that, on the other side?"

"A nightclub. They rent the top floor of the adjoining property, for a considerable sum, I'm happy to say. They were quite happy to design their interior around the wall; the young people like it, I suppose."

"The noise doesn't bother you?"

Rowe reached out and tapped the glass. "Extra thick safety glass on my side. Safety glass on both sides, of course, but double thickness here so that I can have quiet, should I be working late. Roger appreciates it too, I'm sure. Don't you, Roger?" He put his palm on the glass just then, as if trying to pet the shark.

It ignored the gesture, shooting ahead and swallowing a pizza-sized fish in one gulp.

"He does cost us quite a bit in replacing the other fish, of course," Rowe said with a tiny smile. "But it sure felt better than just letting such a magnificent creature die. Now..." He turned Bob's way. "I don't have long, unfortunately, Mr. Davis. But I'll help however I can, of course."

He wandered over towards his desk, by a picture window affording him a view of the bay, and sat down in a leather chair, gesturing to the one ahead of it.

"Hope Street," Bob said, sitting down. "Have you ever run into anything like this drug thing before? It sounds almost too sophisticated for one nineteen-year-old kid, to have a suitcase with special X-ray-defeating inserts. And to move only a hundred K in drugs? That seems a lot of risk."

Rowe nodded, arching his fingers together ahead of him like a mindful psychiatrist. "Indeed, indeed. All questions I might ask myself. Of course, they did catch young Mr. Williams somewhat red-handed, as it were." He seemed almost embarrassed to be discussing it. "I don't mean to condemn; I did not have to grow up in the inner city, as he did, or have the kind of life pressures that would reduce me to... well, to such unfortunate circumstances."

"His sister feels he was set up, that it's just too out of character."

"Perhaps she's right." Then he looked down at his desktop. "It doesn't seem likely, unfortunately. From what the police have told us, that's not usually the case. That's the most disappointing part. I can remember a time, when we started Hope Street thirty years ago, that the sheer idea of using good, Christian people to smuggle drugs would've been... well, it would've been unthinkable."

Eddie Albert, Bob thought. *That's who he reminds me of. The dude from* Green Acres, *but if he was playing a pastor.*

There was something just slightly off about it. *He's the soul of charity, but his favorite pet is a shark? His building is a hub for the downtrodden but shares space with a nightclub and weed stores?*

"It's nice that you take such an ecumenical approach to the local poor," Bob said. "I'm a little surprised, though."

"Oh?"

A few feet away, Rowe's personal assistant shifted slightly in place. Bob noticed he'd spread his feet shoulder-width apart, his hands clasped behind him, as if "at ease." *He's ex-military.* The slight shift in body language had been pronounced, caution rearing its head as soon as Bob mentioned being surprised. He'd also double-knotted the shoelaces of his sensible black Clarks.

"I read a piece on you in *Byte* a few years ago," Bob said. "You started as a Silicon Valley tech bro, didn't you? The Great Disruptor, they nicknamed you in the eighties."

"And like many of us, Mr. Davis, I must concede that I was not a particularly well-adjusted young man. I left that world to the Musks and Zuckerbergs among us."

"Yeah... still, I tried to find an article between the old

days and your move to the charity NGO space twenty years ago in which you actually renounced all that stuff about creative destruction. You know, forced social upheaval to weed out the weak, create a stronger and presumably more blue-eyed America."

Rowe gave him a disappointed look. "Really, Bob? Can I call you Bob?"

"It's finc."

"Blue-eyed America? That seemed an analogy, if I read it right. Bob, do I really strike you as a fascist? I won't apologize for having my beliefs, and those beliefs coming with morals discordant with the way that I used to behave. I can only apologize for the way I used to behave. Do you understand where I'm coming from?"

I mean, more than you know.

The man sounded sincere. He looked sincere.

He just doesn't feel sincere. There' s something... off. But there was no point in raising it until he figured out what; it wouldn't have been the first time he'd misjudged someone for not much good reason. "Okay, Mr. Rowe, my apologies," Bob said. "That was a little harsh, I'll give you that. But you understand my curiosity."

"I'm accustomed to some level of public fascination. I was deeply fortunate to be an early tech billionaire, and that comes with the unfortunate reality of near-constant publicity," Rowe said. "But... as I said earlier, I do have limited time today."

"Just a couple more questions, if that's okay," Bob said. "Did the police ask you about any of your other volunteers or operations?"

Rowe shook his head. "No, not at all. SatMast, the firm I founded, has always had an excellent working relationship with our boys in blue across the country, long before we founded Love and Light. They were very reasonable."

"And you? Are you auditing the remainder of your volunteers or their peers in Colombia?"

Rowe waved a hand dismissively. "No, no, of course not. These are good Christian people, Mr. Davis, folk who take off their own time and give to those who need it most."

That didn't match what Father McKay had claimed. He'd said Love and Light audited everyone.

"Mr. Williams made an unfortunate choice," he continued. "I wish that hadn't been the case, I truly do. But I am most grateful that it was an isolated incident, and that we can continue doing our good work. Now... if you don't object, I am going to be late for a call."

"Thank you for your time," Bob said, rising.

"Sebastian will see you out."

12

Rowe's personal assistant followed Bob all the way to the parking lot. "If you have anything else you need," he said, handing Bob a business card. Bob pocketed it.

"All the way back to my car. You're very attentive," Bob said.

"Mr. Rowe has given all of his employees a chance to better themselves and our society," he said. "That requires a level of respect and loyalty. He is a visionary."

"Ah. See, that's good to know. Because if I didn't know better, I'd think you were trying to identify my ride." He nodded towards Sebastian. "You're ex-military, right?"

"That obvious?"

"Uh-huh. Double knot your boots, and when you stand casual, you're at ease."

"I don't talk about it much," Sebastian said.

"Tough time?"

"No. I enjoyed my service. But many guys didn't, and I

don't really want to hear about it. I find life is more productive when we don't kowtow to weakness."

Ah. Tough guy. He looked young. Maybe he'd have a deeper take on it later on, maybe not. Bob knew both kinds were common enough.

Bob opened the car door. "Well… thanks for your help."

Sebastian crossed his arms but made no motion to leave. "You're welcome."

Bob started the engine and put the car into gear. As the car left the parking garage, he checked the rearview mirror. Sebastian still hadn't moved.

SEBASTIAN KRUG RETURNED to the third-floor office. Rowe was standing by the window, looking out at the parking area, as if keeping watch.

"He's gone?"

"Yes, sir. I have someone following his vehicle, assuming it makes it more than a few blocks. It seemed in poor repair."

"Probably wise," Rowe said. "Best to know exactly who this gentleman is and what we're dealing with before we sort it."

"Of course, sir."

"What else do we know?"

"Our contacts at the district attorney's office said he was there yesterday, and sent us a still image. Definitely the same man. He met with Jim Sheinbein."

"He's the anti-gang crusader type, yes? I see his name in the paper quite often."

"Yes, sir. A good man by all accounts. A good assistant district attorney, anyway."

"Any idea of what they discussed?"

"No, sir, nothing. Sheinbein is quite careful. But the obvious conclusion would be Mr. Bob Davis figured Sheinbein might listen to a friend of Jasmine Williams and take another look at her brother's case."

Rowe frowned and rubbed his chin thoughtfully. "Hmmm. Can't have that, can we? Mr. Davis probably thinks he's doing the right thing or some other noble motivation. But he's interfering with a complex series of plans that are far above him."

It was a novel way of describing a vast smuggling network, Krug figured. But Rowe was a quirky sort of individual. Krug was fairly sure he was gay and as weird as the visitors to his Sunset Cliffs mansion. In civilian life, if they'd met in a bar, Krug supposed he'd have beaten the old man half to death.

But he paid on time, treated his employees well, and respected Krug's opinion on most security matters. He'd been successful at every business venture he touched, and he abhorred weakness. His personal life, Krug figured, was his own business.

"What else has he been up to?"

"We have reliable word from our street subsidiaries that he was carving a path through City Heights. But he wasn't coming after our people. He was looking for Pascal Brown."

"And?"

"We suspect he found him. There was a news report this morning about a police disturbance at Brown's building last night, with an officer being injured."

Rowe winced visibly. "Can't have that. We're patrons of their retirement and disability fund, you know."

"Yes, sir."

"Your assessment?" Rowe turned his way, his watery blue

eyes suddenly seeming darker to Krug, peering through him curiously.

"He's ex-military, so that presents problematic possibilities. The episode last night... we don't know enough to really say. But the fact that he would even try to track down a dealer of Brown's magnitude suggests he'll go to abnormal lengths. Is he dangerous to us? Not really. He's one man, probably with a Don Quixote complex: he needs to tilt at windmills to feel any sense of empowerment now that he's no longer in a squad."

Privately, Krug could admit to himself, the man had made his collar itch. There was something a little wrong with Bob Davis, a quiet confidence maybe. *No. That's not it. It's like the risk aren't even really registering. A man like that might go to dangerous lengths.*

But they'd be dangerous to Bob Davis, Krug figured. At any given time, Rowe had nearly two dozen armed men surrounding him, just in San Diego.

"So you think we should leave him alone?"

"I wouldn't say just that. We need to keep an eye on him."

Rowe crossed one arm over himself and propped his other elbow on it as he scratched his chin again, like a farmer weighing up a bid on a prized heifer. "Right, right." He took a deep breath. "Well... you'll have to kill him, of course."

Krug hid his surprise. But the question just came out naturally. "Sir?" *Did he hear anything I just said?*

Rowe stared out at the Pacific Ocean. "Ohhh, I know. You youngsters always want to look for the best of all possible options. But when you get older, you'll learn that, usually, the most obvious answer is right in front of you. As you said, he's no threat to us because we have the strength of numbers. But given enough time, there are ways to overcome brute force."

"You think he'll gather enough intel—"

"To hurt us? Still doesn't seem likely, I admit," the billionaire said. "But I'm not fond of leaving the possibility open. He's of no value to anyone. Once your man finds out where he lives, set something up. He's been asking around after Pascal Brown all over town. So no one will be surprised by his sudden demise."

Krug gave him a stiff, formal half bow. "Sir." He headed for the doors, slightly perturbed. Rowe had always been exceedingly cautious, but this seemed hasty, an act of a man worrying a little too much.

Eventually, that kind of man would flail around, draw attention from other predators. But not Rowe, he suspected. He had everything going for him, no reason to panic.

Bob Davis wouldn't be any problem. *And if the old man's happy, everyone's happy.*

13

The little café had been a fixture on Fourth Avenue for more than a decade. It had a striped red, white and blue awning above its door and over the larger picture window. It was smack-dab in the middle of the Gaslamp Quarter, amidst hundred-year-old two-story warehouses of red brick and wood, reborn in the pastel shades of the modern age as restaurants, nightclubs and boutiques.

It was also at the same address as one on Bob's list, obtained so many months earlier in New Orleans.

But it sure didn't look like the right place.

He rubbed the newly created stubble on his chin. He'd enjoyed the beard, but it was already uncomfortable in San Diego's relatively dry heat; it would've been brutal in the sweltering conditions of Colombia. He also figured that even if Pascal Brown played ball, there was no guaranteeing his crew would. A change of appearance seemed in order.

The Buttered Crumpet advertised itself in small gold letters on the glass front door as "San Diego's Most

Authentic English Tea Shop." Underneath the scroll was an adroitly hand-painted Union Jack.

Bob pushed the door open. A bell tinkled brightly.

A reception counter and register sat by the front door. Inside, the lights were subdued, a series of two- and four-person tables peppering the hardwood floor space between two walls of booths. At the back, a counter held pasties and sausage rolls, a board on the wall behind the two clerks promising fresh-baked steak-and-kidney pies, Yorkshire pudding wraps and clotted cream with strawberries.

"Good afternoon, sir," the man at the register enthused. "Table for one?"

"I'm a friend of John Butcher," Bob said.

The man's eyebrows shot up, but only for a moment. "Ah, I see." He turned to the woman, who looked easily twenty years younger. "Rosemary, dear, if you'd cover the till for a little bit, I shan't be long."

"Of course, darling." She leaned up and pecked him on the cheek.

The man walked to the deli counter at the back of the room and gestured for Bob to join him. They walked behind the counter and through a beaded curtain. Behind it, a short corridor was partially occupied by a bookshelf. He leaned in and rolled it to one side, the bottom on casters and runners. An undersized doorway led down a flight of rickety wooden steps.

Bob followed him down. In the basement, the café owner switched on the overhead light. The room was mostly filled to Bob's left by a series of plain wooden tables, some older than others, each covered in surveillance gear: video cameras, SLRs, fiber-optic setups, boom mics, shotgun mics, long-range zoom lenses, FLIR googles.

To his right, the man had a drafting table set up at one end of the room, followed by a camera similar to the ones Bob had seen at the motor vehicles department. Nearer the door, a pair of monitors sat atop a corner desk.

"I assume you're here for paper," the man said, his English accent clipped and formal. "One doesn't usually get unfamiliar faces inquiring after gear, and if John is your reference, one must assume you're traveling."

"Right and right again," Bob said.

"And how soon do we need this?"

"Yesterday, basically. As soon as you can do it."

"And we're expecting...?"

"Passport."

"Well, for my best work, we would be looking at three to five days."

That was a long time with Eric in jail, Bob figured. "Too long. What about your 'so good it'll pass anywhere even though it's not my best' work?"

The forger studied him, clearly uncomfortable. "Well, I should say – and this is no criticism of you, by any means – that that is a very short timeframe, indeed. I could, potentially, get you something by tomorrow. But it would take a great many consecutive hours of work, putting considerable strain on my dear wife to handle everything."

"You can skip the why and go right to the 'how much,'" Bob said. The mannerisms and deference were all English middle class, a private school boy who'd somehow found himself supplying corporate spooks and assorted criminals. That and his manner suggested a past in one of the intelligence services.

But he didn't raise it. If he nailed the details the first time, the guy would assume they were known to each other, and that would be difficult, fraught with tensions.

"Thirty-five thousand," the forger said. "Up front, of course."

Jesus H. "That's... Look, I'm trying to help a kid out who's in trouble," he said, knowing before the words left his mouth that it would be futile.

"And I'm trying to maintain my livelihood and keep my rather sensational young spouse happy," he said. "The rate is the rate."

It was almost everything Bob had left. Coupled with a plane ticket to Bogota, he knew he'd be broke before the end of the month, with rent still to pay.

But there wasn't really any choice. If he was going to find out how Eric Williams wound up carrying seven kilos of coke, he was going to have to leave the country.

"Fine," Bob said. "I'll be back in an hour with the money."

Bob headed back out and towards his car. The money was sitting in a "Bob Davis" account, so accessing it wasn't a problem. Collecting it in the first place had been; most of it was left over from a meth operation shut down in California, the rest from a sociopath he'd disposed of in New York.

But windfalls didn't just fall into his lap. There were always people around whom he'd feel just fine robbing – dealers, gangsters, loan sharks – but that was never as easy as just dropping by; they usually protected their cash in the short period they held it before washing it, usually through a front business, casino chip buy or crypto purchase. That meant any place he hit would require facing a team of guys who knew how to shoot. In the movies, the hero could just mention dropping by a crack den and liberating thousands as a throwaway line; in Bob's world, he'd found things typically more complicated than that.

But I can worry about money later. Right now, Jasmine's brother is the priority.

TWO HOURS LATER, he was pulling up in the parking lot behind his apartment building, the only open slot near the road. He put the car into park and shut off the engine.

He had a promise from Charlie, the forger, that his paper would be ready by noon the next day... along with the realization he was going to have to find a proper paying job.

But it had to be done. Going to Colombia without top-class paper was a world of risk. Bad paper leading to him being caught would mean questions about why he had no fingerprints. People would begin making calls, searching databases. Word would filter back, probably to the National Security Agency first, then to the CIA and Team Seven.

And all so I can come back here and start looking for work. If I save this kid, my payback will be giving up the project. Figures. The passport will be one use, too. It'll be NSA-flagged as soon as I get back, which means tossing thirty-five grand in work down the drain.

He got out of the car and crossed the lot. A chair was propped up against the apartment block's back wall, occupied by an elderly man in a porkpie hat and gray V-neck sweater. He was about halfway through a particularly fat cigar.

"Hey, Mr. Fawcett," Bob said. The building's resident manager was pushing seventy and had lived in City Heights for decades. "How're you doing today, sir?"

"Oh, fine, just fine," he said. He cleared his throat and

hawked spit to his right. "That's the smoking, right there. Didn't quit early enough. You don't smoke, do you, Bob?"

"No, sir."

"Good. That's good. That beater I helped you find working out okay?"

Bob looked back at the Hyundai. Just a day earlier, its molded-plastic front bumper had come loose and was hanging slightly on its left side. But it had been cheap and no questions asked, no paperwork trading hands. He sighed, thinking back to the Dodge Challenger he'd had briefly in Chicago. *Now that was a car.*

But he didn't want to disappoint the man, and he'd been on train rides that were pricier. "For a beater, she's real reliable, Mr. Fawcett. Thank you again for that."

As if on cue, the engine emitted a single, large knock sound, like it had been struck with a ball-peen hammer, metal fatigue and heat plaguing the twenty-year-old compact. "As long as she holds together," Bob said, crossing his fingers with a flourish.

"Good luck with your evening, young man," Mr. Fawcett said as Bob opened the back door and headed inside.

HE'D EATEN dinner and packed his bag by the time Jasmine texted back, then followed up with a phone call.

"I saw your note," she said. "Are you sure it's necessary?"

"Yeah, afraid so. We're not going to get anything out of the airport cops that the DA's office doesn't already know. You've been working with Hope Street here for several years, as has Eric, so you'd have some idea if the charity was involved at this end. That leaves Colombia."

"Uh-huh. It does make me wonder though, yet again,

who it is exactly you were before you came to us. This is all... I mean, I thought you'd go back to the neighborhood like I did, ask around."

"Because that worked so well the first time," Bob said. Then he caught himself. She was just nervous. "Sorry, I don't want to be that guy, Mr. Sarcastic. I was in the military; I have training for special circumstances. Your brother being used by drug dealers, quite possibly based in Colombia... to me, that falls right under the heading 'special circumstances.'"

"But... you barely know us. I mean... don't get me wrong, Bob, I've been so glad to have you at the project. And you've been so generous helping the ladies at the self-defense class. My head, knuckles and knees are all lethal weapons now. But... something like this, it could be genuinely dangerous."

Don't let her sit here guilty, worrying about you while you're gone. "I mean... I don't want to burst your bubble, Jasmine, but I've done a bunch of investigative work in the past, and it's usually about as exciting as sitting in a car watching a building or person for hours on end. If you like car radio, it's exciting."

The line went quiet for a moment.

"Jasmine? You still there?"

She tried to hide the worry, but it was definitely there. "Yeah. Okay, Bob. I suspect that's what you'd say no matter what. But... thank you again for doing this. You keep in touch, okay? You make sure you know where the nearest American embassy is, where the hospital is. Do you speak any Spanish?"

"I get by. And like I said, there's nothing to worry about."

14

Bob's flight was ninety minutes away. He sat on the edge of his single bed in the one-room apartment and stared at his packed overnight bag containing a few days' worth of neatly rolled clothes, a spare jacket and an extra pair of shoes.

It had been more than fifteen years since he'd left the country.

Tehran. Team Seven's fateful final mission. He hadn't thought about it in years.

A notion kicked into place. He hadn't been able to place why Rowe's assistant was so familiar. But the memory of Tehran cemented it.

He looks like Edson Krug. Bob's former teammate and nemesis had been dead for more than two years.

He reached into his jacket pocket and took out the business card.

In small, all-cap type, the card read "Sebastian Krug. Executive Assistant." There was a phone number in the lower left, his email address in the lower right.

You've got to be kidding me.

The assistant had to be close to twenty years' Edson Krug's junior. As far as Bob had known, Krug's immediate family were all dead.

But it couldn't be a coincidence, he knew. The resemblance was just too great.

Had the kid projected an air of menace, Bob wondered, or had he just reminded him of the man who'd tried repeatedly to kill him?

He checked his battered old Seiko wristwatch. *Time to get going.*

Outside the back door, Mr. Fawcett was already rocking in his office chair, a newer, longer cigar clamped between his lips, a copy of *Baseball Digest* on his lap. "You're heading out somewhere, young man?"

"Yes, sir. Just getting a few days' break from the city." Bob walked over and opened the Hyundai's rear passenger door, throwing his bag onto the back seat. He slammed the door and reached for the driver's side handle.

"My apologies for your wheels, I suppose," Mr. Fawcett said.

"It's been fine, really," Bob said.

"But you still had to put money into it, which you wanted to avoid."

"Eh?" Bob opened the door. What was he talking about? "Not really."

"Well... Okay, then," Mr. Fawcett said.

Bob got behind the wheel and slammed the door, then rolled down the window, the subcompact lacking air conditioning. "You have a good week, Mr. Fawcett." He put the keys into the ignition.

"You too, son, and hopefully whatever your mechanic friend did holds 'til you get to where you're going."

Eh? What's he talking about? "My mechanic friend?" He reached for the key again.

"This morning, the one working on your ride."

"I didn't..." The implication struck Bob, and instinct took over, his fingers snatched away from the ignition key, his seat belt quickly ejected.

He felt under the steering block.

The object was square and hard, mounted crudely using wraps of duct tape.

Detonator. He leaned down quickly to check the type. It was wired to the ignition, but there was also a thin metal antenna attached to one side.

Bob scrambled out of the car, grabbing Mr. Fawcett under the arm. "We need to move, NOW!" he barked.

The old man struggled to his feet, stumbling behind as Bob half-dragged them around the corner of the building.

The explosion was loud enough to dull his hearing, a bass heavy thump of hot air that lifted the car a half-foot off the ground and engulfed it in flames before gravity brought it crashing back down on the asphalt.

Debris reached back to the building and covered the back road. At the building behind, the concussive force had shaken a couple of parked cars awake, their car alarms bleating shrilly.

"GOD DAMN!" Mr. Fawcett exclaimed, peeking around the corner at the mess. In the middle of the parking lot, Bob's suitcase sat burning. He ran over to it and stomped on the flames.

His passport was in his other soft-side case, his money hidden in his raincoat liner. But he looked down forlornly at the mess that had been his clothes. *Geez. There goes my round-neck Club International jacket.*

"I mean... God daaaamn," Mr. Fawcett said from behind him.

Bob motioned towards the smoldering bag. "Lost my favorite jacket."

The old man turned his head slowly and stared at him for a few moments. "I think you may have bigger things to worry about, son."

Bob took out his phone. He needed to call the fire department and then Jasmine. He kept an eye on the front road, although whoever had set off the device by radio had probably been parked on the road behind them, the radio trigger a backup in case he didn't start the car. They would have already fled.

Someone doesn't want me going to Colombia.

But as far as he was aware, only Jasmine knew. Even if she was somehow involved, she wouldn't have had the time or know-how. He'd been at Pascal Brown's a day earlier, then at Rowe's building that afternoon.

So which one of them followed me back here?

Bob began to pack up his few other possessions in his soft-sided bag. He needed to toss the burner and be out of there before the fire crew showed, with Mr. Fawcett happy to confirm he barely knew his tenant, who hadn't been there in weeks.

15

CALI, COLOMBIA

The flight had gotten in on time, but the town where Hope Street operated its distribution center was a two-hour drive away. Bob rented a fifteen-year-old Ford Fiesta using cash at the airport and bought a new summer jacket in navy blue vinyl, as well as a baseball cap, this time bearing the logo of Deportivo Cali, a local football club.

He stepped out of the terminal with his soft-sided bag slung over his back. The humidity hit him like a wall, temperatures above 100 F. He followed the busy sidewalk to the crosswalk into the rental parking area.

He had aviator sunglasses on but was otherwise dressed simply, in jeans and a T-shirt, his sneakers a bargain brand. He already expected to stand out, so projecting an absence of wealth was important. Bob scanned the parking road in front of the terminal and the parking lot. It was busy, but no one seemed to be paying too much attention.

He knew he had to be cautious. Whoever blew up his car might've tailed him to the airport, seen him board his flight.

It had to be related to Eric Williams's case, which meant the cocaine probably originated in Buenaventura. If they'd taken him that seriously already, they would have men waiting, looking out for him.

Bringing a weapon had been out of the question, Jasmine had made that clear. Besides, he didn't need the hassle at customs. *And she wants me to keep this quiet. So that's what I need to try to do.* She'd been right about San Diego; he'd played things fast and loose, let them get out of hand.

His car was in stall C4. Bob looked at the signs denoting each section and located the right one, halfway across the lot. Another customer was just getting into a similar Ford from the same company.

He followed the row towards his vehicle. Fifteen feet south and one row down, two men were standing near the trunk of an old Mercedes. One of them was reading a magazine, smoking a cigarette. His friend, Bob figured, was a different matter.

Now... there's a man looking for someone specific.

The sunglasses hid Bob's interest, and he kept walking in a straight line, not turning his head but keeping the man in his peripheral vision. *Yeah, he's studying me*. The man drew something from his back pocket, a picture. He held it up, then subconsciously rubbed his own jawline.

Now why... And then it occurred to him. If it was a picture of him, he probably still had a beard.

They'd let him keep walking, he knew, try to use the element of surprise. The rental car was still a dozen spaces away. He kept an eye in each passing car's side mirror as he progressed. Sure enough, two cars later, the two men dropped in behind him, the shorter one turning on his heel once to make sure they too weren't being followed or observed.

The lot was busy enough for them to be nervous, Bob supposed. A row to their east, at least three different families were within good viewing distance. To their west, an older man was loading golf clubs into a Range Rover's rear hatch.

They'll try to keep it quiet. That probably meant a knife, or trying to knock him out and finish him quietly elsewhere.

The car right before his was a Cadillac SUV, tall enough to effectively hide the Fiesta from immediate view. *Yeah,* Bob thought. *That'll work.*

He waited until he was one step past the Cadillac's rear bumper and took an impromptu step sideways, disappearing from their view. The footsteps behind sped up to a trot, the two men desperate to not lose their target.

Bob timed his movement carefully, throwing out an arm right around where he figured the shorter of the two men's necks would be.

His pursuer ran straight into it, Bob's forearm catching him across the throat, his momentum arrested so suddenly that he lost his footing and crashed onto the ground, flat on his back.

The second man was professional enough to not pause, taking a half-step backwards and spreading his feet in a fighting stance, a butterfly knife appearing from his pocket, the man flicking it open with a practiced twist of his wrist.

His friend lay between them. Before the knife man could react, Bob dropped low, grabbing the prone attacker by the collar as he tried to rise, driving his knee into the small of the man's back, holding him, his pain evident, in front of his body. He wrapped a forearm around the man's neck and grabbed his scalp with his other hand.

"¡Le romperé el cuello!" *I'll snap his neck!* Bob cautioned.

If they were friends, they weren't close. The second man ignored the threat and lunged forward, stabbing at Bob's face with the double-edged blade. He leaned out of his reach, letting his captive fall to the floor, kicking down with his right heel as the man's head passed his foot, slamming it into the concrete and knocking him unconscious.

The blade cut through the air in a wide arc, Bob jumping backwards once more. The taller attacker advanced on him, slashing with a forehand, rolling it into a backhanded stab attempt. He bobbed out of its path, reaching down and to his right as the blade passed, hammering the man's elbow joint with a flat-palm punch.

The blade sprang loose and clattered onto the concrete. The knife man's eyes widened, and he turned to run. But Bob was quicker, two long strides catching him up, his weight thrown against his target as he dragged the man face-first to the ground. The man tried to rise, but Bob pinned him with his weight; another open-palm strike slammed into the back of the man's skull, his face caroming off the asphalt.

Bob looked around quickly, both men still out but the first beginning to rouse. They were below eye level, between the rows of vehicles. As furious as it had been, patrons across the lot clearly hadn't noticed or been inclined to raise an alarm. He leaned down and slugged the first man across the side of the chin, crushing the mental nerve, putting him under again.

Bob jogged over to the Ford Fiesta and opened the door, throwing his bag onto the passenger seat. Buenaventura was two hours away, and Cali was inhospitable. Where there had been two, there would be more, and based on the second attacker's lack of concern for his colleague, they'd been well incentivized.

16

BUENAVENTURA, COLOMBIA

Bob looked out the window of his boutique hotel at the small city's downtown. It was a maze of narrow, twisty streets, plaster-sided, flat-roofed buildings, others only partially painted and finished, cinder-block masonry visible all around. Most businesses were fronted by iron shutters.

The conditions seemed as substandard as Bob had expected. Buenaventura had been a violent city for decades because of its Pacific Ocean port, which facilitated much of the nation's longstanding cocaine exports. Buildings were falling apart or half complete. Street corners were strewn with overflowing garbage and casually-disposed-of black plastic trash bags.

The humidity caused the trash to rot and stink, and it meant black mold could be seen on the sidewalks, on the side walls of structures. Roofs had been replaced with rusting, corrugated tin. The sheer number of people hanging out on the stoops of shops and bars suggested unemployment was high. On the streets themselves, he saw what seemed to be ten underpowered Japanese motorcycles or mopeds for every car or truck.

But… there were signs it was a community, nonetheless. The faces on those stoops were friendly, laughing. The old men playing chess outside his hotel were chuckling at an inside joke when he walked in. The hotel staff were professional, courteous.

All the usual signs of people trying, in a place where they don't get much chance to succeed.

Jasmine had been incensed that he was still traveling after the car bomb, even more so that he'd refused to give her enough detail to help police investigate. But she knew she couldn't argue the logic. Both Pascal Brown and Anderson Rowe knew he'd been asking about Colombia, and within a day, someone had tried to stop him.

That meant there was something in Buenaventura he wasn't supposed to know. It also seemed likely Rowe was somehow involved, or his assistant, based on how effectively he'd scared Brown. There was something off about the businessman, something a little feral behind his otherwise kindly eyes.

He'd booked the second-cheapest of the downtown boutique hotels, the kind of three-star place favored by cost-conscious bureaucrats and family making emergency visits. It had a buffet breakfast in its ten-table café. The corridors were carpeted in thin Berber, the wallpaper beginning to yellow from age.

At six two, he was taller than most locals. Living in San Diego, and old-fashioned habits, meant he had a deep tan, which helped somewhat. But it seemed most of the city was either of African roots or, if Latino, well under six feet tall.

His Spanish was fluent, albeit of a formal dialect. He'd stick out as a nonlocal immediately, he knew.

He took out the burner he'd bought just before leaving and dialed a Las Vegas number.

It took Adam Renton twenty seconds to answer, the call routed through redirection and encryption software. "Renton."

"It's me."

"Sir."

"Or, you know, just Bob."

"Sorry, old habits." Renton was former NSA, a top-level spook and signals intelligence expert whom pros hired to get intel others couldn't access. He had contacts across the globe. "How can I help?"

He also charged five hundred an hour plus expenses. "I'm short of cash," Bob said. "I need your assurance I can repay you when I get back stateside."

There was a pause. "Bob... you know my rule on freebies for guys who are operational. It's nothing personal; it's just that you may not—"

"It's one favor, Adam, for crying out loud. I've thrown enough business your way in the last year, haven't I? You made a solid chunk of coin for that dealie in Pennsylvania."

Renton sighed loudly. "There's no harm in asking."

"I need a contact in Buenaventura, Colombia, someone who's solid and knows the lay of the land, the players and places. Someone who does things for reasons other than just money."

"In *Buenaventura!?* I mean, that's not the small request you think it is," Renton insisted. "Even the most charitable local there is so jaded from the narco wars that they accept nothing comes for free. The stuff I've seen in classified files?

If you described a lot of its residents as feeling like hostages, you probably wouldn't be far off. But... I will try, sure. As long as that's it, a contact number. No intros, personal involvement, arrangements or anything that I would normally charge at least an hour to do."

For a guy who worked with mercenaries, Renton sure could be a mercenary son of a gun, Bob figured. "That's all I'm asking."

"When?"

"ASAP. I'm down here meeting with a charity, eh? But my guess based on their years of good rep is that they're not going to have the intel I need, or know what's really going on. It's a smuggling deal, and someone's infiltrated their good graces."

"Ah. Okay... well, hang tight. I have a paying, priority job first," Renton said. "I'll try to get to it soon, though."

"Good talking to you, Adam."

"Sure. Keep your head down, Bob. Watch out and don't cross the Shottas, the Espartanos or the Corsarios. They're the three biggest local gangs in terms of Agency concern, with the nationally problematic Clan del Golfo, the ex-militants, also involved. They've been in a ceasefire off and on for a couple of years and do not take kindly to outsiders who show up and cause problems."

"Noted."

"Ciao." The call dropped.

WASHINGTON, DC

Eddie Stone hated being made to wait.

His CIA boss, Andrew Kennedy, on the other hand, thought nothing of fitting time with his staff around an always busy schedule. Consequently, he seemed unmoved by Eddie's obvious irritation, as he waited for the barber to finish shaving him. He watched his longtime cohort, whom he'd worked with since Vietnam, in the mirror ahead of him, like a gecko studying a particularly lazy fly.

He'd put on a few more pounds, Stone figured as he leaned on the inner doorjamb, and was becoming increasingly rotund. The suit seemed a little more wrinkled than normal.

You're old, Andy. We both are.

"Okay, Kemal, okay!" Kennedy said. "I think if you don't take a break, my friend over there is going to lose it." The barber stopped shaving him. He nodded briskly, straightening up and looking at his client in the mirror. He wiped away a daub of shaving cream from Kennedy's left temple, from just under his rapidly receding crown of silver hair. He reached by him to drop the straight razor into a vial of green cleanser, under the mirror. Then he stepped away from the chair and headed towards the front of the tiny shop.

"He's been cutting my hair and shaving my beard for thirty-seven years, would you believe it?"

"Fascinating," Stone grumbled. "It doesn't explain what was so important that I had to skip an appropriations committee session – you know, the interminable begging and groveling required on the Hill for us to stay active. The session you insisted I attend in the first place."

"They need to see that you're human, Eddie." Kennedy swiveled the barber's chair towards the door rather than get up. "It's not enough that Team Seven remains completely off the books. We're both working on age exemptions, both should've been retired long ago. Maintaining the trust of the key players on the Hill is how we survive, how we keep getting to do what we do."

"I mean... loathsome as that all is, you're making my point for me," Stone said. "What's so important...?" He let the thought trail.

Kennedy used both arms of the chair to push off and rise haltingly. Kemal wandered back over and helped him put on his tweed overcoat. "You made me a promise, Eddie. You promised me after you lost him in Maine that if we got so much as a sniff on Bob Singleton, you'd let me know."

The barber disappeared into the back of the shop.

Oh, for fuck's sake... Kennedy had been obsessed with the last survivor of Team Seven's Tehran mission fifteen years earlier. Stone suspected it was because Bob Singleton knew something that could implicate the deputy director, or Kennedy believed he did.

But two years of hunting him had cost the department millions of dollars and left a trail of dead mercs and contract killers across America. As loath as he was to admit it, Bob had been their best, their best at surviving, at the least. He seemed to have no interest in the Agency or Beltway politics or Kennedy.

None of that seemed to matter. And until he knew what so worried the older bureaucrat, Stone knew he had to play along. "Are you really going to make an issue out of this?"

"Eleven a.m. this morning. It's" – Kennedy checked his platinum Longines wristwatch – "two thirty-eight in the afternoon."

"It was a blurry image that barely crossed the threshold of a potential match."

"HE WAS AT AN AIRPORT!" Kennedy barked. "You recognize the potential implications of that, yes? He could flee the country permanently, perhaps even defect to an enemy. Worse, he could be fully active again, working for someone other than us!"

"Or, knowing how those algorithms work, it could be someone with earlobes that are seventy percent similar to Bob's," Stone said calmly, abandoning the doorjamb and standing up straight, crossing his arms, his body language defiant. "We've worked together for half a goddamned century. Will you let me handle this? Please?"

"How is it that we don't even have a—" Kennedy broke off as the barber returned, looking up curiously on noticing the two men had stopped talking. The barber retrieved a broom leaning against his work counter so that he could sweep up the few remnants of hair on the floor.

Kennedy took out his money clip and peeled off two twenties. Kemal took his cue and propped the broom, then walked over and accepted the cash.

"Thank you, Kemal, excellent as always. If you could give us a minute..."

The barber gave the knowing nod of someone who'd been in DC long enough and disappeared towards the back of the shop once more.

Kennedy put the money clip away. "How is it that we don't even have a decent image from another airport camera yet?"

"Ask your NSA pals," Stone said. "They've been looking since this morning. But he probably checked in using the automated machines, and the angles at San Diego International are really poor there. The software's not getting a hit."

"Don't they get a full facial image at the security gate?"

"They do. Problematically, once again, it has to be automated because of the numbers we're talking about. And the algorithm takes time to break down every pixel from every image. It's pulled out twenty-three potentials so far, all to different destinations. But... again, it wasn't considered a priority airport in the recent federal Homeland Security capital allocation, so their images are lower quality, their cameras a decade old."

"Jesus Christ!" Kennedy barked. "The goddamned priorities in this country sometimes..."

"The problem is, even if we figure out where he went, we have no guarantee he'll come back through the same airport, if he comes back at all. So we need to flag all flights from that destination, nationally, rather than trying algorithmic searches of every airport nationwide."

"Flag? As in..."

"We circulate Bob's picture as an NSA priority catch so that the entire system is alerted, including flagging passport control."

Kennedy shook his head vigorously. "Uh-uh, no, sir. Out of the question. And you know that! You know why."

"Because he's supposed to be dead. If he's suddenly not dead, we have a lot of explaining to do. And we have to let the NSA and probably Homeland poke into Team Seven and Tehran. Plus... they'll arrest him, and you want him dead."

"I want him dead once we know why he left the country... as well as whatever he's hiding from the clean-up," Kennedy corrected. "But... yeah, that's the gist of the problem."

Stone wanted to hit him. But he hadn't survived for so

long by losing his cool. "You're tying my hands, but also asking me to catch a rat. You can't have it both ways, Andy."

Kennedy had clearly been thinking it over before he got there. "Put a team on San Diego. Once we know where he went, concentrate on flights coming back from that destination. If there's one thing we know about Bob, it's that since he fled Chicago, he's been trying to find something, some purpose. We've had stories of him helping people all over the place, which suggests he wants a sense of community. Of belonging."

Stone figured that was a stretch. It was as likely Bob had already concluded whatever business he had in San Diego as that he'd return. "He doesn't usually go back to places," he said. "He hasn't been back to New Orleans or Memphis or Vegas or Bakersfield or Portland."

"Yeah... but they weren't outside the country. This is different for some reason, clearly. And he could've tried it before, so I don't think he's giving up and fleeing for good. But the only way we know for sure is if you pick him up. Keep a team at the airport."

"Fine." Of course, it wasn't fine. Stone knew that, eventually, he needed to find out what Kennedy had really done, what his connection was to a mission that had ultimately cost eight lives and embarrassed the nation.

"Damn right. I know about Portland, Eddie. I know you could've taken him down, interrogated him and removed him from the board. But you fucked around and found out so that you could try for a high-profile win. But you and me, we've always done better when we stuck together."

Kennedy opened the store's front door. "My car is waiting. Keep me up to date this time." He walked out.

Stone figured Bob's real value was long since exhausted, the hunt for him a costly waste of manpower and money. But the more Kennedy seemed to worry, the more Stone wondered why.

Eventually, he's going to drag me down with him.

17

BUENAVENTURA, COLOMBIA

Hope Street's local operation was situated in a port warehouse. Although it was three blocks back from the front line, the building was on stilts and technically over water, a complex mishmash of wooden gangways mimicking a street system.

Bob parked down the street, leaving the car doors deliberately unlocked. In a place where theft is common, he'd learned to leave nothing in the vehicle and the doors open so that windows wouldn't be smashed to gain entry.

The charity's building was large, about the size of a small car dealership back home, its walls of old-fashioned two-by-four planks. The cheap exterior vinyl paint was ancient, peeling and bubbling, permanently grayed by air pollution. At the front of the building on the ground floor, a window opened to the street, slightly elevated, a line of locals stepping up one at a time and being handed clothing, school tools, grocery boxes. A stern-looking nun manned the window, giving directions to a young woman volunteering.

The line watched Bob warily as he opened the front door.

Inside, the floor space was divided into two halves: a warehouse sat behind the giveaway counter, its twenty-foot-high shelves creating a natural room separator. There was a long, narrow room to its right, leading back from the main doors.

Another counter was set back ten feet from the entrance.

Behind it, desks filled most of the room, a door at the back suggesting more office space. A handful of workers were standing behind the interior counter, accepting donations from a woman who'd brought a box of used items, two more in line behind her. A second nun in plain civilian clothes, betrayed only by the coif covering wavy brown hair, was monitoring their efforts. She looked up at Bob and smiled warmly as he approached.

"¿Estás aquí para hacer una donación?" she asked. *Have you come to donate?*

Jasmine had assured him the depot manager, Sister Clara, spoke perfect English. "¿Esta disponible Hermana Clara?" Bob asked. *Is Sister Clara available?*

The sister held up a forefinger to request patience. Then she turned and exited out a door to the back.

She returned twenty seconds later with an older nun, a large woman in corduroy overalls with heavy, round features and thick, dark eyebrows. Sister Clara eyed Bob serenely as she approached.

"Mr. Davis?"

"Yes." He offered a hand to shake.

She gave it one firm pump and bowed her head slightly. "I must be honest that I was quite surprised to get a phone call this morning from our San Diego branch saying you were coming. You have questions about Eric Williams, as I am led to believe."

"That's right."

"Please..." She gestured for him to follow her. She led him down the corridor behind the front counter, between the desks. Along the right wall, a set of metal stairs led to the second floor and her office.

She held the door open for him and gestured with a wave of her arm. The room was spartan, the only art a picture of Jesus on the back wall, above her office chair. He sat down in one of the guest armchairs.

She slipped into the plain typing chair behind her desk and rustled some papers on her desktop officiously before taking up a fountain pen, her other hand leaning on a notepad. "Now... let's see how we can help you, Mr. Davis. You're working on behalf of Eric's legal counsel, I take it?"

"His family. And thank you, Sister. Nosotros podemos hablar español si lo prefieres." *We can speak Spanish if you prefer.*

"No, no, that is just fine, sir. I need practice, of course." She took notes as she talked.

"You knew Eric well?"

She nodded gravely. "I thought he was a fairly open person. He was cheerful, patient with how long things can take to get done here." Sister Clara looked up and met Bob's eye. "I liked him, Mr. Davis. He seemed a kind boy. Working here, in this neighborhood, it becomes important to accept that people will do what they feel they must to survive. There are children far younger than Eric who have done much worse. But... I cannot say that I am not disappointed."

"Did the local police or federal agents approach the charity, to see where he obtained the cocaine?"

"I do not know. Unfortunately, they refused to share much in the way of detail. They had a look at our operation and spoke to some staff next door at the distribution center. But he was arrested in America, and I expect they were glad it was not a local concern. They have more than enough of those for many lifetimes already."

"Is it as difficult as people say in Buenaventura?" Bob asked.

"The people here are tough and resilient and full of God's grace. But years of the port being a political pawn between the government and rebels has been replaced by warring gangs, who are now, in effect, a level of government unto themselves. Indeed, they are often more efficient in helping local concerns than the government in Bogota," the elderly nun said with a shrug. "But they fight, and they squabble, and the hardest of them get into drunken or drug-fueled shootouts, or they kidnap people for a quick and easy payday. It is lawless, in effect, except when the gangs themselves crack down on their own."

There was little emotion attached to the description, Bob figured, despite its vivid cynicism. It must have been hard, working there and trying not to judge the people she helped. It also sounded like the kind of place where smaller, less predictable criminal players would find opportunities. That meant potential havoc around every corner, Bob knew. He'd seen it in Somalia, in parts of Iraq during the war, that breakdown of civility in the face of stark desperation. "So it's not far-fetched that someone might have planted those drugs on Eric?"

She placed her hands together and leaned her top lip against them, contemplating the reality, weighing her words carefully. Then she said, "We spend most of the grant that we receive from Love and Light hiring local security, keeping those very types of people out of our warehouse and distribution center. Is it possible, Mr. Davis? Yes. Does it seem probable? We have been here for ten years, with thousands of volunteer trips either dropping clothing off here or collecting artisan goods to take back to America, and this has never happened before. I leave you to draw your own conclusions."

"Would you mind if I looked at your distribution center?" Bob asked.

She rose and gestured with one hand towards the door. "Please… we will go now."

Sister Clara led him back through the front office and to a side door leading into the warehouse. She opened it, letting it swing wide. "After you."

Inside, the vast room was mostly shelf space. It was hotter, with no air conditioning. The air smelled vaguely floral, Bob thought, like they'd plugged in one too many scent devices. The lights were off near the back of the room, and he couldn't make it out. A man hovered nearby. He had a string vest on, a sheen of sweat on his brown temple, his arms heavily tattooed, his head shaved. A half-inked teardrop tattoo descended from his left eye, and he stared at Bob suspiciously.

Can't see a piece. It could've been tucked into his waistband.

They strolled between the rows. At the end of the first row of shelves, a second man, shorter, in a golf shirt and just as muscular, stood with his hands ahead of him, like a guard. "Are these guys security?" Bob asked Sister Clara.

"As I said, the port environment can be quite dangerous. We have arrangements with local gentlemen to look out for the place, as they know the local players. A security company would likely be based out of Cali and would be accorded no respect, and underpaid. As such, they would not be reliable."

Bob stopped walking. At the head of the third row of shelves, a third guard stood. This one had a shoulder holster, a pistol butt visible. "And would they be members of local gangs, these gentlemen?"

"I cannot say specifically for each man," the nun said. "I do not mean that I won't, I mean that we do not ask." She lowered her voice for a moment and added, "They do usually have their guns in the open, though. They knew I had a guest today."

"Ah." Bob gave her a wry smile. "Thank you for your honesty."

"I have a hope – not realistic, I know, but a hope – that Eric is telling the truth," she said. "Even though it means we have bigger problems."

"Whose men are they?"

"They are provided for us from local interested parties, in this case by Los Corsarios, who some would call a gang, others a 'faction,' depending on your view of local politics. What I do know is that we have not been robbed in more than three years." She stopped walking once they were near the back of the room, out of earshot. "Mr. Davis... it is important for you to understand: for all intents, Buenaventura is a war zone."

"But... people are trying?" Bob ventured.

"People *are* trying. But the civil war between the government and FARC was often waged right here, and in its wake, we have the gangs. Eighty percent of people live in utter poverty despite billions of dollars in trade, illegal and otherwise, going through the port. Here, you are either rich, insulated and powerful, or you are nothing. Their friends and neighbors disappear daily, as is convenient to the gangs. Some are found dismembered within hours; others are never found at all."

"Ah, I see." *So that's why it looks like Somalia. It's facing a lot of the same pressures.* It matched the descriptions of the most dangerous places in which he'd spent his time in the Marines and for the Agency.

He wasn't going to learn much more from Sister Clara, Bob suspected. He needed background on Los Corsarios.

It didn't seem a stretch that organized criminals, with access to regular shipments that skipped customs, might want to take advantage. Sister Clara wasn't asking those questions, but it was clear why. *Why would she?* he wondered. *For most people here, just making it through the day is a success.*

What he really needed was for Renton to come through with a name, a local ally.

His presence would already have been noted, which meant the clock was ticking.

18

Renton, as usual, was as good as his word.

The woman standing outside his room when he got back to the hotel wore a plain black dress and heels. It was longer and formal enough that – even though she could clearly pass for local – anyone spying her there might assume she had money or was a high-end prostitute, waiting for her client.

"Bob?" she said as he approached. She checked the hallway in both directions to ensure they were alone.

"And you are..."

"Adam called me." Her tightly coiled hair was short, her eyes dark. She wore minimal makeup.

"Ah. Let's..." He nodded towards the door. She stood aside so that he could open it, and they both entered his room.

He closed the door. She held out a hand. "Abigail."

He shook it. "Can I assume the cloak-and-dagger routine, meeting me here, was Renton's idea?"

"Mine," she said. "I'm a reporter."

He'd worked with a few before, but Bob's instant reflex was to pull away. "I see."

"Relax. It still means something here. More here than most places, I would guess," she said. Her Spanish was pronounced and accentuated, less rapid-fire than the few Colombians he'd talked to, and he wondered if that was for his benefit. "But maybe before we start trading family vacation photos, you tell me what it is that you need exactly."

"Just like that? Has Renton worked something out, or..."

"He's not paying me," she said. "He helped me on a story in Cali a few years ago, and I owe him a favor."

"It's his currency," Bob said. "But... he's a good guy."

"He seems to be. He told me you might have a problem with drug traffickers. Given that this town literally floats on cocaine money, he supposed I might be able to point you in the right direction."

"Have you ever heard of Hope Street?"

Her dark eyes danced a little as she tried to place it. "No, I don't think so."

No perfume, either. Interesting. In the trade, that would've been deliberate, to avoid being associated with a scent, which made someone more memorable. "They run a charity for the poor here and in America, with a warehouse on the waterfront. I think local gangs might be using it to smuggle drugs to America, to San Diego specifically. A friend of a friend was arrested there while volunteering for them."

She crossed her arms and tilted her head in a manner that suggested she didn't buy it. "That... seems unlikely," she said. "The three largest of the four gangs are all usually in agreement with local charities. They don't want to make enemies of the poor, as they rely on them for recruitment and cheap labor."

"Do I sense a 'but' in there?"

"You do. Lately, there's another player, I think, a new outfit. No one is sure if it's actually new, or whether it's one of the established organizations playing with its enemies. But someone has been attacking their harbor holdings with a string of bombings. They've killed eight men across the Shottas, Espartanos and Corsarios, but only one of those was from the latter. There's some suspicion from the Espartanos that he may have been the bomber, as there hasn't been another explosion in two weeks. But no one is sure what is going on. Perhaps... perhaps this relates, in some way, to your situation."

"Can you find someone who could give us a better idea of what's going on in the warehouse, why they have so many armed guards for relatively valueless contributions?"

She thought about it quickly. "Probably, yes. I have good contacts along the waterfront generally because so much has gone on there, and because I can expense small bribes. More than anything, people here need to survive. How long are you here for?"

"Until I have an idea of what's going on. But as I said, a guy is in custody back home who probably didn't do anything. We need him out of there as soon as possible."

"Okay. Give me a few hours, a day at most, and I should know whether there is anyone to whom we can talk. Give me your number." She handed him her phone, and he punched it in, then handed it back. She headed to the door and opened it. "Ciao, Bob."

He raised a hand to wave goodbye, but she'd already closed the door.

. . .

It took Abigail less than four hours to call him back, this time with a set of directions.

Bob glanced at them on his phone once more, then looked past the rented Ford's windshield to the street ahead. The "park" on Carrera 40 was less park and more unkempt foliage, the broken footings of a building that had become so overgrown with dark green weeds and grass as to be rendered invisible. It sat between two low-rises, one fronted by a three-table café/kiosk, the other a shuttered former hairdresser's.

He parked and got out. Before he could take a step towards the property, a woman in denim overall shorts rose from a two-person table shared with a friend at the adjacent café. She laughed, said something to her friend, then turned down the street. She put on dark sunglasses and a baseball cap, then began walking towards him.

Dressed casually, he almost wouldn't have pegged her as Abigail. She had a sort of amorphous, chameleon quality to her. Bob could appreciate that.

As she neared, she muttered through barely moving lips, "Get back into your vehicle, Mr. Davis."

Bob did as requested. A moment later, she was at the passenger door. But instead of getting into the front, next to him, she climbed in the back.

She slammed the door. "Now, you are just someone giving me a ride somewhere," she said in Spanish. "Drive."

He pulled the car away from the curb. "I take it you're trying to discourage pursuers?"

"You are correct. We're going to drive to my friend's apartment, on the other side of the city. Is that okay?"

"Sure. Do I get a last name, by the way, or…?"

"It's Sanchez," she said. "Most people just call me Abi. I work anonymously, under the byline El Protector."

"Not just an anonymous byline, the male version at that," Bob said. "You must face a lot of threats."

"How long have you been here, Mr. Davis?"

"Please... Bob is fine. About sixteen hours, give or take."

"And your impression?"

"It looks like a war zone. Buildings crumbling, no established local infrastructure, people checking over their shoulders so often they've practically got whiplash."

"Bogota gave up on us a long time ago."

Bob had seen similarly abandoned towns in Angola and the Congo; compared to some lawless communities, even war-torn Baghdad had seemed civilized, with its military police patrols and segmented neighborhoods.

"So tell me about the docks." Bob peered at the rearview mirror. A moped had pulled in two cars behind them and stayed there, even though there was plenty of room in the lane to zip by, as so many locals did.

"They are utterly gang controlled. People outside, they do not understand the gangs. They think they are just violent and evil. But they are a hierarchy in a town that has none. They are a way to move up and gain authority over oneself that these boys, most of them, will never otherwise know."

"You sound almost sympathetic."

"Because I am. My ex-husband was involved in the gangs in Cali. For every one of them who is a lawless piece of shit, there are ten who are just young guys with no other options. And believe me, I know a few; if they found out charities were being used to smuggle, they would probably kill whoever is responsible in a horrible manner. That's why I was doubtful at first. The nuns and volunteers who run them are seen as saints to many in this town."

"Yeah..." Bob said, slowing the car for a working traffic light, the first he'd seen in six blocks. He checked the rearview mirror. The moped was still there. "But that word 'probably' is doing some heavy lifting. Isn't it possible someone else would just see it as an opportunity to hone in or even expand?"

"Possible, yes. Not likely, but possible. And that kind of behavior is why I work in secret. To be a journalist in this town and to be known as such could be a very short life indeed."

"Hang on..." Bob watched the rearview mirror intently once more. "I think we're being followed. Dark-colored moped, to our right rear. He's been on us since just after I picked you up."

"And that," she said, "is why I got in the back seat. People here are desperate, Mr. Davis, but do not ever make the mistake of assuming they are stupid. Some group, some faction or another, has probably been curious about you and keeping watch ever since you arrived. Or some kid has made you as a foreigner and wants your phone and wallet. Take the next right, but don't speed up."

Bob did as requested. "Yeah, he's still with us. He's going to know I'm not a hire car if they've had tabs on me throughout."

"But they won't know who I am, or see me for more than a few moments. My sister's building is a half mile ahead. When we arrive, I will have you pull over and drop me off. You need to lose him before you join me. Apartment 8. Okay? And be sure. The building is doubled-locked, so he's not getting in. But I don't want him even thinking we know each other. Am I clear?"

"As a sunny day," Bob said.

They drove on. After about a minute, they rounded a curve, and she tapped his seat. "Drop me in front of the market stalls to our right. The building is down the street, with a pale orange exterior. You cannot miss it. If the moped tries to pull up next to you before you lose him—"

"Expect a drive-by. I've done a little background work."

Bob pulled over, and Abi scrambled out quickly. He kept an eye on the rearview mirror as he pulled away from the curb, the moped appearing again a few seconds later. *Clever. Now he doesn't even know I'm solo.*

He felt tempted to lead the moped down a dead end, force a confrontation. But his research before flying down had suggested automatic weapons were abundant, and he was on unfamiliar turf, the town's street layout so erratic as to be unlearnable, at least in short order.

He took a left, then a quick right, then another left.

The moped kept pace.

Damn it. The pace of traffic was too slow to evade easily, and the moped could get in and out of jams quickly.

He hung a right and saw his opportunity, immediately turning the wheel further that way, pulling off into a Petromil gas station and parking behind the far pumps, near the mini-market doors.

He watched through the driver's side window as the moped proceeded up Street 6, slowing as it approached the next intersection, the driver letting his feet down on the asphalt as he craned his head from side to side, looking for his target. A car behind him honked, and the moped sped up.

Bob figured Abi could wait a few more minutes. *Let's see who this guy is.* He pulled the subcompact out of the gas station lot and rejoined traffic, falling in three cars behind his follower. After a few blocks, traffic had thinned. Bob pulled into the outside lane, creeping the car up to within a few feet of the moped's rear bumper.

The kid was still looking ahead, still trying to spot any sign of him. Out of his periphery, he noticed the nearby car, craned his neck around slightly and saw Bob. His eyes widened.

He looks about fifteen, for crying out loud. Bob knew what would come next and was a split second ahead, gunning the car and throwing it around the corner, the back end sliding out, even as the kid tried to rev the moped up to speed and take the same route. Bob yanked the handbrake while heel-and-toeing the brakes and gas. The car slid a quarter turn until almost horizontal, blocking the middle of the road.

The kid tried to swerve but was too late, the moped slamming into the car's front left wheel, its driver spilled over the handlebars and onto the hood. Bob got out before he could right himself and grabbed the youth by the collar, dragging him off the hood.

The kid's hand came up and around his body, the flash of blackened gun metal firing Bob's instinctive reaction, his right palm letting go of the kid's collar and slapping the gun hand down and away just as the kid yanked the trigger, the shot chipping the old, worn asphalt. He tried to raise the piece again, but Bob snatched its barrel as he simultaneously kicked the kid's feet out from under him.

The gun stayed put, in Bob's grip. The gunman slammed to the ground.

Bob crouched over him. The boy was wide-eyed with

fear. "Now, suppose you..." Before he could finish the sentence, a rock flew past his line of sight, then another. A larger one clunked into his temple, Bob's head snapping sideways slightly at the impact.

He stood up. A group of street kids had seen the chase and fight and had decided whose side they were on, rocks raining down.

Shit! He kicked the gun away and beat a retreat to the car. The moped rider was still lying prone, fifteen feet away, leaning up on one elbow. Bob tried to salvage something from the situation. "¡No me sigas más!" he said. *Don't follow me again!*

He slammed the car door just as a rock bounced off the side window. He pulled the car ahead a few feet, then backed up, turning quickly and running over the moped's front end. Then he kept going, pulling an inverted U-turn.

It took him less than five minutes to get back to the orange building. There was a spot open at the curb across the road. He pulled over and parked.

She knew what she was talking about, Bob figured. It had taken less than a day to pick up his first tail. It probably wasn't going to be the last.

19

The apartment building's front door was steel, a simple buzzer panel with eight apartment numbers below it offering the only way in. Bob pushed the last black button, keeping his body between the panel and the road, to hide his selection just in case.

"Si?"

"It's me," he said.

The door buzzed, and he entered, making sure it was properly closed behind him before taking the concrete stairs to the third floor. Even in a relatively new block, the stairwell walls were unpainted, rising damp evident from the water stains.

The apartments' front doors were mostly protected by extra iron bars. As he approached 8, an older woman leaned out and hastened him in.

"¡Entra, rápido, rápido!" she said. *Come in, quickly!*

She closed the door behind him. The apartment was warm, the front hall bare other than a handful of coat hooks occupied by light summer jackets. Under them was a series of stacked boxes, as if someone had been packing up.

Abi stood in the doorway to the living room, her body language tense.

"You made sure?" she said.

"I had words with the tail."

"That... is not good."

"It was a kid, probably working for someone watching me at the hotel. He looked pretty spooked."

"They like to use children. It makes prosecutions much more difficult, and people tend to drop their guard. But often, the 'child' is hardened already and armed."

"That would be about right."

Her eyes widened.

"You can relax," Bob said. "He's fine. Just a little less likely to pull a piece next time, I suspect. I've been doing this for a while. I'm pretty careful."

The apartment owner walked past him and stopped, then lit a cigarette. She took a long drag, then stared at him, studying his expression. "In Buenaventura, 'pretty careful' will get you killed 'pretty quick,'" she said.

"Bob, this is Marta. She agreed to meet us because she is moving back to Cali tomorrow anyway."

"And not a second too soon," the older woman said. "A few years too late, I guess."

"Marta worked at the warehouse you're talking about. But her brother, about whom she worries greatly, is rising in Los Corsarios. She thinks whoever is behind the bombs is also perhaps taking advantage of the nuns."

Marta took a long drag off her cigarette and eyed him suspiciously. "You are certain...?"

"It's okay," Abi said. "We have mutual friends."

"Okay." She held the cigarette aloft, one arm across her stomach, pensive. She gesticulated with her cigarette hand as she talked, Abi stepping aside so that she could lead them into the living room. The room was plain, unadorned, a window in the back wall offering natural light. Bob supposed any art or pictures had been packed up in the hallway boxes. A pair of sofas in lime green and candy red probably came with the place, or was clearly being moved at the last minute.

"It is just strange, you know? I worked there for nearly two years. For nearly two years, we have approximately the same number of donations from America come in every week. But in the last six months, they say it has doubled. So... okay. Maybe they do a better job of collecting or something. But at the same time, members of my brother's crew—"

"Los Corsarios," Abi clarified.

"They show up always carrying pistols, shotguns, uzis," Marta said. "They are protecting the cases from the donations like they are more valuable than the donations. And the place, it stinks of flowers, like they are trying to hide the smell of marijuana or something. But I don't see any. I ask one why; he says the cases are special; they cost more because of how much they carry. But to me, they just look like steel suitcases."

"That's a little strange," Bob said. "Seems like overkill."

"Sure. And they have more money all of a sudden, also. The safe in the office behind the storage depot usually has a float with a few million pesos in it. We are not talking about much in American terms, maybe two hundred fifty, three hundred dollars. Now, it has stacks of dollar bills. And I figure, maybe that's what they are actually guarding."

"But... why there?" Bob asked. "Why not in a vault in someone's home or a bank?"

She sat down on the lime-green sofa, then stubbed out the cigarette in a ceramic Holiday Inn ashtray on the table. "I don't know. I just know every few weeks, a man shows up, and they take him in the back. And when he leaves, he is smiling."

Abi sat down next to her, then thought differently, gesturing towards the kitchen. "Should I make some coffee?"

Marta rose quickly and waved her down with both hands. "No, no. I'll do it." She pointed to the lime-green sofa, then flapped a pair of fingers that way. "Sit, sit!" she told Bob.

Bob waited until she'd left. "That must have been tough for her, trusting me."

"Without a doubt."

She sat down.

"Before we talk more, I wanted to thank you," he said. "You're putting yourself at risk for me."

She looked almost parental, as if he'd said something endearing. "Ahhh... that's a very nice way of you to look at it, Bob. But I have lived here for many years now and been a journalist for nearly a decade. I have my own reasons."

"Why? Why do you do it? Why risk yourself in such a dangerous town?"

She took in a breath sharply. "I have a son, Pedro." She reached down into her purse and retrieved a photo, handing it over. The boy was grinning, his hair a little shaggy, freckles on the bridge of his nose. "But because of all of this, I do not get to see him.

"He lives with my mother-in-law in Medellin. His father... I met him when I was very young, just fourteen years of age. I did not realize how cold he truly was. By the time I understood and wanted out, we had a son. And even though he was a criminal, like many gangsters in Colombia, he had people of influence who were frightened of him. So the courts took my son away, awarded him to Benito. He does not know him, care about him or even see him. He only keeps custody to hurt me. But... my mother-in-law is a good woman. She lets me stay in touch secretly, by video call. She knows what her son is."

"That's..." Bob felt a swell of anger, hands tightening into fists. "Is he here in town?"

She tilted her head slightly and stared him down. "I do not like that look, Bob. You looked just then like he used to look before he left the house with murderous intent, or right before he slapped me. No, as I said, he is in Cali. And he is none of your concern."

"Apologies."

"It's nothing. A temper like that, though? You need to be careful."

"I know. Again... I'm sorry."

"It's okay. Pedro... he is why I fight the corruption, the social disorder, as well as I can, with my words."

"And why you're always at risk."

"Every day here is a risk for everyone, in many forms. But... we all die eventually. I'd rather live knowing that risk exists and try to make my time worth it anyway. I have to do this, which means I have to hide in plain sight," Abi reasoned. "Or... I could just walk away, fade into the crowd, disappear amongst it, and join the futility of mass prayer in the face of powerful indifference. That's a different kind of anonymity, I suppose. I know which I prefer."

"You sound at peace with it."

"I am. You, on the other hand, cannot be here long. It

will only take a few days for the questions to turn into resentments or even just an abundance of criminal caution. Or for opportunism, like that boy following you, to come bearing ammunition."

"Then we need to work quickly."

Bob told her what he'd seen at the distribution center, as well as the details of Eric Williams's arrest and the cocaine. She sat listening quietly, not asking questions but taking the odd note.

Marta returned with coffee and joined them. She handed Abi a cup and saucer. "Sugar or cream?"

"I'm fine."

"Do you think you could ID who these guys work for if you went down to the distribution center and took a look as well?" Bob asked Abi.

She nodded. "It's possible. I have known or written about quite a few of them and learned much from Marta, who would just like her brother to quit. There is something off about all of this, though."

"Why?"

"The methodology. For one, based on what you tell me, the smuggling is not really local. Instead of being through the port on a ship or via a disposable submersible, it is picked up here, then smuggled via airplane, which would most likely be via Cali Airport. The local gangs, when involved, are mostly supplying product or guarding it for larger cartels based elsewhere in Colombia and central America."

"So they wouldn't take the initiative, find a new way of doing things?"

"Unlikely. The gangs are bad, but the cartels, the men with the real money, are utterly ruthless. Why cross them when they can work together? And 'find a new way' would be crossing them, believe me. And then there is the question of who they're paying off with the money from that safe. And why."

Abi rose, which Bob took as a cue. "I will give you a call within a day," she said.

Bob turned to Marta and pressed his hands together in muted prayer. "Thank you. I know that wasn't easy."

She waved the cigarette again. "Eh. I'm leaving all of this tomorrow, as she said. Abi has enough fight for both of us, but I am getting older."

Abi looked as worried as when they'd arrived. "You're okay?" Bob asked.

"Please, Bob... This guy following you, maybe we're just being paranoid. But you were very lucky. Chances are, had he surprised you, it would've been to pull up beside your car and shoot you as you waited at a traffic light. Keep your head down. You can't help anyone if you are dead."

20

The warehouse and distribution center were big buildings by port standards. Abi looked up at the worn fascia, the painted letters fading from red to ochre nothingness, the rotting wood-plank siding. She knew she'd been there before but couldn't recall why. A story, doubtless, possibly from before she assumed the mantel of El Protector from a dead colleague.

Outside, a line was shuffling inevitably towards a hand-out window.

She'd prepared carefully, eschewing her jeans, blouse and flats for a flimsy cotton dress and flip-flops. Like most of those in line, Abi was descended from African slaves, and in the bright morning sun, with her fingernails unpainted and no makeup, she fit in flawlessly.

Bob seemed nice, but naïve to local issues. He clearly did not realize how serious the smuggling story could be. The gangs were in a truce; if one of them decided to develop a new drug market and route to the US, the others would demand a cut, at the least, and likely see it as a betrayal. Open warfare had broken out many times before, with gun battles in the streets, and no concern for those caught in the crossfire.

Keeping the port neutral meant everyone being as open as possible about their intentions. Someone had already broken that rule, going after Espartanos' outlets with pipe bombs and grenade attacks. A few months earlier, it had been Shottas bearing the brunt. Each thought the other responsible.

She pushed open the front door, butterflies in her stomach. It was a part of the job she loved, that initial tension. It reminded her that she was working on something worthwhile.

Inside, a customer counter sat near the front of the room. On the left side, the shelves separating the two sides of the operation were filled with what appeared to be local knickknacks: statuettes and carvings, macrame plant holders, "sombrero vueltiao" wide-brimmed hats, hand-stitched dolls.

She clocked the first guard as soon as she approached the counter. He was at the far left side of the room, near a side door to the warehouse.

He had a pistol tucked into his waistband and a stun gun in a belt pouch, neither of which was surprising. Though the charity's holdings appeared to be of minimal resale value, the neighborhood was tough enough for self-protection to be common.

She approached the counter.

"Yes, miss?" the generously proportioned clerk asked. She had a one-piece light green dress on, but it was already

90 F at eleven in the morning, large sweat rings developing at either armpit and her cleavage, where a silver crucifix dangled on a light chain.

"I called yesterday?" Abi lied. "I donated my mother's knit blanket by accident. They said it would be almost impossible to find, as everything is immediately folded and packed, and the clothing is not catalogued, but that I could come and look."

The woman drew in breath sharply, obviously conflicted. She looked around hastily. "Mrs. Perlaza, who runs the counter, is not here today," she said. "You must have spoken with her."

"That's right."

"She is not here. You'll have to come back."

Time for theatrics. "No! Please... miss, I leave for Cali with my family later today. I cannot come back, and... she loved it so much. She died recently, and we do not have enough to remember her by."

"Like Mrs. Perlaza told you, you would probably not see it." The woman gestured behind her. "As you can see, much is packed up, the rest buried in piles..."

"Please," Abi stressed. "You can walk with me. Five minutes."

The woman sighed deeply. "I cannot leave the counter. But..." She reached over and lifted up the flap over the counter opening. "Five minutes. Do not touch anything, or you might spook the security."

The woman looked left, towards the guard Abi had spotted on arriving. She tossed her head backwards towards the shelving, then towards Abi. The man nodded once, then lifted the walkie-talkie clipped to his shirt and muttered into it. He opened the door into the warehouse.

Abi wandered between the warehouse's long aisles. The storage rose up twenty feet; ladders occasionally leaned up against them to reach the top shelves. At the end of the first aisle, a man wandered into view. He had a machine pistol slung over his left shoulder, cradling its stock on his forearm. The half-filled teardrop tattoo was a favorite of Los Corsarios.

She kept looking at the shelves, nodding at him as she reached the end of the aisle. She moved to the next and repeated the process. Halfway down the third, another man popped into view, this time in a white T-shirt and cutoff shorts, again packing a machine pistol.

That's a lot of firepower for clothes and crafts.

At the end of the aisle, she scanned the back wall. In the back left corner, another guard sat on a stool in front of a steel door.

She nodded to the nearer man. "Could it be back there, my mother's blanket?"

The man shook his head slowly, unblinking. As his stare warded her off, the door opened, and another young man walked out, taking the fourth aisle as he walked past them to the front.

¡Suerte! Luck! The man passing was known to her, a gangster who ran a crew on the north side.

"Okay," she said. She moved on to the fourth aisle, then the fifth and last. She made her way back to the counter, feeling their eyes on her.

"I could not see it," she disconsolately told the counter clerk.

The woman shrugged. "I told you. It's a shame, but you should be more careful."

She lifted the counter flap, and Abi headed out the front

doors. She walked up the block, stopping after twenty yards to rustle through her purse. It gave her a chance to check behind her, to ensure no one was following.

21

It took Abi less than her promised day to get back to him.

Bob spent a cautious night not leaving his hotel room other than to get dinner at the tiny restaurant near the lobby. He filled the morning with exercise, running through the top level of the 5BX Canadian Air Force fitness regimen: inclined push-ups, crunches with leg extensions, extensive stretching and five minutes of high-knee, high-intensity on-the-spot running.

He'd just built up a sweat when the phone rang, just after ten in the morning.

"It's me," she said. "I'm at the waterfront."

"You got a chance to look at the place?"

"The distribution center... there's something else going on there," she said. He could hear street sounds behind her, the reporter obviously moving. "I can't talk long because walking around here on a smartphone is just asking to be robbed. But the back of the distribution center is closed and guarded, three men with machine guns that I saw, probably more in the back, one more at the front."

"Any ideas on who?"

"The half-tear tattoos suggest Los Corsarios, but only two of them. The other two, I could not say. I saw a man I know leaving the back area, Poni Alvarez. Well... I say man, but by reputation not much of one."

"You have a pic you can send?"

"I didn't get a chance. Too much attention. But you can't miss him. He's a skinny little wharf rat, my size but wiry, with a false left eye that just stares ahead no matter where he looks. He runs a nightclub on Carrera 21A. He works with Los Corsarios, but he's not a member anymore, more what Americans would call a hanger-on. Word on the street was they literally found him too irritating."

"Yikes."

"Look... I'm going to go to ground for a couple of days," Abi said. "I got a bad feeling from those dudes."

"Okay," Bob said. "Can I help? I can pick you up somewhere."

"No, then they'll connect us. I'll walk a few more blocks, buy some junk food, give anyone who might be keeping an eye out enough time to be sure I'm no threat. Right now, they might be curious, but they're not showing any interest. A gigantic gringo will set them off."

"Call me when you can. Make sure I know you're okay."

"I will. Don't go looking into that place on your own, Bob. You stand out like cauliflower in black beans."

"Duly noted."

She ended the call. Bob had been trying to carefully avoid lying of late. It wasn't the same as honesty, he knew, but it kept people from worrying about him too much.

And when it's the dark of night, nobody stands out too much.

Abi ended the call. Her car was another block away. On the sidewalk nearby, in front of a shop, kids were playing a game involving bouncing a tennis ball off the wall and catching it first.

"Lady!" one of the kids yelled in Spanish. "Lady! You want to buy some maracuyá juice?" He had a small table set up outside the door to the convenience store. "I squeezed it myself."

Abi grinned and chewed her lower lip, struck by the sweetness of it, with so much trouble around. She glanced over her shoulder quickly but didn't see anyone.

She turned toward the boy. "How much is it?"

"Two thousand pesos."

She fumbled in her purse, looking for a small bill.

The squeal of tires behind her prompted a quick turn, the sound so close she half-expected to witness an accident.

Instead, two men were bailing out of a car.

One was from the warehouse.

She turned to the street ahead to run, but had only made it a few steps when the rubber truncheon came down across the back of her skull, the world spinning into darkness.

22

The Maracaibo Club was trying, Bob figured. It really was. Built on stilts along the north edge of the city, it looked out over the water and, in most other places, would've been bucolic, relaxing. A large wrap-around balcony on the second floor afforded drinkers a view of the city and shore, as well as the vast stretch of jungle to the north. A backlit glass sign had survived the decades of turmoil.

But the place was old, wood warping and fading in the extreme humidity, the plaster exterior walls chipped and cracking, weeds coming up through the tiny adjacent parking lot's asphalt.

Bob kept an eye on the building as he approached from the south, along 5 Street. He parked the rental car and walked up the hill, looking for anyone paying attention as they milled on stoops or sat outside businesses at card tables. Someone was playing a song by Juanes, fervent Spanish vocals blended with intricate rhythm guitar, set off starkly by thumping pop drums.

The club itself looked busy, even in the early afternoon. Men in shorts, jeans and golf shirts milled around the bottom step to the front doors, smoking cigarettes. Others were on the upper balcony, drinks in one hand, cigarettes in the other. A few were smoking blunts, marijuana joints packed into cigar wrappers, just another sign that law enforcement didn't carry much weight.

He'd asked Renton about a fake ID, something federal and official enough to make people nervous. The former NSA man had just chuckled and said no one from the federal government makes people in Buenaventura nervous. "Forgotten, yes. Nervous, not in the slightest."

He took the first three steps, passing a small group of three men, two seated on the other end of the wide steps, the other leaning on the rail.

"You want something, man?" the standing one asked, nodding his way.

Bob pointed towards the building. "Just a drink."

His interrogator stood up straight. "No, no. That's not how it works. This is a neighborhood place. You're not from the neighborhood. You want to drink here, you have to pay the cover charge." He took a few steps towards Bob, his two friends also rising. All three were young, muscular. Two of the men had the half-teardrop tattoo Abi had described.

Bob gave them a show of nervousness, letting his gaze flit between them. "How... how much?" he asked, stammering.

"How much you got?" The three men closed on him, one reaching for his front pocket and the bulge of a wallet.

Bob's left arm shot out, grabbing the man by the lapel, pulling his head down even as he drove his knee upwards, slamming it into the man's chin. He collapsed on the stairs, his two friends frozen for a moment in shock. Bob kicked the tall man in the testicles, hard, and he fell to his knees.

The shorter Corsario went for a sheath knife at his waist.

Bob clocked the move, hopping up one step and turning his body even as the man swung the knife, the extra distance ensuring the blade's arc was short. He struck downwards, driving the heel of his right hand through the man's shoulder, the arm popping out of joint, the attacker screeching as he dropped the blade and fell onto his backside, gripping the dislocated limb.

Bob wheeled around, anticipating another attack. Instead, the patrons on the balcony were static, shocked, the entire fight taking less than thirty seconds. To his right, the man who'd initially harassed him fell over sideways, cupping his bruised genitals.

He kicked the knife down the steps. "¿Alguien más? ¿Alguna tontería más?" Bob demanded loudly. *Anyone else? Any more bullshit?*

In a lawless town, Bob knew, allegiances tended to be pragmatic. They'd clearly confronted and harassed him, and they'd paid the price. He hadn't killed anyone, so revenge wasn't on the table. The other patrons went back to their drinks, the fight clearly not the first the place had seen.

He opened the front door and walked in. The interior of the club was more empty, just a half dozen drinkers at tall tables and a bored-looking bartender. The walls were pale pink, decorated with black-and-white movie posters. He nodded Bob's way. "You in the right place?" he asked.

"If you serve beer, I'm in the right place," Bob said. He sat down at the bar, a decorative mirror on the far wall affording him a view of the entrance, just in case. Above, a giant ceiling fan kept the room cool.

"What do you want?" the barman asked. He clearly didn't like unfamiliar faces, either.

"What do you suggest?" Bob asked.

"That you find another place to drink."

"Hah! Point taken. But I meant beer," Bob said. It didn't matter. He hadn't had a drink in months, since his relapse in Maine. And that wasn't going to happen again; for the first time in ages, Bob figured he'd beaten the liquor demon back permanently.

The man grumbled a little. "We have Aguila, and we have Heineken. You look like a Heineken guy."

In the mirror on the far wall, Bob saw the front door open behind him. The short, younger man from the stairs strode in, a look of pure malice on his face. He had a pistol in his right hand. Bob reached down and grabbed the cut-glass ashtray on the counter, turning in one smooth motion and flinging it side arm, like an overweight Frisbee.

It slammed into the bridge of the man's nose, breaking it, blood spurting from his nostrils, both hands coming up to his face as he stumbled backwards. Bob spun his stool and jumped up, sprinting towards the gunman. As the target regained his balance and pulled a hand away from his face, Bob dropped into a slide on the tile floor, the sole of his right shoe driving through the man's ankles, his feet flying out from under him.

The young gangster crashed to the ground, his pistol flung from his grip. Bob hopped to his feet, took two steps left and picked up the gun, shoving it into his waistband.

At the bar, the bartender had retrieved a sawed-off shotgun from beneath the counter. But the young man wasn't getting up, his bell rung. The barkeep kept the shotgun in hand, pointed at the ceiling.

"My apologies," Bob said in Spanish. "He and his friends decided to try to rob me outside."

The bartender didn't move except to reach out with his free left hand. "The pistol, please. No weapons in the bar."

Ah, hell. Bob had been hoping to hang on to it, just in case. He handed it over.

Along the far wall, an office door opened. The man leaning out was short, wiry. He looked around the room, craning his neck, one eye bobbing from side to side as the other stayed perfectly still.

"WHAT THE FUCK IS GOING ON OUT HERE?" Poni Alvarez bellowed. The room turned, the half-dozen patrons already heading for the door, suddenly distracted. From behind him, two other men walked out of the office, both in tracksuit pants and T-shirts.

Poni looked across the bar, to the unconscious gangster by the door. Then his gaze flitted over to the bartender, holding a pistol in one hand, a shotgun in the other. Then they fell on Bob.

His eyes widened in recognition. "That's the dude! KILL HIM!" he bellowed.

23

The barkeep turned back towards Bob, realizing what he was supposed to do, his face a mask of aggression.

Bob leaned in before the man could raise either gun, grabbing him by both lapels. He drove his forehead into the barkeep's chin, knocking him cold even as he held him upright, twisting hard as he reached across the bar, turning the man around and crouching behind him as his colleagues opened fire.

The barkeep's left arm dangled, the shotgun hanging from his trigger finger. Bullets struck the unconscious man high on his chest, plumping muscle, driving him backwards, blood spraying from the wounds. Bob hopped slightly to reach over the bar, yanking upwards on the man's forearm, the shotgun flopping backwards towards him. He grabbed it with his own left hand and pulled the trigger, a spray of buckshot hitting the first bodyguard center mass, knocking him off his feet.

The second gunman tried to dart sideways, looking for

an angle of attack. Bob leaned left, pivoting the barman to the right, two more gunshots striking him. He tossed the shotgun a few inches into the air and caught it by the stock, working the pump with the same hand, repeating the maneuver, the second blast taking down the other guard.

Behind them, Poni shrieked a high-pitch yowl of terror, then sprinted into the office and slammed the door. Bob heard a lock click into place.

He wondered if any would even bother calling the cops. The two guards were both awake, one moaning, clutching a chest riddled with buckshot, his wind gone. It was painful, but he wasn't going to die. A few feet away, the second guard had flopped onto his stomach and began to crawl toward the pistol he'd just dropped.

Bob walked over and kicked it behind the bar. He looked at the lifeless bartender as he slid into a seated position, his gaze vacant.

Damn it. He hadn't shot the man, he knew, but might as well have. He leaned down next to the crawling man, also winded. "You're not going to die, buddy, but I need you out of the picture for a few. Sorry for this." He leaned down and hit the man with a short, hard right cross, driving his knuckles through an imaginary point an inch past the mental nerve in the side of the guard's chin.

Across the room, the door opened a crack. He drew the pistol, then realized it was the boy who'd charged in, staggering out. He stored the pistol back in his waistband.

He hopped to his feet and moved over to the bar. A pile of cloth towels sat under the counter. He picked one off the top and ripped it in half, then wet each half under the bar tap. He moved back to the first man, who was trying to lean up and look around.

"Sorry about this," he repeated, hitting the man square on the side of the chin, his eyes rolling back in his head. He rolled the man over and bound his hands behind him with the wet cloth, the knot held tighter by the moist material. He repeated it with the second guard.

What would a solid response time here be, anyway? He looked back at the door. They were likely to be interrupted, at least by other gangsters, Bob figured.

He sighed a little. He didn't really want to, but...

He jogged over to the dead bartender and grabbed his corpse under the arms, dragging it out from behind the bar. He dragged the body across the room and propped it up against the wall across from the double doors, the man's eyes wide open but dull, lifeless, his string vest stained crimson.

There. That should deter anyone from further rescue attempts.

There was no sign of police, no sirens. He wondered if gunshots alone would be enough, or if, in the neighborhood's war-torn state, anyone would be brave enough to even make the call. He doubted it.

Bob walked back to the office door and pounded on it three times. "PONI ALVAREZ! WE NEED TO TALK!"

Then he stepped to one side.

Sure enough, a moment later, a chunk of the door disappeared to the crack of a .357 Magnum. Bob leaned over and looked at the hole. It was right about where his head would've been and a good four inches around.

Dude must be standing pretty close.

A warbling voice spluttered, "Don't try to come in here! I'll kill you, I swear! Don't you fucking know who I am!?"

"You've got five more rounds in that .357," Bob replied

loudly. "If you want to plug the door a few more times, I can wait."

He leaned down slightly and craned his ear. He could hear Poni trying to call reinforcements. "Why isn't anyone answering?!" he demanded.

I need to remove his options. "This is a nice place," Bob barked. "But if you're not out here in twenty seconds, I'm going to set fire to it. And I'm going to stay here to make sure you can't get out until it's out of control."

Silence.

He chanced a glance through the door hole. Poni was at the back of the room, by an open window. He was shaking the security bars. "Mother of God, why don't you open?!" he bellowed.

"Okay," Bob called out. "Have it your way." He glanced over at the bar, then back at the door. It gave him an idea.

He trotted over to the bar and grabbed a bottle of vodka. He soaked both ends of a towel with the alcohol, then shoved the towel into the bottle. He repeated it with another towel and bottle. Then he walked back to the door, placed one bottle at his feet, took out his Bic disposable and lit the other.

Then he tossed the bottle on-end through the hole and ducked away from the wall. It shattered, getting Poni's attention, two more shots perforating the entry.

"I can keep doing that until something else catches and the booze doesn't burn off quickly enough," Bob said. "But you can only shoot the door three more times." He lit the next makeshift Molotov cocktail and tossed it into the room. The lack of a gas additive meant they'd be ineffective as explosives, but the room was going to get uncomfortable very quickly.

A few seconds later, the door flew open, a gun jutting out, clung onto by a skinny forearm. Poni attempted to turn around the corner and check for Bob's presence. But Bob timed the straight right hand perfectly, the punch catching the gangster square in the nose, breaking it. "Nnnhhhh!" The gangster dropped the pistol and slumped to his backside, clutching his broken beak. Bob leaned past him and picked up the .357, pocketing it.

"That didn't go how you'd hoped," Bob suggested. "Now, you and I are going out to my car, with my gun jabbed into your ribs so that your friends outside don't get any stupid ideas."

"I don't know nothing!" Poni exclaimed.

"You know enough. Be straight with me, and you'll survive the day. Go on, get up."

The gangster rose, morosely, to his feet. Somewhere in the distance, an emergency siren blared. "Is that for us?" Bob asked. Poni shot him a look of futility. "Nah, didn't think so."

The gangster's eyes flitted quickly again to the corner of the room.

Now that's interesting, Bob figured. He followed the glance. An old-fashioned, three-drawer, green metal filing cabinet sat flush in the corner, partially disguised by an ornate lamp.

He wandered over. *Could be booby-trapped.* "Open it. Slowly."

Poni skulked over. He knelt down and opened the drawer. There was a white plastic bag inside. "Take it out."

The club owner did as demanded. Bob peered into the bag.

Timers and Semtex. Now that's really interesting. Poni Alvarez, what have you been up to?

24

Daniel Rivas paced back and forth on the faux-Persian rug in his office, hands behind his back, contemplating his options, trying to determine his best approach to dealing with the woman.

He was an exceedingly careful man. He had to be. As a former propaganda officer with FARC, the rebel group that had fought the government for decades, he had been at the forefront of promoting its recruitment message.

But he was not an imposing figure, at just five feet six inches, with a thin frame, a bony chest, thick eyeglasses below his mop of brown hair.

He relied on intelligence, information, foreseeing problems before they could blow up in his face. He maintained a professional exterior, always wearing a suit and tie and using a driver. He was respected by his men for his planning, but also for his blunt honesty.

They feared him for his ruthlessness.

It had been an issue during his time with FARC; when pardons had been issued and peace talks held, he'd expected a reward for his decade of service, his contribution to the cause. He'd fought like an animal for the revolution, even become one.

True, his family had been monied, had advantages. Had his behavior as a young man not embarrassed them and burned bridges, he might not have looked to the rebels for a new home in the first place. He knew that.

But he'd done everything they'd demanded, crossed every boundary between man and monster for them. And they had abandoned him.

"AIIIIIIGGGH!" From the next room, a blood-curdling scream practically shook the connecting door. "POR FAVOR!... NO MAS!" a man bellowed gutturally. *Please. No More.* "POR FAVOOOR... AIIIIGGGH!"

Two of his men had been torturing the man for four hours. A career criminal with his own small crew, they'd been instructed to make his first day agonizing, but not terrifying: they were burning him with hot pokers, without doing quite enough damage to risk the man's life.

On day two, they would waterboard the man, shoving a cloth down his throat and soaking it, the sensation of drowning inducing sheer, nerve-breaking terror in even strong men.

By day three, the man would be begging them to stop. Rivas would visit personally at that point. Tell the man his only hope was to understand that Rivas was his sole salvation. That pleasing him was the only route to making his suffering end, abandoning his gang and swearing fealty to his new master. And then, when the man showed the usual initial reluctance, he would cut off the pinkie finger on the man's weaker hand with a blunt breadknife, sawing slowly as the man screamed once more. The stump would be dipped in hot tar, to cauterize the wound as painfully as possible.

On the fourth day, they would let him rest for a few hours longer, as if the torture had ended. Then they would start again. Only when he stopped screaming, stopped fighting and was resigned to death would they relent.

It usually took no more than ten days to break a man completely, to have him so grateful for an end to the torture that he would do anything and feel genuine gratitude for the opportunity. At that point, Rivas would comfort him, offer him a sliver of compassion.

And then, instead of killing him, he'd become a loyal servant, a dog bent to my will... only one who already has a pack of his own.

He knew the only way up in Buenaventura was power. His still relatively small crew did not have nearly enough to challenge the Shottas or Espartanos, or even the Corsarios, although he'd already co-opted three of their local neighborhood captains without them realizing it. But by adding more men, more crews, slowly and without warring, his power base could spread.

The bombings had been accidental genius, Poni Alvarez's idea to get revenge on a rival club almost setting off a war between the Shottas and the Espartanos, neither even ready to consider that a small player like Rivas might dare attack them directly.

Timed explosions meant he'd expended only the minimal manpower required to set them, with Poni – barely even an affiliate – standing to take the blame if his man was caught.

The woman, however, could not be treated with such manipulation and disdain.

He did not know whom she worked for, but she was too

poised, too calm to be a mere spy for another crew. She was either police or government or media, of that he was sure. His men had found her strolling around the Hope Street distribution center and followed her, seen her head towards a man in a rented Nissan, then break off at the last second.

It had to be the man San Diego had warned him about, the man they'd said would come down on behalf of the arrested American's family. They hadn't seen the license plate, but the description of the car matched what the boy following the American had seen.

But the woman was definitely local: the diction, the knowledge of how to smoothly lie her way past the woman at the counter, her appearance. It all added up to one problem: he couldn't just torture information out of her. He had business partners, cocaine suppliers who didn't need the extra attention. One of them visited the location regularly to pick up his fee.

Killing a journalist or lawyer – or worse, a government agent – would bring hell down on the city from Bogota, which seemed to always be bristling for an excuse to unleash the military. They already hated him for his time in FARC despite his willingness to save his own neck by turning over his former brothers-in-arms.

He stopped pacing at his desk and pressed the intercom button on the phone. "Joao, bring her in."

He sat down behind his desk. He had a few moments before they brought her from her temporary cell in the basement. He checked the lapels of his navy suit jacket and cleaned off a piece of lint fluff.

His intercom buzzed. "Chief, the little piece of shit passed out again." It was his torturer, an enthusiastic former military intelligence interrogator. "We were almost done for today. Do you want me to send him back downstairs?"

"No. Wake him up. And go hard for the next half hour. I have a guest coming who needs to hear it."

He hung up.

There was a brief knock on the door.

"Enter!"

Joao was a short, stocky former FARC guerrilla, a veteran of the drug wars, who'd been in firefights before Rivas was born. He had the woman's upper arm in a vise grip. Rivas nodded to the chair ahead of the desk.

The guard plonked her down in it, then stood behind her, hands ahead of him, feet shoulder-width apart, making it clear escape was impossible.

"You know who I am?" Rivas asked her.

"I do." Usually after the better part of a day captive, Rivas had found, women were more compliant. But her eyes flashed indignation.

"YEEEEEAAAAARGH!" From the next room another guttural scream.

Well timed, Rivas thought. "Then you know I will not hesitate to kill you, to kill your loved ones, if you are not straight with me."

"I know your reputation," she said coolly. "It does not include extreme stupidity."

"You work for the Shottas, yes?" he said.

He could've sworn he noticed her lips curl up ever so slightly, like she was holding back a smile.

"Interesting," she said. "You've grabbed me off the street, but you have no idea who I am."

In the next room, the prisoner screamed again. It caught

her attention, her head flitting that way ever so briefly. Rivas saw an opportunity to shake her calm exterior.

"You like that sound? No? It does not take much effort to make a man scream like that," he said.

She looked nonplussed. "He should try giving birth sometime."

Rivas got up and paced behind his desk. "You project an air of bravery. But if you were brave and from Buenaventura, I would already know who you are. Instead, you are a mystery. This suggests either a government agent or media. I don't think the local cops would have the balls to snoop around my business. I pay them too well."

"Interesting theory."

"And, if true, a problem for you," he said. "Because if nobody knows who you are, nobody that I need to worry about will miss you."

She was smirking at him, Rivas decided. He stopped pacing. "What?" he demanded.

"You don't build a crew like yours, rapidly, without business agreements already being in place. If you're like ninety percent of the crews in Buenaventura, that business is selling cocaine, probably to someone bigger than you but... cut from the same cloth."

"And so?"

"So you must defer to their wishes on such matters," she suggested. "If you are correct – and I'm not saying you are – you know the kind of attention killing me would bring down. And so... you can waste your time making the man next door scream, as sick as that is; but it won't change what I do or don't decide to tell you."

Rivas felt a stinging irritation. She was, of course, correct. His cocaine was sold back to the same Mexican cartel from which his contact routinely stole the coca and precursor chemicals. The Mexicans had been under federal siege over the number of journalists they'd killed and would not appreciate such attention.

But he had become accustomed to extracting information without killing people, breaking their spirit using pain and coercion. He would push gently today. Tomorrow, he would begin to apply pressure. Eventually, tired, hungry and aching, she would tell him what he wanted to know.

He had grown patient in FARC, expecting a bullet around every corner.

He had grown patient as the federals closed on him, time and again, only to fight his way back to respectability.

He had grown patient expecting to die, and as a consequence, Rivas always walked away.

25

Abi stared Rivas down, but her stomach was doing backflips. There had been rumors of a new player in the gang war for months, but no one had even considered Rivas, the former FARC interrogator who had gone to ground. At least, no one that her sources knew.

And she knew little about him except his reputation, as a butcher, a warlord who saw himself as a refined man. Gangsters were usually cut from the same cloth and could be handled, manipulated even. Rivas was a different kind of animal, unshakably cruel, with no hint of concern for others.

At his desk, Rivas rifled through her purse. "No ID, no wallet, no old receipts. Not even a gum wrapper. Just a recorder, a stun gun, a notepad, and a change purse with some folded bills. Not even a lipstick."

"I've always thought I looked better without much make-up," she said calmly. *He skins people alive. Oh God... what have I gotten myself into?* She loved her job, loved the impact it had, however impermanent. Loved that she ultimately helped people. She'd accepted the dangers. But Rivas's time with FARC was well known, with many astonished he'd avoided prosecution.

"I look at this collection, it makes me think you're a reporter. If you were a federal, they'd assign you a cover, which you would exaggerate. You would have IDs in that name, business cards. Instead, you can take notes. And... that is it."

"That's one theory."

He reached over to the other side of his desk and picked up a piece of paper. He held it up, a printed-out digital image of Bob. "Who is this man?" he asked her.

She frowned, accentuating her utter lack of recognition. "Don't know."

"A sincere statement, yet I still do not believe you." Rivas nodded to his men. "Take her to the lab." He turned back her way. "I have a video-conference call to make, and the wireless in this building is, regrettably, insufficient. But we will continue this discussion there after my meeting."

From behind the chair, Joao's oversized fist grabbed her dress collar and pulled Abi to her feet.

She had to stay calm, she knew. She needed an escape window, and that would require patience.

Poni Alvarez drove nervously, his hands gripping the wheel at ten and two like a stranded swimmer holding a flotation device. He craned forward, towards the windshield, his eyes flitting between it and the rearview mirror, perhaps hoping for a last-second save. Occasionally, he'd glanced down at the gun Bob was holding in the passenger seat.

"We'd better be close," Bob muttered. He wanted the gangster nervous, but not so nervous that he forgot his task.

Poni reverted his attention to the road. "It's the big building at the end of the street."

Bob's instructions had been simple: to be taken to whoever was running coke out of Hope Street's charity operation. Poni had tried, briefly, to convince Bob that his employer was not a man to try to reason with. In fact, Rivas had been a former commandant and interrogator with FARC, the rebel group that had waged a civil war in Colombia for decades.

Which was about what Bob had expected.

The lab building had parking behind it, Poni said. But a glance at the map had suggested to Bob the parking lot had only one exit, making it ideal for a trap, or at the least to box an opponent in. Instead, he had him drive past the front of the office block, which looked about half the size of a football pitch, two stories of whitewashed cinderblock with only a few boarded-over windows.

As they passed, Bob spotted the sign above the front door, "Logistica Tavares, S.R.L."

"Tavares Logistics?" he asked.

"They were a geotechnical surveying company for the oil industry before the worst of the troubles. Listen to me: do you really need the gun, my friend? I am just a club owner—"

"Who tried to put a .357 bullet between my eyes," Bob said. "Just be glad I'm letting you live. Pull over here, ahead of the delivery truck." They were far enough from the front doors to avoid general suspicion. Bob checked the rear- and side-view mirrors. The street looked empty, just the odd car coming and going.

Poni did as asked, putting the old Renault 4 into park using the wheel-mounted shifter.

"Get out, but do it slowly," Bob ordered. "If you run, know that I can hit you accurately from fifty paces, and you won't get twenty feet."

Poni nodded nervously. Both men got out of the car. Bob used the pistol to signal Poni around the back of the car. "Open the trunk."

He did as told.

Bob looked both ways. There were kids playing on the other side of the street, an elderly pair of friends at a card table in front of another building. But the street generally seemed quiet. The taller delivery van parked behind them was cutting off much of the road view, which helped. "Get in," he said.

"Hey... it's nearly dark. You could just let me go. I could say I saw nothing..."

"If I have to ask you again," Bob warned, "I'm just going to shoot you in the back of the head and let you fall into the trunk. Does that sound better to you?"

Poni reluctantly followed through. The hatch was barely large enough for luggage, let alone a man, and he had to curl into a near-fetal ball to fit. "Man, this is not right. It's very hot in here."

"Like you said, the sun's going down. You won't suffocate before I get back. But here's the deal: if you yell or scream or make any noise at all, you'd better hope someone else lets you out. Because if I hear noise when I get back here, I'm going to put four or more bullets through the lid of the trunk and see if that shuts you up. Do what I tell you, and when this is done, I'll let you go."

"Okay... but what if I came up with some money? What if—"

Bob slammed the trunk shut and locked it. He checked

the street again, but it was still quiet as the sun slipped below the horizon. He opened the driver's side door and retrieved his soft-sided bag from the back seat, slinging its long strap over his head so that it rested against his back like a knapsack.

He reversed direction and headed back up the road.

26

The Tavares building was in reasonable condition, the off-white spackled plaster and small rectangular windows mostly intact. It was just two stories, like so many industrial blocks in the Colombian town.

Bob circled the building. There was easy ingress in front and back, along with a side window on the alley between it and its neighbor that looked just about reachable, the ledge eight feet off the ground.

He checked both ways down the alley, then sprinted forward, kicking off and up the wall, steely fingers grabbing the ledge so that he could pull himself up and look inside.

Washroom. Perfect. He pulled himself up and clambered over the ledge, dropping onto the room's cold concrete floor. He looked under the two stalls to ensure he didn't have company.

He heard an exterior door close abruptly, from right outside. Bob stepped behind the washroom door and pushed himself up against the wall. It swung open a moment later, then closed, a janitor in blue overalls and a denim ball cap heading directly to the pair of sinks to wash his hands, pushing a bucket and mop.

He was taller, thin as a rail. *He's... what, six foot? Six one, maybe?* No one ever paid much attention to cleaning staff, Bob knew. It was a bold idea, but...

He stepped out, the man's attention on washing his hands thoroughly. Bob tapped him on the shoulder, and the man looked up in the mirror in front of him first, then realized, wide-eyed, that he didn't recognize the person about to assault him.

The janitor tried to turn. Bob timed the right hook perfectly, catching the man on the button, his legs turning to jelly.

He slumped to the floor. Bob moved two paces to the door. There was a wooden wedge behind it, probably used by the cleaner to prop it open. He shoved it under the door in case of any arrivals while he worked.

Then he knelt next to the man. He took off his shoes, unzipped his one-piece overall, and carefully pulled it off over the man's feet, leaving him in an undershirt and underwear.

He'd managed to grab a few things from a shop near the hotel, including extra shoelaces. He pulled the man's hands behind him and tied them together with one lace and slapped a piece of duct tape over the man's mouth. Then he used the second lace to tie the man's right thumb to his left big toe, the victim on his stomach, the line taut.

For both digits, he used a handcuff knot: dual loops that tighten when pulled. It was an old Mossad trick useful for restraint with no cuffs or ties. Any pulling motion would both tighten the knot and tweak the painful medial plantar nerve, sending agonizing pain through the foot arch, as if it had been stabbed.

The man tried to roll over. The lace pulled on the toe nerve, his eyes suddenly wide, his screaming through the tape utterly muffled.

"Don't move, or it will hurt like hell," Bob said in Spanish. "I'm going to borrow your overalls and hat." Then he grabbed the man by the collar and dragged him, stomach first, across the floor and into the first stall, heaving to shift the man's hundred and sixty plus pounds.

The man bellowed once more.

"Sorry, unavoidable," Bob said. He closed the cubicle door behind him. "Apologies in general. I know you probably just work here."

Bob put on the overalls and cap, then retrieved the mop and bucket from beside the sinks.

He moved to the door and peeked outside, realizing there was a short hallway and a second door to a ladies' room. He opened the door at the end of it and looked around the corner.

The first floor of the building was busy, dozens of tables covered in bricks of light brownish puttylike material. At the front door, two guards stood facing towards the street. In the center of the room, three giant boilers were connected via steel chimneys to the building's internal ductwork. Around each table was a series of navy-blue plastic drums, each looking to be around forty gallons.

He walked out slowly and positioned the bucket by the near wall, then began mopping the floor. He was a good twenty-five feet from the nearest table, hopefully enough that no one really paid attention.

Bob had seen Agency photo sets of cocaine processing and recognized coca paste almost immediately. Each table featured a two-person team in white lab coats, goggles and ventilation masks. One cut the blocks into smaller bricks in metal trays, then mixed in some kind of solvent, based on how much gas they were releasing. After a few minutes, the second man took each of the trays, one by one, to one of the three boiler-style separators.

They're making cocaine hydrochloride. From what he remembered, the solvents would cause the cocaine to partially crystallize. The units that looked like boilers would be used to remove any remaining solvent from the crystallized cocaine hydrochloride, which would then be dried and finally broken down into powder before being packed into solid bricks for shipping.

The final stage of the process was the most dangerous part of making cocaine due to the caustic solvents, but it looked like the only activity in the place. *So he's getting the paste from somewhere else, converting it here and selling it on.*

He kept mopping the floor, but let his eyes drift across the room. Each table was nearly full, stacked with product and just enough room to work. There had to have been tons of coca paste. How many kilograms of cocaine would be drawn from just what they had there, in one afternoon?

He thought back to the street in San Diego, to those ten-year-olds being forced to risk their lives just to hook more desperate people on the stuff. He remembered Jasmin's despair at her brother's plight.

Bob's hand tightened on the mop, and he suppressed a swell of anger at the notion.

This place is shit, and it should burn to the fucking ground.

Then he took a deep breath and centered himself.

Not now, Bobby. Priorities.

He reached into his left pocket and withdrew his phone. He started the camera app without raising the device, holding it low. Then he crouched, as if adjusting the handle on the bucket of dirty water at his feet. He secreted the phone behind the bucket for cover, then turned it side on and took a series of pictures, slowly raising the phone about six inches to get a variety of images. Then he stored it back in the side pocket and stood up again.

Along the left wall, there were two open doorways at each end with three steps up to them. He pushed the mop and bucket that way, the casters rolling smoothly. Bob glanced through the door.

The next room over was divided in two by a central wall. It was full of long tables, each staffed like a factory assembly line. A man at the front was passed a metal suitcase, which he opened and placed in front of the first worker. The worker then stripped the interior lining from the case and its natural cardboard separator before passing it to the second.

The second worker took a new piece of material and began stitching it into the case, then another, as if adding two dividers. The room had a strange smell, he noticed. *What is that? It's floral. Why would they be pushing the scent of flowers through the room?*

The fake lining they found in Eric Williams's case. He checked the lab workers to ensure they were occupied and that the guards hadn't turned. He took out the phone and snapped two quick pictures.

The worker passed the newly altered case to the end of the next table, where a man placed eight bricks of wrapped cocaine into it, then shoved it to the next worker, who rearranged them until they were flat and held tightly between the two decoy linings, like the contents of a sandwich between two slices of bread. To the outside viewer, the only visible content would be the top of the "bread": a molded, 3D image of a suitcase interior.

The cases go back to the charity because the charity has a customs waiver. In the event of a spot check, they X-ray the bag and see a benign interior. It was clever as hell, Bob figured, but relied on the bags never being actually opened and checked.

He suspected the airport worker who'd manually opened one probably intended to steal, and was as shocked as anyone to find himself holding seven kilos of coke.

How many bags had Hope Street brought in through San Diego alone? Jasmine had mentioned shipping fifteen to twenty cases of clothing down per week. If the same number came back per shipment – and with branches all over the country – it was potentially hundreds of kilos per week, tons per month. In the rare chance of a manual intervention, like Eric's, they could point to a relatively unvetted volunteer as the culprit.

The flowery smell had to be something. It was too pungent to just be coincidence and seemed to be emanating from the suitcase room.

One of the men on the case line looked up in his general direction, and Bob took it as a cue to move on. He pushed the bucket along the wall, past the processing tables, until he was by the second door.

The next room over was occupied, a man leaning against one end of a long conference table. Bob stepped back to avoid catching the man's peripheral vision and listened.

"... If we're careful, we can increase production sixfold by this time next year."

"I see. That seems a large number."

Bob recognized the second voice immediately. *Anderson Rowe.* He took out the phone again and hit record, holding it low by his side, palmed but the mic end facing out.

"It is. But we need to strike while we've still got an advantage," the man at the table said. "The same contact supplying the paste is also in charge of tracking it, so the Corsarios won't notice any shortfall. At the volume they move, that's not surprising. But eventually, someone might compare overall production costs here and elsewhere in Colombia and realize they are subsidizing a competitor out the back door. At that point, things could get ugly quickly, and the percentage play will be to shut this down."

Out the back door? He's stealing the paste from a competitor. That's why this is so profitable; his production costs must be less than half a normal lab's.

If that's Rivas, he must have balls of steel.

"Fine, do what you need to do," Rowe said. "I'm hosting a charity event this weekend and cannot be reached. Ideally, once we've cleared up the other problem I mentioned, we will not need to speak again."

"Ideally. I've been working on our vigilante situation, by the way."

"Then he's there?"

"Somewhere. I had a youth follow him, but he was spotted, and he lost him. But we have some leverage now, so..." He let the thought trail.

"Fine. You can contact my PA if you need any further direction. Our business for now is done."

The man at the table stood up straight, the call evidently ended.

Bob glanced back at the lab room. He could feel the weight of his soft-sided bag against his back. He had photos of the suitcase, tape of Rowe talking to Rivas. Surely that was enough, at least for Assistant District Attorney Sheinbein to make a case that Williams had been set up.

But maybe not. Even if he lets Eric go, would it be enough to indict Rowe? *Probably not.* Recognizing a voice was a nebulous tie, at best, and it wasn't as if Bob could testify to it. An expert might testify it was him, but again, that wouldn't even be enough to indict.

And they'll find another way to smuggle it in. If the too-clever-for-itself smuggling loop drew attention, they'd doubtless revert to disposable fiberglass submersibles – mini subs – like the other smugglers in Buenaventura. It would be more costly, but they could do it.

And they will, because they can't resist a cheap source of expensive coca paste.

The Semtex in my bag isn't doing anyone any good just sitting there.

He glanced at the boilers and separators, doubtless under pressure. They were being fed by natural gas lines that ran up their stack to the ductwork fifteen feet above. A charge placed against one of them? It would be a hell of a blast, and the natural gas lines would feed fire back to their storage tanks, probably out back or in a basement.

He looked around again quickly, then began to roll the bucket along the wall, towards the center of the room, his decision made.

There was a certain symmetry to using the same bombs Rivas had used against his competitors to destroy the place.

It wasn't why he was there, and there was always danger in going off-mission. But the notion of doing nothing at all didn't seem acceptable in the moment, not when an entire city was hostage to the trade.

He'd fire off a few rounds from Poni's .357 a minute before the timer was due to blow, give the workers – most of whom probably knew no better – a chance to get out.

But then this place is coming down, and Rowe's dirty product with it.

27

Bob rolled the bucket and mop back to the far end of the room. The gas lines ran up, through the floor, along the side of the separator chimneys, which gave him options. Placing a timed charge on the separator units would mean wandering into the middle of the work floor, amongst the staff. They'd get a closer look at him, which would bring questions about why he was unfamiliar.

But on the second floor? Being above the target wouldn't matter; the gas lines guaranteed that any blast would travel back to the first-floor equipment. He glanced over at the stairs, in the corner of the room.

Of course, there was no telling who or what was up there. And the target constituted unnecessary risk. *I could just get out of here now; with the evidence I've got enough to help Eric Williams. It's probably not enough to convict Rowe, but Rivas would be toast, done in by the feds or rival gangs.*

He glanced back at the tables covered in coca paste. *Make up your mind, Bobby, or head out the bathroom window.* He wasn't there to fight the drug war, much of which he figured could've been solved by legalizing and restricting it, like booze and pot.

But without that option available, gangsters like Rivas were in control, with nothing between them and the often naïve, emotionally damaged kids who'd get hooked.

The little voice in the back of his head was telling him not to diverge from the mission. But he ignored it. *You need to do this, for everyone's sake.* He kept his head down but his eyes raised, peeking out from under the janitor's denim ball cap to ensure no one was watching as he approached the stairs.

Twenty feet behind him, he heard the scuffle of shoes on concrete. He glanced over his shoulder. One of the workers was heading directly toward the bathroom where the janitor was tied up.

Ah, shit. You stretch recon into action and this is the sort of thing that happens.

The employee reached the bathroom door.

If he opens that, I'm probably done.

His hand stretched out for the doorknob.

"Hey!" Both men's heads turned to find the source, on the far side of the room near the front doors. A guard was waving at the worker. "No breaks. Get back to work."

Bob exhaled deeply, turned back to the stairs and headed up them, the bucket in his left hand.

At the top of the steps was a landing. The upper floor had evidently been management offices at one point, a series of glass cubes divided by a central corridor. It appeared empty, the lights out. Bob followed the corridor to the floor's midpoint. He glanced in each office as he passed. They'd been stripped of anything of value, the furniture gone.

In the middle of the floor a support column ran up to more ductwork ten feet above. The gas line was attached to its back side. Bob removed his soft-sided bag and opened it at his feet, crouching to remove the three explosive charges. The Semtex package on each was large, nearly brick-sized. There was a good chance that, if the central column collapsed, the entire roof and second floor might come down with it. Even if it didn't, flames feeding back down the gas lines would hit the pressurized separators within seconds.

And then everything goes boom.

He placed the first two charges against the chimney, taping them down by wrapping the duct tape several times around it. Even if discovered, it would take several minutes to cut the tape away and reset the timer, minutes they likely wouldn't have.

He hesitated with the third charge. If there was some sort of emergency cutoff or safety valve, it was possible the explosion wouldn't backflow to the equipment. Ideally, he needed to place a charge on the natural gas tanks themselves.

He set the timers on the first two charges to ten minutes and packed the third back in his bag, which he slung over his head. He took the stairs back downstairs quickly. He checked at the corner landing to make sure no one from the lower room was near the stairs, then trotted back to the bathroom as quickly as seemed safe.

Inside, he placed the half-full bucket against the bottom of the door to discourage quick entry, then headed to the window. In the toilet stall, the janitor struggled and tried to talk through his gag.

Bob checked the alley both ways, then hopped out to ground level.

He followed the side of the building to the back parking area. It was quiet, no movement. Most of the two dozen spaces were occupied by mopeds and small-engine motorcycles, with a cube van and a Toyota sedan the only cars.

The dual natural gas storage tanks were in a mesh-enclosed area next to the building's back wall. There was a loading dock that, by position, emptied into the back room, where the suitcases were being prepared. He kept an eye on its roll-up door as he made his way to the enclosure.

He had no wire clippers, and the gate was locked. The top of the fence was protected with old-fashioned barbed wire, rusty from years of humidity. He checked his perimeter again, then stripped off the one-piece janitor's overalls, tossing the denim garment over the top of the fence to cover the barbs. He repositioned his soft-sided bag, then took a few paces back.

Bob ran for the fence, kicking off it and up with his right foot, his hands protected by the double layer of denim as he vaulted it. His feet came down on the soft soil by the tanks.

He took out the Semtex charge and placed it against the bottom of the first tank, taping it in place. He set the timer for forty-five seconds later than the first two, a guarantee that if the central column didn't collapse, the conference room and Rivas would still be hit.

He checked the mesh door and drew its simple latch-driven deadbolt. A moment later, he was heading back towards the corner of the building and the alley to 4 Street.

The truck rounded the corner without warning, the sound of its big engine disguised by the alley's high walls.

Bob flattened on the ground in front of the cube van. He raised himself up to a crouch and watched around the van as the truck crossed the lot to just ahead of the loading dock. Its reverse alarm chimed steadily as it backed into the raised dock.

The tailgate opened. A man jumped out onto the dock.

Bob didn't like the idea of more people inside. The plan was to go back through the bathroom, fire a couple of shots in the general direction of the guards, causing panic among the staff. They'd begin to flee. The charges would begin to go off, clearing the rest out and giving Bob his cue to exit.

More people inside meant more risk, particularly if they were in the back rooms. But the staff on the floor were just workers, people who needed the money to survive and probably had no other options. He had to make sure they got out safely, he knew.

The men getting off the truck were carrying weapons. They'd likely be in the conference room with the former FARC man. *They're not your concern. They're not Rivas, but they're not taking his dirty money under threat. Stay on mission, Bobby.*

Four men had entered the building. He gave it another ten seconds to ensure the driver and cab passenger had joined them. He rose to his feet, then quickly dropped back to a crouch, one more guard stepping off the back off the tailgate.

His left hand was grasping a woman by the upper arm, pulling her along.

Abi.

Shit.

He checked his Seiko wristwatch.

Six minutes and this place blows. He turned and ran back towards the alley and the bathroom window.

He needed to get her out of there before that happened.

So much for doing things quietly.

28

The guard half-dragged Abi into the building. Beyond the loading dock, a short corridor led to a back entrance into what appeared to be an old-fashioned conference room, a long wooden table taking up most of its space.

Daniel Rivas stood on one side of the table, leaning against it. "Good, you are here. Now, we can finish our talk, and I can tell you a little about this place."

She looked around. She could see out the room's main door. It appeared to be a lab, as he'd said at his office, people in safety masks working at a series of white tables. "Let me guess, you process cocaine here."

Rivas straightened up and began to pace back and forth on his side of the table. "Yes, yes. That would be the case. But do you know how it is made?"

"Roughly," she said.

"Then you know one of the most important stages is to separate the cocaine crystals from the material we do not need. To do this, we use highly caustic substances:

hydrochloric acid, sulfuric acid, acetone. Have you ever seen what sulfuric acid does to human skin? I have, many times. It is quite horrific in its own lovely way."

"Charming."

"We have barrels of the stuff here, you know. I have often wondered how long a human could survive if they were slowly lowered into it, so that their skin and bones began to dissolve from the feet up."

"You've 'often wondered'?" Abi replied. "As in, you sit around fantasizing about melting people alive, like the bad guy in *Roger Rabbit*? That makes you kind of a sick bastard, don't you think?"

His expression shifted from cockiness to irritation in a heartbeat. "I did not ask you to poke your nose into my business, you silly bitch! What happens to you now is your own doing. But we can make it a lot easier if you—"

In the next room, they heard gunshots. People were screaming, the floor shuddering slightly as if a herd of animals were about to stampede through the room. Rivas nodded to his two guards by the door. "Find out what's going on," he demanded.

Abi felt a swell of hope. Perhaps he was being attacked by rivals. Whatever it was, she knew it might be her only chance to escape.

BOB OPENED the bathroom door a crack and checked the lab's main floor. Behind him, the janitor's muffled demands echoed from the toilet cubicle.

"Sorry, friend, really. It's not about you," Bob offered in Spanish. The janitor ignored his good intentions and kept kicking.

The front door guard was facing them again. The staff would see him, and he wasn't disguised anymore. But if he'd gauged the operation correctly, they were too scared to speak up or raise an alarm.

He left the bathroom and approached the corner stairs. He'd thought about climbing them and turning off the timers, but he'd wrapped them down so tightly he likely didn't have time. He checked his watch again.

Three minutes. Subtlety isn't going to cut it.

He kept one eye on the guard as he followed the wall to the first door, the suitcase room. He leaned in. At the far wall, as he'd expected, was a second entrance to the conference room next door.

Bob ignored the staff's curious stares as he walked the length of the room and opened the door just enough to check inside.

Abi was standing near the conference room's main entrance, a guard on either side. The man he assumed was Rivas stood on the other side of the table. He was lecturing her, it sounded like.

Time's running out, Bobby. Time to stir things up.

He turned back to the roomful of assembly-line workers, drew the pistol from his waistband and fired two shots over their heads.

The staff panicked, several shrieking, all bolting from their stools, a mass heading for the open doorway in unison. He ran behind them, firing two more shots into the far wall of the main room, the panic spreading like gas on a fire as they overwhelmed the two front entrance guards and began spilling outside.

Bob turned and ran back to the conference room's second entrance. He pulled it open and ran inside. The two guards beside Abi were looking back out the main door into the front room, trying to figure out what was going on. Rivas was crouched behind the table, hiding.

Bob shot the first guard through the back, center mass. The second turned, too late, the pistol spitting fire twice, bullets striking him in the shoulder and rib cage. Both men went down, clutching at their wounds, one on his knees, the other prone.

Bob turned towards Rivas but realized he was rising from his position, gun drawn. He sprinted sideways, tackling Abi, throwing both of them through the door into the next room, their bodies rolling over the side of the short stairwell to the concrete floor as the gangster emptied his mag at the empty doorway.

The first charge blew, a thunderous roar that shook the entire building as he helped Abi to her feet. The room was three-quarters clear, but people were screaming, still pushing, trying to get through the main entrance.

"We've got to go, NOW!" Bob yelled. He grabbed her by the collar and yanked her to her feet, half dragging her towards the bathroom door.

A massive chunk of metal ductwork crashed to the ground a few feet away, and they froze for a split second. Bob pushed her through the swinging door, into the bathroom. "Go, out the window, now!" he yelled. "Just GO!"

She climbed out. Bob turned back to the main room, where most of the staff had fled, but others were trying to get past the remaining guard. He was standing ahead of the wide-open front doors, waving a pistol wildly to keep them back.

Bob took careful aim and shot him through the left thigh, the guard collapsing instantly, clutching the wound.

The remaining workers streamed over him like he wasn't there.

They'd be out in seconds. A chunk of ceiling tiles smashed to the ground beside him as he waited for the crowd to thin enough so that he could get out.

The janitor.

Bob didn't wait to see if the guard was still breathing, turning and sprinting for the bathroom. He flew through the swinging door shoulder first.

Bob turned to the first stall and kicked the door open. The janitor was still prone, unable to free himself. Bob picked him up in a fireman's lift, taking his dead weight over his shoulder, the man's bulk almost driving him to the ground. He tipped the body out the window, dropping the man clear.

The second charge blew, fire running back up the gas lines to the separators, the equipment exploding a split second later, an even bigger shudder as the building's roof began to cave in, a fireball spreading outwards, a column of heat throwing open the bathroom doors, blowing Bob out the window before he could raise a foot, consciousness lost before he'd hit the ground.

29

Poni Alvarez woke violently, wrenched from the black void of nightmares about his childhood orphanage by the impact of the tiny Renault 4 being flipped onto one side, his body slamming into the trunk lid.

It popped open, and he rolled out onto the road.

His ribs ached. He could smell smoke, hear screaming and panicked voices. He opened one eye, the world a sideways mass of legs as dozens of workers rushed by the overturned car. He struggled to one knee.

The building's roof had caved in and was on fire, great columns of flame twisting and turning their way through any wooden fuel. The windows were shattered, the front doors still there but blown wide open. A chunk of brick and plaster the size of a vending machine lay next to the car.

He'd been stuck in the trunk for nearly an hour, fiddling with the lock from the inside, trying to spring the latch unsuccessfully. Eventually, he'd given up and fallen asleep.

But... what happened?

The gringo. The American has blown the place up. He shook his head as he gaped at the smoldering wreck.

Movement to his left caught his eye. Someone was staggering down the alley to the rear parking lot, limping, backlit by the flames, right hand by his side clutching a pistol.

Rivas.

His boss had a gaping wound in the top of his left thigh. He saw Poni gawking and nodded his way. "What?" Rivas demanded, as if nothing behind him was shocking.

"Boss... you're bleeding."

Rivas looked down at the open gash. "It was a hunk of glass. It's nothing." Then his eyes narrowed as he studied the bruised club owner. "Why are you here? Did you have something to do with this, little worm?"

Poni shook his head vigorously. Being a survivor meant avoiding the wrath of the powerful. He'd always understood that. As spiteful and mean as Rivas could be, he was the ultimate survivor. "No, boss! I was hurt, my ribs broken, I think. I was trying to stop him." It wouldn't hurt, Poni decided, for Rivas to think he was heroic.

"STOP WHO?!" Rivas snarled.

"The American! The American, boss, I swear—"

Rivas looked around, scanning the crowd, searching for any signs of a target. "Where? Where is he?"

"I don't know, boss. I fought hard, but he must have had help," Poni said, improvising. "I had him at gunpoint, but before I could pull the trigger, someone hit me from behind."

Rivas shook his head in disgust. "Incompetent!" He closed the few feet between them at a furious limp and cuffed Poni behind the ear. "You let him do this!?" He scanned the crowd furiously again until he spotted another of his men. He staggered over and grabbed the man's pump-action shotgun, then turned it on Poni.

"Boss, no, please!" Poni cowered, throwing his arms up in front of his face.

Rivas pulled the trigger, but there was no shell in the pipe. He tried to pump the breach, but there were no more loaded. Angered, he threw the gun at the smaller man, Poni half ducking out of the way as it clattered to the ground.

"No matter," Rivas said. He nodded to the man whose gun he'd just discarded. "Get a car. We go to the warehouse; we load up. We find this guy, quickly."

Poni tried to interrupt. "Boss, what can I—"

Rivas cuffed him again. "You shut up, asshole! You're going to stay here and tell the police what you did, how you forgot to check the pressure on the equipment. How this is all your fault. If you don't, I guarantee you, by next week no one will know you or your family ever existed. You got me?"

Poni nodded furiously. He'd seen what Rivas did to men who disagreed.

A HAND on his arm woke Bob from a furious dream, the details fading to nothing as soon as his eyes were open.

He sat up suddenly, jerking his body away from the person's touch. Then reality kicked in, and he realized he was lying on a sofa, light muted in a postage-stamp living room.

"Shhh! Shhh... it's okay," Abi said. "You got hit in the back of the head by a brick, I think. But you're okay."

Bob flexed his neck muscles, feeling them creak from stress. "Feels taut, almost like a little whiplash." He looked around. The rest of the apartment looked equally undersized, someone's one-bedroom, the living room drapes drawn. "Where are we?"

A man walked through the opposite door, carrying a tray with three mugs. "I made us chocolate," he said in Spanish.

It took Bob a second to place him. He lowered his voice and said in English to Abi, "That's the guy I knocked out. The janitor."

"I speak English." From up close, without mission focus interrupting, Bob realized he was older, probably in his late fifties or sixties or, perhaps like many in Buenaventura, just aging prematurely. "You saved me from the explosion. So when you were unconscious and your friend was worried, I said I lived near."

"I don't get it," Bob said, sitting up and almost immediately regretting it, his head beginning to pound. *Ah hell. Concussion, I think.* "I'm the one who blew the place up."

"I supposed as much." Their host set the tray down. "I am Miguel. This is my place. It is not much, but it is okay. Please… take a chocolate."

Bob and Abi each retrieved a mug of the hot beverage, but neither tried it, unnerved by his hospitality. Bob looked around the room. It was spartan, but homely, with family pictures on a side table, a large crucifix attached to the wall just above it.

Perhaps sensing their reticence, Miguel leaned forward, retrieved the third mug and took a long sip. "Hmm. Dark and good."

They tried it. The hot chocolate was bitter, dark, unlike what he'd experienced in the past. "Why are you helping me when I assaulted you and destroyed the place you work, Miguel?"

The older man sighed. "I am sixty-eight years old. I

know… Everyone tells me I do not look my age, for which I am grateful. But we all know what Rivas and his men are. Those of us from here, we do what we have to in order to survive. It does not mean we approve. Me? I follow the word of my Lord and Savior, Jesus. And he demands we both turn the other cheek and embrace those who try to do good. I don't have a job no more. But they figure everyone got out, and to see Rivas's bad works taken down a level? I cannot fault you, so I must embrace you."

Bob felt flushed, a swell of embarrassment hitting him. *I don't think I've ever been that generous in my life.* "Thank you. I'm not quite sure what to say."

Miguel shrugged. "It is enough. As I said, you saved me—"

"I endangered you."

"True, but Rivas and his dirty chemicals endangered everyone. At least he stored them carefully, in a lead-lined room in the basement. So they will have some protection, the fire crew. But he is an awful man."

"Is?"

"When we were leaving, I saw my cousin Nestor. He said he saw Rivas stumble across the parking area just before the final explosion."

God damn it. Apparently, everyone gets mercy today. "A shame," Bob said.

"It is not for us to decide." The old man waved a hand dismissively as he said it, as if nothing ever really was.

Abi was making eyes at Bob, jerking her head subtly towards Miguel.

"What?" Bob asked quietly.

"He's lost his ability to make a living. Help the man."

Bob looked around the room. "My jacket?"

Miguel rose and retrieved it from a hook near the front door. The back of the left sleeve was badly scorched. "I was going to see if I could patch the hole that is starting before you woke..."

Bob took the jacket. "No... please, you've done so much more than enough already, sir." He reached into the inside pocket and found the small slit in the lining, then retrieved the wad of bills tucked inside. "I keep this for emergencies..."

Before he could expound, Miguel's palms rose in deterrence. "No! Please, I cannot possibly."

"You can, and you will," Bob said, handing him the folded wad. "It's not much, just a few hundred dollars, but hopefully..." He let the thought fade, the janitor's embarrassment obvious.

"I never taken no handout before," the man said.

"Not a handout," Bob said. "Rental on our time here, and compensation for my knocking you unconscious earlier. If you can be generous to honor your belief, I can be fair to satisfy mine."

Miguel pondered that, then pocketed the money. "This will go further here than you realize," he said. "I thank you."

Bob half turned to set the jacket down next to him on the end of the sofa. His ribs screamed at him, stabbing pain running up through his armpit to the nape of his neck. "JESUS H!" he bellowed.

Miguel winced. "*Por favor*..."

"Sorry," Bob said. "I've cracked my ribs on the left side too many times. Each is a little more harsh than the last." He realized Abi hadn't said anything and gestured her way. "You okay?"

She nodded quickly but had both arms across her body, as if looking for security. "I'm okay. What you did back there... it was incredibly dangerous and not what we talked about."

"I know. It was an operational decision, made in the moment. I saw how much cocaine was being produced in the place, and it reminded me of where most of it ends up, in the inner city back home, hurting the people who can least afford it."

"So you figured you'd blow up a building?" Her tone was icy.

"I got the workers out first."

"You created a panic, and they got out, yes. But only by seconds, Bob! You could have missed people, or they could have been trampled!"

"But I didn't, and they weren't."

"Even now, the neighborhood is still burning, and the few resources to fight fires in the city are all there, which means if something happens elsewhere, someone could lose their home."

"It was a calculated risk," Bob said.

"But that is in the past," Miguel interceded. "Rivas, he hardly paid any of us. He knew all of our families, made it clear everyone in the neighborhood worked for him whether we liked it or not. There will be people upset and worried that they have no money rather than little money. But we will survive. The gangster, though, he will have problems."

The janitor was hinting at something, Bob figured. "Why's that?"

"I hear much, cleaning a place. No one pays attention to the man who cleans up their messes, but I hear. He spends much money to buy his 'paste' from a man who works for the Mexican cartels. He owes this man all the time and pays him when they sell, because he is always expanding. So he has no real…" Miguel turned to Abi. "How you say '*movimiento de efectivo*' in English?"

"Cash flow," she said.

"If he can't pay the man who brings the paste, that man can't pay his bribes at *la fabrica*… the factory. He talk big money, thousands of US dollars per week. Now, maybe there will be war between them. But at least it will not be in this neighborhood."

"That's something, anyway," Abi said, shooting Bob another cold look. "Did you at least get the evidence you need?"

Bob nodded. Then his eyes widened. "My phone!" He grabbed the jacket and found it resting safely in the left-side pocket. He opened it, then texted Abi what he'd gathered. "You're going to get an audio file and some pictures. Keep a separate copy of these just in case, as a backup. Until I get home and hand all of it to the assistant district attorney, we have to assume Rivas will be looking for us."

For the first time in the evening, Abi's lips curled up into a slightly satisfied smile, a sense of amends made. "Then your friend will be exonerated, yes?"

"I think so." He had his usual trepidation, his sense that another shoe had yet to drop. But Bob had to admit it to himself: for once, everything had gone to plan. "Usually, when I've had to help someone in the past, things have gotten complicated and fallen apart. It's a nice change."

In the other chair, Miguel made a hasty sign of the cross and muttered something quietly. Then he saw their perplexed expressions. "I say a prayer, that it is as you say."

"Now what?" Abi said. "I still need to do work for my story on all of this. I will need as much paper as I can get on the buildings, ownership, how it relates to Rivas. And I will need to talk to your young friend by phone."

"I figure that can be arranged once I'm stateside," Bob said. "El Protector gets another big scoop, the gangs all take a hit, and Eric gets to go back home. But until I get there, you have to go to ground."

"I have work to do," Abi protested.

"For a couple of days, you don't," Bob stressed. "For a couple of days, you need a place you can go where they won't think to look. There's no point you working on the story if you're not alive to file it."

"But—"

"No buts," Bob said. "Trust me on this. Rivas will be out for blood. And I have to be able to fly home knowing you're safe without me here."

She squinted a little and tilted her head, her face withering in disapproval. "Yes, because until you got here, I wasn't managing on my own."

Bob pinched the bridge of his nose. "I didn't mean it like that. I—"

Her expression softened, and she grabbed him by the upper arm again and gave him a little push. "I know."

"I'll be out of town within a day or two," Bob said. "I want to get an idea of where else the charity is sending cases. It's national, according to my friend Jasmine. If I can follow some of the cases back to the source, I have a second example to give to the district attorney, and maybe I can pin down Rowe as the person ultimately responsible. His talking to Rivas on tape combined with his charity being caught red-handed in more than one city would probably be enough to ruin him."

Bob rose, his muscles and ribs aching.

"Please!" Miguel said. "At least stay and finish your chocolate."

Abi smiled at him broadly, beaming for just a few seconds. The contrast from a day earlier, when she'd told him about losing her kid to a gangster, was stark. It wasn't going to get her son back, but it had helped her fulfill her purpose, her vow to get rid of as many of the bastards plaguing her community as possible.

Sometimes, Bob figured, *this shit is actually all worth it.* And that made him smile a little, too.

30

Villa Del Mar sat on the outskirts of Cali, a hilly neighborhood of middle-class, low-rise homes and successful small businesses. The common lack of exterior decoration or even paint made it look a lot like Buenaventura, Bob figured... minus the debris, trash, broken buildings and hopelessness.

Carrera 66 was just as busy as the streets in the coastal city, mopeds and motorcycles dominating traffic, kids in shorts listening to music on earbuds, neighborhood moms pulling small, wheeled carts to the grocer's. "A lot of people," Bob said. "You're sure they don't know you here?"

"My cousin only moved here four years ago," Abi said, guiding her little Fiat along the narrow thoroughfare. "And his family lived in Bogota before. Nobody knows him in Buenaventura."

They'd stopped by Bob's hotel to grab his things, Bob waiting in the car, Abi confirming two men in the lobby checking out everyone coming and going, one with the familiar half-teardrop of El Corsarios.

On the way out of town, Bob had dumped the penultimate of six credit cards supplied by his deceased former fixer, Nicky Velasco. It had been used to hire the rental car, which was a burning husk.

The card was no longer viable, and Bob knew the last card – set up, as had been Nicky's pattern, against the accounts of known organized criminals in the US – had just a thousand dollars preloaded onto it. The "Bob Davis" passport he would have to toss as soon as he returned home, as it could be red-flagged by the NSA on entering the country. It had cost all but ten thousand of his remaining funds, and he already owed Adam Renton another five thousand.

Trying to do the right thing was getting pricier by the day, it seemed.

Abi gestured to an upcoming street, the homes unadorned, but also in pastels of orange and blue. She clicked on the left turn signal. "This is it. When we meet Alex, be cool. He's what you would call very strait-laced. He also does not like America because of the country's influence on our politics and economy. But he knows you're helping me, and he knows I'm a reporter."

"You said you haven't seen him in some time," Bob mentioned as she pulled the car to the curb and parked. "You're sure he's safe?"

She gave him a sharp look, but it softened almost immediately, acknowledging that he was just being careful. "We played together every day as kids, and our parents are very tight. He's family. You don't have to worry."

Bob undid his seatbelt. "I'm going to get a cab downtown. I'll have a new burner by this evening and will call you, okay?"

She nodded. Bob opened the door. At the last moment,

she clamped a hand down on his left shoulder. "Bob... be careful."

He nodded. "I will."

"I've learned not to ignore my intuition, and we are both fortunate to be alive after yesterday. Keep a low profile until you are back home, and I will worry less."

"I'll be on a plane tomorrow."

"I'll hold you to that."

"If I can confirm Rowe's charity is moving bags of coke through any other port, I have a tie to Eric's case, and Rowe has a lot to explain to the cops."

He got out of the car, retrieving his soft-sided sports bag from the footwell. "You take your own advice, okay? I know you want to tie Rivas to owning those buildings, but keep it low profile for a couple of days."

She nodded. "Good luck."

Bob closed the door and headed up the street. There was a store a block away. *Maybe grab a clipboard and an ID holder. A confidently carried clipboard opens all sorts of doors.*

DARIEN, COLOMBIA

EVENING HAD SET IN, the sun an orange crescent above the jungle tree line. His leg hurt like hell, but Daniel Rivas stood stoically in the living room of his mansion, ahead of the sixteen-foot floor-to-ceiling windows, watching darkness approach.

The mansion had been "liberated" from a competitor a year prior in the town near Cali. Rivas was hardly ever there, even though he loved the quiet of the small community, the giant swimming pool and mountain views. Work governed his life, and his work was in Buenaventura.

In the moment, however, that was beside the point. Rowe had sent an envoy to take charge, and that meant playing the genial host despite the pain in his leg and the bitterness in his heart.

The stocky young man in the tan suit, sitting calmly on the white leather sofa fifteen feet away, had introduced himself as Sebastian, an assistant, nothing more or less. His task was to ensure damage control. To that end, he had said on introduction, police and federals had been bribed already, and his supplier paid off.

That meant they were no longer partners, Rivas realized.

It meant that from now on, effectively, he worked for Anderson Rowe.

"I just do not understand how it profits us to wait here for word from others," Rivas began to say.

The man on the sofa crossed one leg over the other. "That's what the man wants. It will go better for you if you don't challenge that reality. We have two dozen men from two top security firms in Cali looking for 'Bob Davis' and his female accomplice. Somebody will have seen something, and our teams will know about it in short order. The kind of work they do... they can't really afford to fail someone like Mr. Rowe."

"And then we kill them both," Rivas said.

"Once we know what they know, yes."

Rivas stopped pacing and wagged a finger at his guest. "No, take my advice. I made this mistake already. We find them, we kill them. We worry about the details later. If I did that yesterday, I would still have my laboratory today."

The lab fire had made every newscast in the country,

pillars of flame kissing the sky as firefighters tried to keep the fire contained. They'd begun by pouring liquid concrete over the burning foundation before the flames could reach the basement storage room and the heavy pollutants stored inside.

Two years of work, Rivas thought. *Two years, undone in a matter of minutes*. His anger was white hot, incendiary. But he knew he had to rein it in with the American present, not dare show an ounce of his real rage.

The fire would draw attention from the other gangs, too. They might even connect him to the other explosions, their missing captains. Everything he had built was teetering on the edge of destruction, and this man wanted him to just hang around his house, doing nothing.

"Just let us handle it, okay, sport?" the American said. "The boss has kept you alive so far. And you're going to pay for that protection. That starts with respecting the man's wishes. So" – he gestured towards the other sofa – "take a load off. We're going to be here until this gets resolved."

Sebastian reached inside his suit jacket and withdrew a 9mm Smith & Wesson from a shoulder rig. He checked the load, a serene smile on his face.

Whatever had him so confident, Rivas hoped it was going around.

31

Abi watched the sun go down through the tiny window of her cousin's second bedroom. It had been another long day in a series, but she was grateful to still be there and fighting.

She wondered and worried about Bob. He was clearly doing things for the right reasons; she just wasn't certain they were the right things. The lab fire had made the news, which reported two dead, both guards. As most of Rivas's men were former Corsarios, and most Corsarios were former orphans, it seemed unlikely anyone would mourn their passing.

But it's still not what we wanted.

However insanely crude his methods, Bob had gotten results. The audio was clear, the photos telling. She knew he'd wanted her to hold off before working, but she'd managed to get into a government tax database that listed the property's numbered-company owner. The next step would be to write a first draft of the story, then start chasing reactions.

A lot of people had seen her face and would put two and two together. She'd worked over the phone, anonymously, for so long that the sheer speed with which they'd figured out she was media had startled her. Now, "El Protector" would have to be retired. She'd have to use her own byline and live with the potential fallout.

But it will be worth it to take down Daniel Rivas.

She looked at the clock radio by her bed. It was just after midnight. She contemplated staying up to write the first draft.

With any luck, Bob would get back home the next morning, and his friend would be free shortly thereafter.

It seemed like she'd never be free of Buenaventura's problems. She reached into her purse and took out her son's picture, a warm glow filling her.

But he will be. As long as I can fight for him, he will be.

Bob left the motel early, hiking the quarter mile to the airport instead of calling a car, the hood on his sweatshirt pulled up, his soft-sided bag slung over his back.

Even at just after five in the morning, Cali was already busy. Traffic was steady if not heavy, the city still lit for darkness as the sun began to skirt the horizon. At the airport, to the whine of a jet landing, he stopped near the gated freight entrance, well before the departures doors.

He took the soft-sided bag off his back, unzipped it and took out the ID holder, now containing his Bob Davis driver's license and the clipboard, a thatch of paper from the motel shoved into the clip. He repositioned the bag, then slung the ID around his neck with the attached lace. He gripped the clipboard in his left hand.

Bob approached the gate. A guard was standing two feet away in a sentry box. He looked bored. Bob flashed the ID quickly, then pulled the clipboard in front of it and flicked through the pages. "Doing a freight check for our clients," he said in Spanish. He looked up and met the guard's eye. "Charity freight? Should be a bunch of cases going out today from Buenaventura. I'm just checking the numbers."

The guard nodded for him to go through. "They're number six, I think." The guard leaned around the sentry box and looked back at the freight area. "Wait. No, five."

"Thanks."

Bob strolled over to depot five like a man in no rush to get back to the office. Inside the corrugated-roofed, open-fronted hangar, an airport worker was loading a series of cases just like those at the lab onto a luggage cart. "From Hope Street?" Bob asked.

The man nodded. "Yes."

Bob made a motion to count them, lips moving. At the end he said, "That's all of them. This is the San Diego shipment, correct?"

The worker looked puzzled. "San Francisco."

"Of course." Bob shook his head as if mad at himself. "It's too early in the morning to be auditing shipments."

The other man gave him a grim smile, then got back to loading bags.

It took Bob about five minutes to walk back to the front of the terminal and departures, and another five to get to the counter. The terminal was almost empty, only the most frugal business travelers awake at that hour.

"Can I help you, sir?" the counter attendant asked cheerily.

"I sure hope so," Bob said. "I need your next available seat to San Francisco."

ABI WAS ENJOYING HER MORNING. For the first time in a week, a few minutes spent in a neighborhood market felt relatively serene and safe, and she'd browsed for nearly an hour, flitting between stalls of fruit and veg, after promising Alex she would make him superlative breakfasts for as long as she stayed.

He'd taken the day off to make sure she settled in okay. Now, she was sitting at a rickety old card table at a market café stall, on the cobblestones, drinking a superb dark coffee with just a touch of sugar.

The bags at her feet contained some smoked ham, potatoes, flour and some mixed fruit for a cocktail, to end the meal perfectly sinfully. It was easy, watching others come and go, shopping bags in hand, to imagine living back in Cali, giving up the fight in Buenaventura. To go back to her first newspaper job, a junior reporter handling local social announcements and obituaries. To return to a newsroom with colleagues, the clatter of hard work and the tapping of fingers on keyboards.

Then I could do this just about any morning, without worrying about whether someone will blow my head off.

But she wondered to what end. When she'd had her son, when her ex-husband, Benito, had been with her, the idea of an idyllically empty and lazy day seemed absolutely brilliant. Now, her only real purpose was to fight for normalcy, even if she could never find it herself. Even if she'd never get her boy back.

She downed the rest of the coffee and rose. *No point*

wallowing in self-pity, she supposed. *He loves his grandma and is happy and safe. That's what's important.*

She had to get back to the house, feed Alex and get back to working on the story, Abi knew. As much as they already had, more would shake loose as the story was exposed, more people willing to talk, more reaction from the community and officials. She kept a cautious eye on passing cars as she made her way up the street.

At Alex's, she got a slight chill at the front door despite the muggy heat, the hairs rising on her neck as if being watched. She turned quickly, checking the dead-end street in both directions. She paid attention to the parked vehicles, looking for movement in the cabs.

But there was no one in sight.

And that's what this job does to you; it makes you see danger around every corner.

She opened the door. "I'm back!" she called, letting it swing closed behind her. She put the grocery bag down and set the deadbolt, then the emergency door chain. She picked the bag up again and made her way into the living room. "They didn't have the robusta beans," she called out, "so I got the—"

She stopped the sentence short. Alex was seated on the sofa. A stocky white man was sitting next to him, one arm around his shoulder. "Your cousin and I have been having a little chat about your work activities," he said.

Abi bolted, dropping the groceries to run for the door, the butt of an assault rifle striking her in the side of the head before she could finish the turn, consciousness lost instantly.

32

SAN FRANCISCO, CALIFORNIA

Bob walked down the long, wide stairwell from the second level of Harvey Milk Terminal 1, the baggage carousels coming into view halfway down.

His flight had been four hours after he'd seen the bags being loaded in Cali. He'd expected more complications in America, where airport security continued to be treated as if terrorism was common. Instead, the woman at the gate had told him that there was a shuttle at the end of Terminal 3 that would take him directly to Field Road, on the edge of the property, where the cargo hangars sat.

For once, everything had gone his way in the aftermath of the lab explosion. Bob figured if that trend continued for another hour, he'd be able to head back to San Diego with enough proof to make Anderson Rowe's life difficult and get Eric Williams out of jail.

At the base of the stairs, he dumped his Bob Davis passport in the nearest trash can. It would take the Homeland Security team at the airport less than a half hour to flag the

NSA, another twenty to thirty minutes to scramble a team of dogs from the CIA branch office downtown, five miles away.

He didn't plan to be around for that long.

A few minutes later, he had a pep in his stride as he headed across Terminal 1 to Terminal 3.

He was near the double sliding doors at the end of the vast concourse when two men stepped in behind him, at either shoulder. He felt the stab of a barrel pressing against his kidneys. He glanced down. The man had a light coat over his arm and the gun.

"Everyone keeps calm, nobody gets shot," the gunman said quietly. "We're going for a little walk."

"Took some balls, pulling that in here," Bob suggested, buying time as he looked both ways, trying to gauge how quickly he could put either man down. They were both big, muscular, their expressions utterly nonplussed, wearing sport coats over a golf shirt and turtleneck respectively. Either could've been a college dean or a boxing promoter. "Now... what are you two going to do if I make a fuss, with all the security and police around here?"

They stopped walking. The second man reached up and used one hand to turn Bob's chin, slowly, towards him. He kept his voice low, just above a whisper. "We'll fucking kill you, then we'll walk out the doors over there, and in short order, we'll be ghosts. And there will be lots of screaming and crying, and they'll have images that are of no use because neither of us has a criminal record of any sort. By the time they put a name on either of us, we'll be gone to ground, and you'll be rotting in a morgue."

Okay. So... no nerves, then, Bob figured.

They resumed walking, the two men keeping an eye on passersby. Near the doors, a policeman was talking to a customer by a magazine rack. He saw the group, and it caught his eye.

Gunman Number Two gave the cop a confident nod and a smile. The policeman's attention went back to the yammering customer.

"Where are we going?"

The double doors ahead of them slid open. The day was hot and dry, a subtle shift from Cali's humidity. Beyond them, a black Ford Crown Victoria limousine sat at the curb. "The man wants a few words," Gunman One said. He walked ahead and opened the door. "Take the jump seat," he ordered.

Bob climbed in.

Sebastian Krug sat on the leather rear bench seat, hands clasped calmly ahead of him. He showed no visible reaction to Bob's presence as the other two men climbed into the back and the front passenger seat.

The man up front turned halfway so that he could keep his gun trained on Bob.

"Mr. Davis," Krug said, "I must say I am most disappointed to see you again, albeit not surprised."

The close confines of the limousine cab presented possibilities. It would be harder to control him in a tight space without them hurting one another, Bob knew. But the man in the front seat likely had that barrel less than six inches from his skull. So much as sneezing too hard would mean a bullet to the brain.

Speaking of which... "So... why all this?" Bob's index finger made a circling motion. "Why take me to talk to Rowe when you could just shoot me and dump the body?"

"We'll get to that," Krug said. "He has some questions."

He seems unflappable. But if he's like our Krug, he's got a short fuse, Bob figured. He nodded toward Rowe's assistant. "Your last name: you wouldn't be related to Edson Krug, by chance?"

Krug's eyes widened in shock. He realized he was playing his cards open and returned to a stoic expression. "He was my uncle."

Of course. Krug's younger brother had died before he left the military to join Team Seven, as Bob recalled.

"I knew him," Bob said.

"He was a hero," Krug said. "He died saving the vice president from an assassin at Dulles Airport in DC. And that was after earning a medal in Iraq. I highly doubt he even knew a piece of shit like you by name."

He seemed energized at the mention, as if a moment of hero worship had woken him up. "Well... that's one version," Bob said.

Krug's expression ran coldly blank. "What?"

"Nothing. Not how I remember things, but you do you."

Krug's eyes were contemptuous slits, his chin up as he stared Bob down. "You know nothing about me. And your transparent attempt to force a confrontation or distraction will only end in your death. So shut it." He turned his gaze directly ahead, as if Bob had vanished.

"Okay, then."

The limo slowed. Bob looked through the tinted glass. They'd parked outside a long hangar, surrounded by others, sizable gaps between them allowing cargo vehicles to come and go from the adjacent runways.

A series of luggage carts were strung together at the far end of the building, each loaded with suitcases similar to those in Colombia, tops just poking over the sides of their trailers. Another was parked at the curb, its trailer seemingly empty.

Anderson Rowe was standing in the middle of the hangar, hands in the trouser pockets of his navy-blue suit. Bob clocked three more guards... and one more surprise.

Abi sat in a molded-plastic chair, just ahead of Rowe. Her arms appeared tied behind the chairback. A guard stood next to her, a revolver held to her head.

Bob half rose out of his seat before the car had even stopped rolling.

"Just... keep it cool, Mr. Davis," Krug said. "I think your going off half-cocked has done enough damage already, don't you?"

They got out of the limousine as carefully as they'd entered, the man up front staying put, his gun on Bob, until the others were clear.

Anderson Rowe turned to acknowledge their arrival. "Ah, Mr. Davis! You're here, finally."

He sounded near chipper, Bob figured. *Rowe must have a private jet, to have beaten me back here.* It made sense, he knew. Billionaires didn't tend to fly commercial.

"BOB!" Abi exclaimed.

"Don't worry," Bob told her. "We'll figure this out."

"I assure you, you will not," Rowe said. "Please, Mr. Davis: don't give the poor lady false hope. That's most unseemly. Your phone, please."

Bob took the burner out of his pocket and tossed it to him. "It won't do you much good. I haven't even linked my accounts yet, and I just bought it ten minutes ago in the terminal."

Rowe looked at the phone with distaste, then handed it to Krug. "Make sure he's telling the truth." He turned back to

Bob. "You're going to tell us where you've sent or hidden any evidence, Mr. Davis."

"Because?"

"Because if you don't do so voluntarily, Mr. Krug will apply considerable zeal in ensuring you do so involuntarily."

"And then you're up shit creek, and the nearest paddle is miles away," Bob said. "You don't know what we've got, Rowe, that's clear. So you can't do a god damn thing but make idle threats. For all your outer cool, your cheerful 'TV kids host' vibe, you're just another gangster. You're just less honest, is all."

Rowe approached him, getting within striking distance. Bob was tempted to take him down before the others could react, but Abi was sitting ten feet away under guard.

The software titan leaned in, speaking softly, his voice utterly calm. "You think you have everyone figured out, don't you, Mr. Davis? But I'm afraid you've got me all wrong." He stepped away and walked over towards the nervous journalist. "You think I'm putting on some sort of front to cover up someone horrible, don't you?"

"Well... aren't you?"

"Not at all!" Rowe said, smiling warmly. "I really am quite happy and cheerful, most of the time. It has a disarming quality on the witless, to be sure, but if they're happy, well, then I'm happy. You see, in a moment, I'm going to shoot your young friend here in the head, killing her. Can you imagine how hard that would be for someone hiding their true self? I mean, at the very least, it would seem an angry act. But the truth is, I feel nothing for Ms. Sanchez. It appears not many do, given how easily her cousin sold her out."

"You threatened his—" Abi began to interject.

"QUIET, BITCH!" Rowe turned, anger flaring for the first time, his face instantly red, veins standing out on his neck, the sudden transition shocking Bob and making Abi flinch in her chair. "YOU WILL SHUT UP! Women will *speak* when *spoken* to!" He turned back to Bob, his features shifting in a moment, kindly Dr. Jekyll making an appearance. "You see?" he said gently. "Who wants that sort of thing? Anger helps no one, Mr. Davis, even though women always seem to want to provoke. What *always* works is leverage."

He walked over to Abi and stood beside her, taking the pistol from his guard's hand. He placed the barrel against her temple.

"Like most of her gender, she has little value unless giving birth or cleaning up. In an ideal world, the notion that this... 'female' would have the temerity to take a man's job in a man's world..." His head shook slightly, as if the sheer notion of being interrupted by a woman had been traumatizing. "The name of your email carrier, along with your password and login, Mr. Davis. Mr. Krug will take note."

"With that attitude towards women, your mother must be proud," Bob said. Abi shot him a wide-eyed glare of disapproval that said *don't provoke him*.

Rowe took a deep, slow breath, a daydream expression taking over as he cast his mind back. "My mother was an ungrateful whore who died when I was young. She accepted my father's ring, a place at his side, the trappings of his family's wealth and holdings. And yet when he exerted his husbandly rights, she fled and took up with a farmer, of all people, a country bumpkin. My father slid a knife between the man's ribs and made her watch while the life seeped from him. And then a year later, the dirty slut killed herself, depriving his son of a mother and him a caregiver." He took another deep breath. “On the other hand, you clearly value the opinions of the weaker sex far too greatly. Your account details, Mr. Davis.”

On cue, Krug produced a phone and prepared to tap in the details.

“Kill us and you don’t get your evidence,” Bob said. “You’re not going to—”

Rowe pulled the trigger, the .40-caliber bullet deafening from close range, Abi’s head jerking to one side as the bullet tore through her brain, blowing out skull and viscera, the concrete hangar floor splashed with gore.

“I only need one of you alive,” Rowe said, half-yelling to account for the ear-ringing gunshot.

Abi slumped to her right, her gaze vacant, her life over.

33

Bob felt the wind leave his chest, his legs suddenly wobbly, his mouth dropping open, the shock of seeing her die somehow different than those who'd gone before. He thought instantly of the photo she'd shown him, the boy she never got to see. "Oh God..." he managed.

"Surely not, Mr. Davis," Rowe said, handing the gun back to his guard and wisely keeping his distance. "I highly doubt he's ever been on your side."

The open wound had exposed arterial ruptures, blood running fluidly, like a slow tap, down the side of her neck and onto her blouse, down her arm, curling like a crimson tendril around her wrist, dripping onto the floor. Her eyes stared ahead, unseeing, the light gone.

"What's going to happen now, Mr. Davis, is that my men are going to put you in the back of my jet, where we have a locking room ideal for transporting troublesome individuals. Once we're back in San Diego at the building, Mr. Krug is going to torture you using interrogation techniques he learned with the Navy SEALs, and he's going to find out where you've hidden your safety net. That's all it is, at this point."

"Get fucked."

Abi. Jesus Christ. He shot Abi.

"And there's the tough guy again." Rowe sighed a little, as if disappointed by a loud pupil in the back of a classroom. "I know you think it's keeping you alive; in fact, it's just making your death longer and more painful. I am a billionaire several times over, Mr. Davis, a bringer of jobs, a man who shakes up entire societies. A winner. I crush or raise the fortunes of others daily. When a man loses his employment for a reason he does not understand, causing him to hang himself from the living room chandelier, it's because I will it, I profited from it. When another rushes home to tell his excited brood of future SatMast workers that they're getting an in-ground pool, I'm the one who fills it with water. To them, I practically walk on it. You, Mr. Davis? You're a pest, a footnote in one of my employees' unreadable self-published biographies."

"You're already dead," Bob said quietly, unable to take his eyes off Abi. "You just don't know it." It came out in perfunctory fashion, something that had to be said, even though Rowe barely existed in the moment.

Her eyes gazed lifelessly past him. *She trusted me. She trusted that I was going to protect her, do right by her. I promised her she'd be okay.*

And he just wasn't that kind of guy.

But he told me, he told me who and what he really was, and I didn't listen.

I didn't listen.

A hand grabbed him by the upper arm.

"Oh, I'll be sure to make sure my insurance is all

current," Rowe said. "But I don't expect you'll be any more bother." He dropped the smile for a moment and turned to his men with a snarl. "Not unless anyone else wants to join the dead bitch in the chair."

The smile returned. "Now, Russell and Grant will take you over to runway 19L and my Gulfstream 5 while I have a chat with Mr. Krug. We'll leave shortly."

The tycoon looked over at Abi's lifeless body without a hint of emotion. "And someone clean up that mess."

The guard dubbed Russell waved his pistol towards a luggage cart at the curb. Its white plastic trailer had high sidewalls, enough to contain luggage two rows deep.

He nodded towards it. "In."

Bob complied, swinging one long leg over, then the other. "Now what?"

"Sit," the guard said.

Bob did as told. The two men climbed into the cart, its molded-plastic shell slightly bigger than the golf variety. The man Rowe had called Grant turned in his seat to train a gun on Bob. "It's a three-minute trip. Give me any shit, and I will shoot you. The man wants you able to answer questions, so it would suck if I accidentally shot you and you fucking died. Okay?"

Bob stayed silent. Grant's mouth was moving, spittle flecking the corners of his Marlboro Man mustache, but Bob wasn't really listening. Instead, he gradually worked the wrist ties from side to side.

No internal resistance. No steel-band construction.

They're standard ties, not reinforced restraints.

The cart pulled away from the curb and onto West Field Road, heading east towards the runways. He'd put the grisly scene behind them out of his mind already; the only way to sufficiently suppress his rage at Abi's murder was to begin concentrating on the next step.

Stay on mission. Get free, take these two down; that's step one. Because you don't get to be angry. You put her in this situation and got her killed, Bobby.

Now, the job is payback.

The numbers were badly against him, he knew. He kept an eye on the man up front, Grant. Eventually, being half turned like that in his seat was going to prove uncomfortable. Bob wondered if he went into a fetal position, as if overwrought, how the man would react. He dropped onto his side and tucked up his knees, staring aimlessly at the sidewall of the trailer, but keeping his peripheral vision on the guard.

After a few seconds, Grant turned to face the road.

He had no time to waste, the plane fewer than two minutes away. Bob pushed his shoulders down and back, stretching the ligaments as far as they could go, pulling his feet and knees as tight to his chest and torso as he could, straining to swing the loop of plastic under his buttocks and the soles of his feet.

He felt his shoulders slip out of joint, the partial dislocation on his left side leaving the arm nearly dangling, with an agonizing stabbing at the center of the cartilage. His stomach muscles crushed together to the point it felt they might rip. Something was going to snap, and sweat beaded on his brow as he tried to withstand the pain.

The pressure gave, the trailer shuddering slightly as his arms came free, hands coming over his feet. He lay for a moment, panting from the simultaneous exertion and pain, hands still in front of his knees.

No time to recover. He glanced up at the cart just as Grant looked back.

"Don't fuck around back there!" he yelled over the wind and the whine of the cart's undersized motor. He turned back to the road ahead as they turned off onto a track adjacent to the runways.

Bob looped his bound hands over his knees and pushed off the cart as well as he could, trying to get his torso up off the surface. It was only a few inches, but it was enough, the combination of his weight and downward pressure from his kneecaps snapping the plastic wrist restraint.

The cart jolted to a halt. Bob was up on the soles of his feet instantly, sprinting forward before the two men had even cleared the cab, leaping over the side at Grant, his left arm clotheslining the stocky guard across the throat, feet knocked from under him. Grant slammed to the ground, back first, his pistol skittering away from him.

His partner tried to get a bead on Bob with his pistol from the other side of the cab. But he stayed low and behind its front end, reaching the pistol as the other man sprinted around to get a clear line of sight. He rolled sideways twice, coming up on his back, the gun outstretched over his head to shoot backwards, two bullets hitting the driver in the upper chest.

Russell staggered and collapsed, falling over backwards and then onto his side, clutching at the wounds. Bob heard a scratching sound ahead of him. Near his feet, Grant had made it to his knees and was rapidly scrambling towards him. Bob kicked down and out, hard, his heel slamming into the other man's face, Grant rolling over onto his back, clawing at a broken nose.

Bob rose to his feet and shot the man twice as he lay on

his back, any notion of tempering his actions with mercy utterly out of the question. Once he'd stopped moving, Bob shot him through the temple. Then he walked over to Russell and shot him twice in the head as he moaned.

He looked back to the road. There were lights perhaps a hundred feet back.

The Crown Vic? Possibly. For a fleeting moment, he thought about staying there, bunkering behind the luggage cart and seeing how many of Rowe's men he could pick off, maybe get a shot at the man himself.

Don't be selfish. Don't let anger decide. If you stay, you might get some measure of revenge, but they'll protect Rowe, and the numbers are against you. There had been four more guards, plus Sebastian Krug. *Six on one isn't going to end well, not in an open environment.*

This isn't about you, Bobby, his conscience counseled. *You can't get her justice or free Jasmine's brother if you're dead.*

He looked west, to the area south of West Field Road. The nearest hangars were busy, a massive shipping operation, the parking area filled with trucks, cars, luggage carts and trailers.

Bob took off running, his feet pounding the asphalt as he tried to turn back the clock, find enough speed to reach them before the car caught up. The image of Abi lying there, her expression horrified but also empty, devoid of life, filled him with rage, and he channeled it, knees higher with each stride as he tried to find speed, his stomach muscles still screaming.

The headlight glow grew until it passed him slightly, the car's engine audible as the driver accelerated towards him. Bob turned and sprinted sideways, between the rows of parked vehicles, brakes screeching as the Crown Vic tried to back up.

He cut between two rows and headed for the hangar proper, a pair of workers in orange jumpsuits and safety helmets watching, puzzled, as he turned a corner and headed around the building.

On West Cargo Road, a depot twice the size of a football field was surrounded by razor-wire fencing. But the main gate was open, just a manned barricade bar to prevent unwanted vehicles. Bob ran towards it and ducked under the bar.

The bored-looking security guard had been seated with his chair tilted back against the gatehouse. He scrambled to his feet. "Hey! You can't go in there!" But Bob was already by him, running north parallel to the tan stucco building as the headlights from the Crown Victoria pulled onto the parallel road heading south.

As he rounded the northwest corner of the building, the wall turned to concrete, the other side invisible, the razor wire still featured. An alarm started to sound somewhere behind him.

He sprinted across another car park. The wall and razor wire loomed ahead. A car was parked in a slot directly against the wall. Bob ran up the front bumper, over the hood and roof, feeling the soft metal give slightly, leaping for the wall's top edge, a two-inch strip of concrete on either side of the sharpened metal. He used both hands to vault him over, the razors just nicking the palm of his left hand as he cleared the wall, his feet coming down balanced, on the balls of his feet, on the West Cargo Road median.

Across the road, a Singapore Cargo facility looked less

busy, just a handful of cars ahead of it. A man was getting out of a pickup truck. Bob pulled the pistol and leveled it at the driver as he sprinted towards the truck. “KEYS! NOW!” he yelled.

The startled driver tossed him the keys in mid-stride. “BACK AWAY!” Bob commanded. The man took a few steps from the truck as Bob jumped behind the wheel. “Apologies,” Bob said. “I’ll leave it nearby.”

He started the engine and threw the truck into reverse, backed out, tires screeching on the warm asphalt. He gunned the engine, hoping his vague memory of the airport’s layout was good enough, driving south, then turning west, then north again, the truck’s back end sliding out as it found West Campus Drive. It emptied directly onto North McDonnell Road, running under the freeway.

Bob checked the rearview mirror. The Crown Vic was nowhere in sight. He waited until the opposite lanes were clear, pulling a hard U-turn, the truck crashing through a flimsy chain-link divider, tires finding traction on San Bruno Road, heading west.

34

Bob dumped the truck on a side street in San Bruno, the suburb adjacent to the airport. At a Regency Inn, he waited in the lobby, grabbing a free newspaper off a side table and hiding behind it as he gauged the guests coming and going.

A man in a cowboy hat was loudly accosting the front-desk staff about his wake-up call times.

"If I miss my god-danged flight because one of you don't make the call on time, then it's up to the god-danged clock radio, and that ain't enough, you see?" the loud man insisted.

Bob leaned past him. "Sorry, buddy... quick question for these fine folk," he said, bumping the man as he did it, his left hand expertly slipping the man's wallet from his back pocket. "What time does the restaurant open in the morning?"

The cowboy-hatted customer shot him an annoyed look. "Can you not see we're talking here?"

Bob held up both palms. "My apologies." The man was

still stuck in the one-sided argument as Bob walked out of the building.

He walked back up the street to a second hotel; he'd spotted a convenience store on the lower level in passing. It was smaller than the Regency Inn. He checked the wallet en route. It contained two hundred and fifty dollars in small bills, a couple of credit cards and a debit card.

In the store, he bought the cheapest burner they had to keep the purchase under $100, a knockoff flip phone with one hundred and twenty free minutes, so that he could use the debit machine's tap function, as well as a map of San Francisco, because the phone had no data plan, and he didn't know how long he'd be without cash.

In the hotel's lobby, he oriented himself. There was a car-rental place a block away, but he had no ID. A block further still there was an auto shop with secondhand car sales.

Worth a look. He turned up San Mateo Avenue. There was a string of auto shops, but the place he was looking for fairly announced itself. Scott's Fine Cars was surrounded by a razor-wire fence not unlike the one at the airport. The array of vehicles ranged from old and decrepit to new and never valuable, an array of subcompacts, compacts and cars that had probably been written off at least once.

Now there is a man who'll do a half cash, half cards deal for something cheap, with no questions asked. And if he wouldn't, Bob figured, he could be convinced.

He walked past the auto shop and continued on for three more blocks, the road busy with traffic but the sidewalks nearly empty in the early afternoon heat. He found a café that was still open. The clock behind the long, old-fashioned lunch counter said it was nearly eight thirty at night.

He ignored the counter and took one of the four

booths, nearest the back of the room. The seat was red vinyl, soft, the adjacent front window smudged by dried soap residue, partially obscuring his view of the road. A waitress delivered a plastic menu. "Special's Salisbury steak and mash," she said. "Coffee?" She had a pot in her other hand.

"Tea, green tea if you've got it."

She frowned at the need for a second trip. "All's we got is Lipton breakfast tea."

"That'll do," Bob said, though he didn't really mean it.

"I'll give you a few minutes to decide," she said.

The waitress departed. Bob took the burner out of its box and prayed it was charged, as the guy at the store had claimed.

It flickered to life.

Adam Renton answered on the third ring. "Go ahead," he said, no name used. He clearly didn't recognize the caller.

"It's me. The situation's fluid and dangerous, and I need an evac. I have no ID, cards or contact, but I think I've got a line on a used car."

"Where are you?"

"San Fran, in San Bruno, near the airport."

"Okay. Don't even think about the rental, for one. Regular car thefts are way down due to ignition codes and engine arrest, so police have manpower, and those guys have heat all the time. I'm assuming you've broken a few laws to be in the situation you're in?"

"Several."

"Yeah. Whichever dealer or rental place you've scoped, they'll report you the second you're out the door, no matter how much you sweeten the deal. Hang tight for a second..." Renton drifted away from the call. He'd be doing quick research, Bob recognized, figuring out whom he knew in San Francisco, how to best serve his client.

"Okay," Renton said on his return, "here's what you do. There's a rapid transit station just down the road from you. You're going to take the Red-N line to San Jose Avenue and Randall. You'll cross the pedway to Mission Street and start walking north. At Twenty-Sixth Street, you're going to hop on the number twelve bus. It will take you to the Greyhound station at 425 Mission in about thirty minutes. Understand?"

"Check."

"Across the street is a cocktail bar, Madarae. In the men's room, there will be a package in the toilet tank farthest from the door with money and ID. Do you need a piece?"

"No, I'm good."

"Okay. I'll get it underway. It should be there by the time you arrive. A ticket – you're heading back to San Diego, I assume..."

"Correct."

"A ticket will be waiting at the Greyhound depot. Bob... this whole deal isn't going to be cheap. Along with the five hundred for my hour, you're going to owe me for the cash drop, and it'll be probably double the thousand I'll have him leave. Can you handle that?"

Bob considered his near-empty bank account and that rent was due in less than a week. "Not a problem," he lied. He'd have to make good, he knew. Handlers like Adam Renton didn't grow on trees, but they did disappear when the money dried up.

"I'll be by the phone," Renton said. He ended the call.

Bob pocketed the phone as the waitress arrived with his tea. "And what can I get for you?" she asked, taking his menu.

"A to-go cup," Bob said. "I have to run."

She sighed as she turned and headed back to the counter.

Bob rose as she returned, and took the Styrofoam cup. He filled it with hot tea and left a ten-dollar bill on the table for her troubles. Working at a diner in the evening probably wasn't a whole lot of fun.

He headed back out to San Mateo Avenue and towards the station. Rowe would doubtless be back in San Diego before him, but that didn't matter. In the moment, Abi's death still fresh in his mind, the trip could've meant walking for days across a desert and he'd have done it.

35

The bus ride to San Diego was twelve hours long, with a stop in LA for a bathroom break and a paperback. Bob had maintained his grim focus for the first few hours, but that motivation waned as the miles crawled on.

It wasn't her death stuck in his head, that brutal final moment and image of her lying there. It was the frozen image of her in her sister's apartment, in Buenaventura, that glow of pride in her eyes as she discussed her little boy.

She'd lost her boy, her marriage, her ability to be herself in public instead of hiding behind a byline. But instead of giving up, she'd fought like hell, every day, to make life better for a town that didn't seem to want her help.

In the end, it hadn't mattered. That was as bad as her being dead, the notion that because he'd failed her, he'd also rendered all of her work somehow disposable, forgettable.

The bus was too warm, the windows unable to be opened. It was loud, crowded, with kids bickering. Even in the few moments of quiet respite, the sound of the wheels on asphalt droned steadily through the floor. Someone had been warned to stop vaping by the driver twice in the first three hours; the back of the bus, where Bob was seated, reeked of black cherry smoke.

None of it even registered. He'd overnighted in ditches, sewer drains and swamps with the Marines and later with the Agency. He could still shut out the background noises, the pointless distractions, the cacophony of self-interest.

But he couldn't shut out the image of Abi focused, intent, seated on a lime-green corduroy sofa, elbows on knees as she listened to Bob.

She'd said it herself. She could've gone back to Cali and her regular job at the paper, a rank-and-file reporter, no memorable bylines, no big front-page stories. If they'd helped change anything, it could've been without her involved and at risk.

But she was better than that.

Mistake number one had been to keep her involved, Bob knew, even after learning she had a child. Not a dependent, true. But kids need a mother when growing up, and she'd made arrangements through her mother-in-law to be there for him, even if it was only online.

"Jaden, Marshall! You both sit down and be quiet!" Across the aisle and a seat ahead, a mother was scolding two young boys. One of them ran past her seat, ignoring her and stepping on the toes of the man seated behind her.

He winced and sighed loudly.

"Sorry!" she said with a little wave. "They're usually so good."

Bob had never had a sibling, had never really felt the pull of parenthood. He wouldn't have wished his childhood on anyone. It felt almost selfish to consider, in the moment, knowing how much Abi had loved her son.

The boy in the aisle stopped running and looked up at him, his face becoming serious for a moment, dark eyes trying to peer into Bob's soul. The kid frowned, then walked quietly back to his seat by his mother.

Do I look that bleak? Probably. It reflected how he felt. In Chicago, two years earlier, helping Dawn Ellis and Marcus Pell survive a hit squad had felt liberating even as it forced him to go on the run. In New Orleans, he'd helped save an entire community.

And then things had become more complicated. Old enemies had resurfaced, and the Agency had shown a ruthless desire to take him off the map. He'd had to make hard, desperately difficult decisions about who lived and who died.

And in trying to save some, he'd been unable to help others. Ellie Grainger, a lovely woman with a grieving husband and friends in Memphis; Professor Richard Jenkins, dumped in a desert hole by a dirty cop who'd paid the ultimate price for his murderous choices; Bob's friend Justin Hayward, reduced to a shadow of his former self in Philadelphia thanks to two bullets to the head.

Tom Peters, a traitor to his country, but a man full of regret, trying to get his daughter out of a dangerous game of sleepers and assassins in Portland, Maine, but instead lying dead against a pine tree on a remote island, the rain spattering his lifeless eyes.

And now Abi Sanchez, so close to her latest worthy goal of stopping a bombing-driven gang war in a lawless town, but so far from ever being a happy mother again.

Bob hung his head. He hadn't cried many times in his

life; he'd learned long ago to push that sort of sentiment down deep, bury it where it couldn't get in the way.

He felt a tear rolling down his left cheek. *Stupid*, he told himself. *Stupid to wallow. Just means you feel sorry for yourself instead of them, you selfish prick.*

Stick to actionable objectives.

Maybe his remorseless former Team Seven cohorts Edson Krug and Eddie Stone had both been right all along.

Maybe you were never really built for this.

He glanced at the soft-sided bag on the empty seat next to him. It wasn't his old Puma bag, which he'd had for decades but had finally lost. Instead, this one was pale blue and a little smaller, shiny polyester with a Champion Athletic logo down one side. But it served its purpose. He took the burner out of his pocket and thought about calling Dawn. She didn't have his new number yet, so she had no way to reach out for help.

Not that she probably needed it. The danger she'd faced as recently as his time in Maine had shown that, once again, the only reason the Agency would threaten her was to get to him. So he'd stopped talking to her about his life, what he was up to. He'd restricted calls to updates on her progress at her clinic, and her church group, and in helping Marcus through college.

Dawn would know what to do, how to handle it all. She always did.

But he knew eventually she would pay a price just for knowing him. They always did.

With his fiancée, Maggie, seeing his selfish side for an evening had been fatal. She'd stormed out of an argument, one that he'd started unnecessarily, and driven angrily, hastily. He could've stopped her, but he'd let her go.

And she paid. She paid the Bob toll.

It had been different with Abi, who, for all intents and purposes, had been a work colleague. But the result had been the same.

He'd been angry when he'd boarded the bus, riled up enough to ignore the cramped confines, the loud kids, the illegal smokers. But quite suddenly, the ride felt claustrophobic, the view obscured by smudged windows and ambient light as the bus pulled into the station in Los Angeles.

He'd texted Abi the photos and recording from the factory, so a copy still existed somewhere other than on the burner phone Rowe had confiscated. Had he thought to mail it to Jasmine, as well...

But you were in a drug lab, remember? Like Dawn says, Bobby, focus on the real, not the worst-case scenario. Maybe she stashed a copy somewhere else. Maybe that's still out there.

He had to hope, because Eric Williams's life probably depended on it. That was his next problem. He'd have to explain it all to Jasmine. She'd been horrified merely by him wounding some of Pascal Brown's men.

The notion that a journalist had been killed because of his efforts would be too much. She'd feel compelled to involve the police, and that would immediately flag the NSA, which would already be searching San Francisco, his passport photo having tripped their surveillance software.

What am I even doing? This was a simple case of the wrong guy being arrested. Now Abi Sanchez is dead, a neighborhood half burned to the ground. And I haven't actually solved anything because the evidence was still on my phone, and Rowe has it.

Why? Why did I blow up the lab? Without that, maybe they make less effort, maybe they're days behind us instead of hours.

What in the absolute fuck is wrong with me?

"Stop will be a half hour, so feel free to use the facilities or get a beverage. We depart again at one-oh-five," the driver announced.

He looked out the window. Less than thirty feet from the bus was the sign for a tavern, offering "Cold Beer."

You were a better man as a drunk. At least then, nobody got hurt. Maybe what you really need is a drink.

He'd been so diligent, he knew. *But what has it gotten me? More death, more alienation. More grief. Jesus H. I just...*

I just need a fucking break from it. I have to turn it off.

Bob got up out of his seat. *Just a couple of beers, to take the edge off.*

36

Adam Renton paced the living room of his Las Vegas high-rise apartment. Beyond the balcony door, the lights of the Strip and the casinos afforded the city an additional glow, and even fifteen stories up, he just had to open the door to catch the sounds of a town that never slept.

But Vegas was the last thing on his mind.

He should've called back by now.

In the far corner of the room was his workstation, a giant, L-shaped desk featuring five chained monitors and two connected keyboards, along with three rows of cellphone chargers, each bearing a different phone and number, each number taped to the phone to remind him of its particular place and purpose.

The third phone began to buzz, as if on cue. He tapped his earpiece to connect to it. "Go ahead."

"Wazzup, wazzup, wazzup! What's happening, dude?"

He kept his cool despite Clem P's bro demeanor. The former Army infantryman was a security guard now at the courthouse in San Diego, with access to a wide array of documents and criminal records. He had value despite his unctuous personality.

"Oh... you know. The usual happenings," Renton said. "Where's our boy?"

He'd sent Clem to keep an eye on the Greyhound station. Bob had been expected to show there six hours earlier. Now it was nearly midnight with no sign.

"I'm telling you, dude, he's flaked. No sign, and no word the cops arrested anyone off a bus between here and San Francisco. I checked with LAPD as well, and to be sure, I checked hospitals to see if a matching John Doe had made an appearance. Nothing. Nada. Bupkus."

"Where are you watching from? You've got eyes on all buses from LA?"

"It's not the most popular form of travel anymore, dude. It's not hard. I'm telling you, he hasn't come through tonight. You want me to hang here?"

"Yeah. Tonight and tomorrow."

"Dude... I have plans."

"You owe me, Clem. This is about the cheapest way to pay that off that anyone who knows me is going to encounter. I'd encourage you to take advantage."

The other party sighed, resigned to it. "Fine."

"I'll get you out of there before the day's done, okay?"

"Yeah... yeah, all right, dude. Let me know."

Renton ended the call just as another came in. "Go ahead."

"Adam."

He looked at the number and realized it was LA. "Chuck, what's happening, my man? Did you get a chance to check out the depot for me?"

"I did. You owe me for this one. I was supposed to be bowling tonight. League semi-finals."

"I've got a box of Cubans with your name on it, bud."

"I think I found your boy."

Renton's posture pricked up like a meerkat on a scent. "Talk to me."

"That's just it… I THINK I found your boy. He's at a shelter a few blocks from the bus station. But every time I get close to him, he holds up his hand and says, 'You really don't want to do that.'"

"He look sober?"

"Hell no. I waited outside, and he showed about an hour later, hit the liquor store down the block, headed straight for an alley a few doors down. He'd drunk half the pint by the time I approached him again."

"And?"

"Same thing. Held up an index finger and just said, 'Don't.' It was the way he said it. You just know sometimes when it's a bad idea to push it."

Damn, Bob. What the heck happened? "Understandable. Send me the deets, okay, Chuck?"

"Will do. Good talking to you."

The call dropped.

Renton tried to avoid getting involved in his clients' lives.

But this felt different.

Bob was different. There was no doubt about that. Most of the men he worked with were good at one thing: killing people. He didn't ask them about their work, and he didn't ask where the money came from, or why they needed intel.

And that had been Bob, for a long time. He'd seen the man's CIA and NSA files.

But it sure as hell isn't who he is now.

Somehow, in the two days prior, he'd lost sight of that.

Bob's file hadn't filled in all the gaps. But he knew they'd hunted for him, hunted for multiple former clandestine operations staff. He knew they'd found him living rough, drinking himself senseless daily.

Renton hated getting involved. Direct involvement meant exposure, risk, with little additional reward.

Not that it mattered in the moment. He headed for the front hall, to retrieve his suitcase.

I'm not being soft, he told himself. *He owes me eight thousand dollars. This is just protecting an investment.*

RENTON'S FLIGHT didn't leave for another hour. He sat in the Las Vegas International terminal and watched his fellow passengers as they tried to stay awake, the clock by the boarding desk clicking over to one forty.

Most of them were on their phones. He kept his in his pocket; he already lived on it. Any chance at downtime, offline, was always appreciated.

His phone rang. He pulled it out frantically, half expecting to see Bob's number. Instead, it was an unfamiliar caller from Alexandria, Virginia. He answered, "Go ahead."

"Mr. Renton, we haven't met, but I suspect you know me. My name is Ed Stone."

Renton felt a chill run through him. Stone had featured prominently in Bob's file, and a few others besides.

"I can't say I expected you to call, Mr. Stone. Certainly not at this time of night."

"It's been brought to my attention that you know a few of the same people as a former colleague of mine, Bob Singleton."

"Okay. And?"

"It's also been brought to my attention that he may be working in California right now, having just returned from a trip out of the country."

"You don't say."

"Oh, I do. And you're at Las Vegas International at just about two in the morning."

Renton's head swiveled around. He was unaccustomed to being the person watched.

He didn't like it.

"Cheaper flight," Renton said. "Take the red-eye, you save a couple hundred bucks, easy."

"To Los Angeles, no less."

To know that, they had to know he'd just bought the ticket. The card he'd used had been anonymous, preloaded. That meant they'd had to witness the purchase, which meant...

He looked around again, spotting the nearest dangling surveillance camera high above. "Really, Mr. Stone? From what I understand, to have me on live, you'd have to be working with my former NSA colleagues. That seems a lot to bother with."

"There aren't many handlers in America Bob would trust anymore, Mr. Renton. I suspect you're one of them. That, and having some of the same friends, means you might even be working for him right now."

"I'm going to a comic-book convention. You can look that up, as well," Renton said. "Starts tomorrow at the LA Convention Center. You can come along, I guess, but it doesn't sound like your speed. Not by reputation, anyway."

"It's nice to know I still have one in my dotage. Probably a good idea if you remember that and let me know, should you see him."

"I'll keep that in mind."

"You know... you're not doing yourself any favors working with him. You're famous for the legwork you do, the hard graft and research."

"Thank you."

"It was a statement, not a compliment. Me? I don't see it. To me, someone as meticulous and careful as you're reputed to be wouldn't come within twenty feet of Bob Singleton. Because you'd know what tends to happen to his friends. I'd expect that man to be more worried about his future. And Bob? Bob doesn't have a future. He's only alive because he's had extraordinary luck, with others bailing him out, time and again."

Renton snickered a little at that.

"What?" Stone demanded.

"Well... you think you've got such a good handle on who he is. But you don't seem to have considered why that happens, why people always want to help him, even when it's dangerous. I've always been a transactional sort of person, Mr. Stone, never too wedded to needing attention or a group. Maybe it's because my folks died when I was young, but I like being on my own."

"I can respect that," Stone said.

"But it's not for most people," said Renton. "You? You're no different from Bob. You're... what, seventy-three? Something like that. You've been at the CIA so long, you need a waiver to stay there. But you do because it's your tribe, your community. Until I got to know Bob, I didn't really understand that."

"Really? We're going to go all hearts and flowers, are we?"

"It's not just sentiment, Stone. Having a family, a community... it's an agreement. To look out for each other, to stand up for righteous choices that keep us collectively safe and happy. He gets that. Maybe I do, too, now."

"Pftttth..." Stone tsk'd. "Sentimental bullshit, Renton. See? This is what I mean. He's got you thinking like a civilian. But what I do? It's important. To this country. To our security. You can save your goodwill speeches for those who need them. But take this warning: working with Bob Singleton will get you killed."

"I'll keep it in mind."

"You do that. Enjoy your weekend, Mr. Renton."

The line went dead. Renton stared at his phone for a few seconds. He'd have to toss it, of course. With a known cell, the Agency didn't even need cameras to track him. The phone's own transmission ID would be enough.

And that's why I travel with spares.

Still, even then, he had to be careful, he knew. They'd try to track him out of the airport using its security network, just in case he went running to his client.

Find him, figure out what went wrong, and get the hell home.

37

Bob stared blankly out the smudged window along the homeless shelter's back wall, a few feet from his temporary cot home. Rising sunlight glinted off a railcar on the flyover tracks as the day broke.

He glanced back at the shelter's main room. It was filled with cots bearing paper-thin sheets and worn blankets, each about five feet from the next, in rows. Each cot had a small side table, but they all appeared unused, the occupants perhaps not trusting their meagre possessions were safe in the pen. The place was mostly full, some sleeping, others sitting on the edge of their cot or a neighbor's, chatting or playing cards.

He stared back out the window, relishing the slight warmth of the early afternoon sun. Beyond them, the vast Los Angeles River viaduct stretched for miles, nearly three hundred feet wide but bone-dry save for a twenty-foot strip of greenish water running straight down the middle.

Dawn wouldn't have approved of him taking out

Anderson Rowe. Neither would Jasmine. Even sharing the notion was out of the question.

Decency suggested he call Jasmine, tell her what was going on. But he was bereft in his misery, weighed down by the pointless brutality of a leaden-hearted world.

Rowe didn't deserve to live, to kill someone else like Abi, to frame any more charity workers, to keep financing Daniel Rivas's debacle in Buenaventura.

But chances were, he'd fail at that too, he supposed. With Abi dead, the evidence he'd sent her was lost. Unless he was a complete idiot – and history suggested otherwise – Rowe would've destroyed his phone by now and the only other copies.

The booze, however, hadn't helped so far, hadn't worked. Hadn't done its job. Something had changed, it seemed, in how his brain received its intoxicating glow. Sure, it had given him a few minutes of sleep and distracted peace. But for the most part, it had just blurred the edges of a terrible reality.

His buzz was beginning to fade. The shelter smelled of dirty socks, the room too warm from so many bodies. He couldn't stay at the shelter forever, he knew. He'd expected it to be a comfort, anonymity amongst the lost and forgotten. But it was hard to find respite in a room full of murmured conversations and snoring drunks, the muted overhead lights lending a sense of hopelessness. Instead, being surrounded by misery had ramped up his depression.

He wandered back to the cot and sat on the edge. *One more night. One more night and one more pint. Then I can... what?*

What came next? He wasn't sure he could go back to San

Diego, face Jasmine. But just walking away felt like a cowardly betrayal.

"Bob."

He looked up, his brain registering the untimely familiarity a moment late. His eyes scanned the rest of the large, open room to see if the man had any confederates.

"Relax," the guy said. "You haven't recognized my voice yet, and we've never met in person."

"Adam!?"

Renton looked around for eavesdroppers, then sat down on the edge of the cot next to him. "Bob… what are you doing?"

"You came looking for me?"

"I had to protect my investment."

Bob shot him a sour look. "Really?"

"Yes, really. If I let guys just stiff me, I'd get an unworkable reputation. That doesn't mean I'm just here about that, though."

"Yeah? You worried about me?" It came out about as bitterly as he'd intended. "Don't bother."

Renton just nodded, lips pursed, absorbing the insult without comment. "What happened? I tried calling Abi yesterday and today, and you. And then my man in San Diego said you didn't show or pick up the cash drop."

"She's dead," Bob said. "A guy named Anderson Rowe shot her in the head right in front of me. I was right there, and I couldn't stop him. I didn't even believe he'd do it, Adam. I really fucked up. And whenever I fuck up, somebody dies. Usually someone who doesn't deserve it."

He glanced over at the handler. Renton looked suddenly despondent, probably because he'd known her longer, and it was just hitting home.

"You wanted to know what I was doing," Bob said. "I'm getting out of the fucking way. That's what I'm doing."

Renton didn't say anything right away. A cot away, a neighbor shuffled off, perhaps hearing more than made him comfortable. Eventually, Renton slapped himself on both knees with his hands. "Nope. No, we're going to get out of here, and you're going to get on the next bus back to San Diego, finish what you started."

"Jesus... Adam..." Bob shook his head gently. Didn't the man understand?

"Bob... Abigail knew what she did for a living. She knew it was potentially fatally dangerous."

"Not now, Adam, please. Not that load of shit."

"No, NOW, Bob. I'm your handler on this, and part of that is looking out for your mental health. You can't get shit done if you're wallowing in second-guessing and low self-esteem. And right now, you sound like you want to eat a fucking bullet. Okay? It's not going to help Eric or his sister, and it's not going to bring Abi back."

"Yeah, but—"

"No buts. When you were in the SEALs, scouting in Afghanistan—"

"You do your homework, don't you?"

"I do. And I know about Kandahar, about how many times you almost lost your life there and how many of your colleagues were killed. But you persevered, for the mission. Justin Hayward once told me you were the most stubborn motherfucker he'd ever met – but nearly always for what you figured was the right reason. So you persevered."

"It would've been an insult to their memories to do otherwise."

"So how is this any different?"

Bob shot him a hard stare. "Are you serious? She wasn't a soldier, Adam."

"Ohhh, I see now. It's not because she's dead. It's because Abi was some poor, frail woman who needed big, bad Bob to bail her ass out. Right?"

"Please..."

"Or was she fighting the same fight you are? Was she a cliché in a skirt, Bob, or was she a warrior, fighting the good fight? Fighting for what she fucking believed in! HER fight!"

It wasn't an act. Renton seemed genuinely annoyed.

Bob remembered Abi's expression at the factory, when he'd burst into that conference room and gunned down her two guards. Most people would've been panicked, terrified by the immediacy of death, frozen in that fear. But her eyes had widened and flashed with intensity, her focus absolute. She'd been in the game, and at least for those few moments, she'd found her place.

And all without pulling a trigger.

Then she'd done what he would've done and helped drag a comrade out of the fire and rubble and danger.

He's right.

Jesus H. He's completely right.

Mourn later. Beat yourself up later.

For now, she deserves better.

"Point taken," he said. He sucked in a lungful of stale shelter air and looked around, recognizing where he'd been for two days at last. Then he looked over at Renton. "I need another favor."

"You have balls the size of a Mack truck. You already owe me eight grand, and that's not counting this little trip. Your old employers are looking for you, by the way."

"They usually are. They threaten you?"

"Sort of. More of a warning about your general unsuitability as a colleague."

"Okay… so just being practical, then."

Renton smiled but reserved comment. Instead, he wagged an index finger Bob's way. "Just don't forget, I'm counting all of this as billable hours. So you're either going to owe me a sizable chunk of change, or we're going to make another arrangement."

"You know I'll make good."

"And you know that's not usually how I work. So I'm already doing you a favor."

Bob stifled the urge to lecture his handler. Renton was the best freelancer out there, but he'd always been open about his ruthless take on the trade. *He hadn't lied. If anything, like he said, he's been doing you favors on his dime. He's flown out here on his time to straighten your pathetic ass out.*

"Okay, how about this: your regular billable rate, and I'll owe you a job," Bob said. "NOT… not anything black. Nobody dies. Get that off the table right now. But protection, extraction, infiltration, you've got me for one task."

Renton knew it cost ten times as much to hire a good freelance merc as a handler. A job of any significance would be worth tens of thousands to him, maybe hundreds.

"You'd do that?" Renton eventually said.

"I'll do that if you find out what happened to a file I sent to Abi Sanchez in Cali. I texted her from a burner, and the burner was later destroyed." Bob gave him the name of the carrier.

"They'll have a backup copy somewhere, as it's standard cell text," Renton said. "So even if I can't find out whether she stashed it or sent it on, I might be able to borrow the backup off their servers. Man… not easy. Phone companies are diligent about their security; their staff aren't typically falling for an easy generic phish or talking too much in local bars."

"We need this. We need something," Bob said. "Rowe has my phone, probably her phone, too. So he's got copies; he knows what I know." He knew his desperation was beginning to show through again. He frowned as a fragment of a memory popped back into his head. "And we need to know why that drug lab reeked of flowers."

"Eh?"

"The one thing I haven't figured out yet. Place reeked like a grandma in her Sunday best, lilac or lavender or something. And I'll need some help in San Diego," Bob admitted. "He's got at least a dozen men at that building, maybe more, and Edson Krug's nephew is his personal bodyguard. A distraction, something to draw them away, leave him exposed."

"Edson Krug!? You're kidding me."

"Nope. I'd say it's a small world, but when a guy traipses all over the country, he's bound to bump into familiar names and faces eventually."

"Does he know?"

"That I killed his hero? Hell no. It didn't seem politically astute, eh? With a gun to my head and all."

"*You* killed Krug? I heard he got dusted by some nutjob attacking a senator or something."

"There are multiple versions. How well did you know Edson?"

"Barely. You know I worked for the NSA after the Army?"

"Yeah, of course."

"We crossed paths a few times when he was with Team Seven. He overstepped his mandate by pressuring US relatives of an overseas target, and someone in our head office had words with your head office. He didn't have the best reputation for charm or civility."

"That's about the politest way of saying he was a sociopathic asshole that I've heard in some time," Bob suggested. "Either way, Krug Junior will be a handful, I figure."

"But... you don't really know anyone in San Diego, do you?" Renton said. "Your files say you barely spent any time there with either the Marines or the SEALs, and most of your Team Seven tenure was overseas."

"I know basically nobody other than Jasmine and a few other home-building volunteers. But I did run into a guy recently who might be able to help."

"The drug dealer, Brown?" Renton sounded dubious. "The guy whose apartment you basically stormed, and whose guards you shot up before prying him off an exterior window ledge fourteen stories up. That guy?"

"Well... I didn't say it would be an easy sell, did I? But if you've got any tips, I'll take them."

"Yeah," Renton said. "Come up with another plan."

38

SAN DIEGO, CALIFORNIA

The lights were low at SatMast International Communications' waterfront building. A desk lamp fought back the shadows as Anderson Rowe paced his gargantuan office.

Occasionally, he would stop to look up at the fish swimming around the sixty-two-foot-wide, floor-to-ceiling aquarium separating them from the adjacent nightclub. Sometimes, the blue shark would appear and, despite being fed meat multiple times per day, would choose to swallow several of the smaller breeds before disappearing into the larger aquarium that sat behind the building.

He'd paid more than $8 million to ensure the office side of the tank was made of a Kevlar derivative that was both soundproof and shatterproof. He could see the flickering color changes from the club's dance floor cutting through the water without having to listen to the thumping abominations they called music.

Give me a Brahms concerto any night, he thought wistfully. *Instead, it's thump-thump-thump.* Young people had always been stupid, Rowe supposed, but now more than ever. The bass subwoofers in the club were probably ruining their hearing. If they didn't pay him a fortune in rent, he'd have evicted them years ago.

But the aquarium wall was a hit, paying for itself in less than a decade.

He'd always had a knack for profit and for grandiose gestures. When he'd led funeral services for his former mentor and partner, the company's founder, he'd arranged for him to have a Viking burial, his body atop a pyre on an open wooden boat off the coast, set alight with a flaming arrow.

That he'd had the man slowly poisoned over the five years prior, having already arranged it so that only he could purchase the outstanding private SatMast shares, was no reason to scrimp on the big day.

Rowe had not lied to the pugnacious thug at the airport in San Francisco, Bob Davis – or whatever his real name was. He'd been completely calm for most of his life, essentially unflappable. But he did have an internal sense of security, like any person. And his was finely attuned. It rarely steered him wrong.

And Mr. Bob Davis made him slightly nervous.

Not only was the man's name clearly a cover – they'd exhausted their state and federal contacts looking for some clue as to who he was – but he'd had his fingerprints professionally removed at some point, according to Sebastian Krug, suggesting he'd been a field operative for an agency. Clearly, he wasn't working with the federal government, or he'd have had more help.

But the look on his face after the woman had gone down had chilled Rowe for a split second, a core level of dread he hadn't experienced since childhood, waiting for a beating from his father's switch.

There was a knock on the office door.

"Come."

It opened, and Sebastian Krug entered. "Sir, you asked me to check in before eight."

"News?"

"We... have yet to locate any sign of him in San Francisco. As I said previously—"

"Yes, yes, I know your thoughts on the matter. You said he'd be back here before the day was out, as I recall. But no sign so far. And no sign there, either."

"We are trying, sir," Krug said.

"Redouble your efforts, Sebastian." He stared into the younger man's eyes. "You know how I feel about failure, my boy, even someone I trust as much as yourself. That trust comes with a caveat that you must serve your purpose, like all of us."

"Yes, sir, of course. I still think the long-haul bus routes—"

"This is a man of action, Sebastian, a ruthless man. He blew up a drug lab; he dragged young Ms. Sanchez into his problems without a thought to her being of the weaker sex. He will have obtained a car quickly and easily and would not rely on someone else to get him from point a to point b. Don't waste our time!"

"Of course, sir."

Rowe looked at his watch. "It's... seven-oh-four. I expect you to check back in with status updates every two hours. I shall have Rogelio drive me home at midnight. By then, I want something concrete. Understood?"

Krug nodded. "Absolutely, sir." He headed for the door.

"Oh... and Sebastian?"

Krug turned as he opened the door. "Yes, sir?"

"Pop next door and feed the shark, would you? Poor thing looks starving."

Bob stepped through the doors to enter the bus terminal, the other passengers ahead slowing his pace. The ride from LA had been sobering, a study in considering how much he remembered of Rowe's building, of Krug and his men.

He knew he had to heed Renton's warning. The fact that Eddie Stone had contacted the handler directly did not bode well. It meant he was taking the hunt seriously again. They'd have grabbed an image of him at the airport even if the NSA hadn't flagged his passport, he supposed.

That meant they'd have people in San Diego, waiting for him to return. Stone was nothing if not thorough.

He scanned his surroundings. People were using ticket machines, a solitary service window providing real human assistance. Past them, a small line was shopping at a news kiosk. Along each wall were fixed plastic seats for people waiting for their rides.

The hairs on the nape of his neck stood up immediately, but he wasn't sure why. He scanned the room in reverse.

By a water fountain, a man with a newspaper under his arm turned his head a little, away from Bob.

He's tense. And as I don't see anything else problematic about to go down, maybe he's looking for me.

He'd known leaving the country would bring heat. Stone had made it clear in Maine that they'd hunt him to the ends of the Earth if need be. But the Colombia trip had been unavoidable.

Bob kept an eye on the nervous traveler until the exit. He watched the door swing closed behind him. Bob headed south, towards East San Ysidro Boulevard. He needed to grab a cab and get back to City Heights.

The man stepped out of the alley as he passed, falling in behind him, the stun gun jammed into his lower back. Before he could pull its trigger, Bob dropped low into a tight crouch, the would-be kidnapper caught off guard, tripping over him, balance lost. The man slammed to the sidewalk on his right side.

It was late enough that foot traffic was minimal. Bob leaped back to his feet and grabbed the man by the collar of his jacket before he could react, then dragged him into the alley, his grip lost on the stun gun.

Bob hauled him to his feet against the wall. "Talk. Why are you—" He didn't get a chance to finish the sentence, the man's knee shooting upwards towards his groin, Bob blocking it cross palmed, a reflex. He spun a quarter turn on his heel, then threw his elbow backwards, catching the man on the chin.

His adversary slumped, dazed, to a seated position. "Now. Let's talk about—" From behind him, Bob heard the scratch of dress-shoe soles on concrete. He threw himself sideways, the dart from the tranquilizer gun flashing past him, its sharp tip burying itself in his colleague's shoulder.

"Oh, shit!" the seated man cried.

Bob ran forward, dipping at the last second to pull the dart out, turning and throwing it backhanded, counting on its feather flights to keep its line true. The dart struck the second man just below the carotid artery. His eyes widened, and he dropped the tranquilizer gun to clutch at it.

The shooter pulled it out, but he'd taken some of the

drug, his balance suddenly precarious. He staggered sideways, his left foot crossing his right as all equilibrium deserted him, and he thudded to the ground, unconscious.

Bob crouched beside the first man. His eyes were glazing over as well, but he was still awake. "Agency?" he asked.

"F-fuck you," the man blurted.

"Let me guess: Eddie Stone wanted me alive because he's curious why I left America. Something like that."

The man's eyes swam in their sockets. "I... I jush..." His voice tapered off, and he looked around the alley, confused. "Where 'm?"

Bob gave him a pat on the head. "It's okay. Shhh." Then he hit him on the side of the chin with a short right hook. The man's eyes closed, his breathing regular as he slipped into dreamland.

Bob rifled his jacket. He had a CIA staff badge, as well as nearly eight hundred dollars in mixed bills and a set of car keys. Bob held them up and studied them wistfully. It would be nice to have a convenient set of wheels again for a few days.

Nice but out of the question. The car would have a transponder in it, making it easy and quick to locate. He pocketed the cash. He searched the man's waist and found his service pistol, a Glock 19. He left the tranquilizer gun by the second man; Rowe and his ilk didn't deserve a nonlethal option.

He walked south from the alley, calling for a taxi as he made his way down the street.

39

The cab lingered at the corner of Fairmount Avenue and Dwight Street even after the light had changed. It was late, nearly ten o'clock.

"Well, wat'chyou think, mon?" the driver asked. He had thick dreadlocks and a green, yellow and red knit cap. The cab smelled strongly of marijuana smoke, a Peter Tosh song playing on the sound system. "You good here, or we need to go elsewhere?"

Bob looked through the front windshield toward the block containing Jasmine's apartment building. There were at least four people who seemed out of place; the woman on the bus shelter bench was older, perhaps in her fifties or sixties. Instead of being on her phone or reading a book, she was holding that morning's paper and pretending to be engrossed.

A dozen feet away, a parking attendant had checked the three meters in front of Jasmine's building at least four times, but not before aimlessly walking to the next block and back on each occasion.

And am I not supposed to notice she's working at ten at night? The obvious policy demand that the surveillance team "blend in" had been taken literally, but they were relative amateurs. They were doing an awful job as a consequence.

Half a block in the other direction, a man was standing at an intersection, waiting to cross.

"So?" the driver asked.

"A few more seconds," Bob replied.

He watched the man cross the street, look around to gauge if anyone was watching, then cross the side street to the next block. After less than a minute, he'd walked in a square pattern, returning to his original corner.

Bob took out his phone and dialed Jasmine's number, the only one in San Diego that he knew by heart. After five rings, it kicked over to voice messaging.

Damn it, pick up! If she was screening calls, or even out for the evening, he had no way to tell her that her place was being watched. The voice message ended, and a beep sounded. "It's me," he said. He read off the number for the burner. "Hit me back as soon as you can. You have company around your building."

He ended the call. "Okay, I've seen enough. Can you take me downtown?"

The Rastafarian cabbie nodded with a sideways shake. "Sure enough, mon, sure enough."

They hadn't been CIA. They wouldn't have been that sloppy, Bob knew, or so bluntly direct in their methodology. That meant they probably worked for Rowe. He knew Bob was heading back to San Diego because the billionaire had killed Bob's friend. And he knew from before he'd left for Cali that he was working with Jasmine.

So they figure I'll have to make an appearance here eventually.

"Wha' gwan, mon?" the driver asked. "Ya got an address, or what?"

"Yeah, it's on Third Avenue, near Harbor Drive. Just find the nearest corner."

They'd expected him to visit Jasmine. Bob doubted the same would be true at Pascal Brown's apartment tower.

THE GUARD at the security desk was a different man from a week prior. Bob's patience was running thin and his energy flagging even more. But he kept a pleasant demeanor as he sauntered up.

"Evening. Can you call up to Mr. Brown on floor 14; tell him Bob Davis is here to talk."

The guard held up both hands in a "ah, shucks" motion. "Can't do it, pal. Sorry about that. There's a no solicitations policy that—"

Bob interrupted him by taking the pistol out of his waistband and setting it on the counter. "You were saying?"

The guard looked at the gun, then at Bob's expression, then at the gun again. "I'll just call up, then," he said.

"And if you trigger a silent alarm or something, you'll cause a big scene," Bob added. "So maybe wait to see what he says first."

The man's hand hesitated above the console ahead of him. Then it drifted right and picked up a phone. He punched three digits on a number pad.

"Yes, sir, my apologies, it's Kieran at the security desk. A Bob Davis says he needs to speak with you, I think rather urgently. Uh-huh... uh-huh... yes, sir, please just hold on a second."

He handed the phone to Bob. "He wants to speak with you."

Bob took the handset. "Hey."

"I thought I was going to be fortunate and that you weren't going to grace me with your presence yet again." Pascal Brown sounded weary, which made sense. It was getting late, and his prior visit had been eventful.

"It's a fluid situation," Bob offered. "I'm just taking things as they come."

"Okay. Well, be that as it may, I've got four guards here who would both very much like to cause you immense pain and who are, I suspect, somewhat worried that you might kill them."

"Annnd... do you suppose I'd have called up and announced myself if I came here to kill anyone?"

"Possibly," Brown said. "You don't strike me as the kind of man who's overly nervous. Ever."

"And assuming you were straight with me the last time I was here, do I have any reason that you could think of to want to come here and take on five gunmen?"

"Again, not sure the danger would worry you, but... no. One doesn't come to mind."

"Then you're thinking straight," Bob said, "which is a good thing, because I've got an offer I don't think you're going to refuse. I'm going to help us both solve a mutual problem."

The pause wasn't long. "Okay, head on up."

Bob handed the phone back to the man at the desk. "You don't want to know," he said. "It's not worth whatever this place pays." He took out the money clip he'd lifted off the

CIA man at the bus station and peeled off ten twenty-dollar bills. “For your trouble.”

The guard picked up the bills and briefly fanned them, to speed his count. Then he pocketed the money. “And you have a nice evening, sir.”

40

The clock's minute hand had passed ten o'clock. Sebastian Krug stared up at it, then at the elevator to the third floor, then at the clock once more.

It was time to update Mr. Rowe, but he had nothing new to tell the man. A team had been scouring the city for hours, with no sign of Bob Davis. He'd ignored Rowe's advice and sent a man to the bus terminal just in case, and there were enough police and what looked like feds around for them to have been there for a reason.

But whatever that reason was hadn't been obvious, and their federal contacts hadn't called back to enlighten him.

The crew at Jasmine Williams's apartment had seen nothing all night. She'd returned from work and, he suspected, bunkered in for the night. There had been no sign of visitors, and the disguised watchers had no inkling of anyone watching them in return.

He was unsure of his next step but had an idea. He needed Rowe's approval, because he needed Rowe's approval to go ahead with anything. The man was a generous employer, but he micromanaged to the point of inducing terror in his staff.

That in itself didn't bother Krug. His father had taught him – as his grandfather had taught his two sons – that the man who was ruthlessly self-assured and self-protective would always win over the self-assured socialite, the man who sought power in popularity and acceptance.

But he owed Rowe, for giving him a chance at a career after he'd been washed out by the Marines. For giving him an ethos, a reason to exist in the civilian world. All because of some little rag-head urchin, some piece of shit who probably would've stuck an IED in their convoy's path five minutes later had Krug not shot him as he begged by the side of a road near Khartoum.

It hadn't been callous murder; the boy's hand had flashed to his shoulder bag as the first vehicle passed him; they'd been attacked by militia while protecting humanitarian convoys multiple times.

It was reasonable then, and it's reasonable now.

The Navy didn't see it that way, of course. His court-martial had been aggressive, a prosecutor trying to get him an extended prison term back home. They'd bargained it down to an error in judgment of being threatened and a dishonorable discharge. He could still remember the JAG lieutenant staring down at him, like he was nothing, telling him he was lucky, that he deserved far worse.

All for protecting our team.

The fucker.

Rowe, on the other hand, paid his men well and treated them with respect. He was the kind of man his hero, Uncle Edson, would've wanted him to emulate. He was sure of it.

He hit the up button. The elevator pinged a moment

later, and the doors opened. It took less than a minute to reach the third floor.

Rowe was standing in the doorway to his office when the doors slid open, waiting for him. "Well?"

"We could waste hours searching, sir, but it's a huge city, and he's one man and possibly not even in San Diego. But I have an idea."

Rowe crossed his arms like a schoolteacher about to scold a pupil. "It had better be a good one."

Bob glanced up from his perch at the far end of Pascal Brown's sectional sofa. The three guards were all big men, all armed, all familiar faces. They sat less than fifteen feet away on a recliner, a stool and the edge of a flower box, respectively. The fourth remained by the elevator, down the hall.

Each glared angrily at Bob, their focus unwavering despite an array of head and facial bandages, one with his arm in a sling, each with gun drawn, resting on each man's lap to save the time of drawing them later. "They can put those away, there, Pascal," Bob said. "They've got no need to worry about me, no, sir."

Brown sat in a semi-relaxed pose; he was leaning against the sofa back but had his arms crossed defensively. "Uh-huh. You know, just because you didn't kill me the last time you were here does not mean I'm going to assume the same this time," the dealer said. "And they've got every right to be pissed off. Two of them only just got out of the hospital."

Bob offered them a quick wave of his left hand. "Yeah, gents, real sorry about that and all. Didn't want to be inhospitable, but some folks figured your boss here was up to no good."

"Uh-huh." Brown was nodding, but his face was still shrouded in doubt. "You see, from my perspective, you don't come across as the most stable of individuals, Bob. The men you shot at that house on Central, they like you even less than my crew. Turner needs a bridge for his lower molars, and he's only nineteen."

"Understood. But... I could easily have killed you, and them, but I didn't," Bob said. "That has to count for something."

Brown stared at him again, dumbfounded. "I mean... Sure. It means you could be crazier. It does not mean, in terms of stability, that you're an aircraft carrier readying for an F-15 landing. You feel me?"

"Consider yourself felt," Bob said. Then he frowned. It hadn't come out right. "You know what I mean. Point taken, eh?"

"You mentioned a mutual problem," Brown said. He leaned forward and rubbed his hands together nervously. "Perhaps we could skip over the catch-up and just get to that."

"Surely. You're a drug dealer."

Brown rolled his eyes. "I'm—"

"A businessman, sure, sure," Bob said. "But the business is, largely, cocaine. We've already established this, because you've already told me about your new competition."

"Yeah." Brown leaned forward and rescued a water bottle from the table, taking a sip. "And I sort of figured, from the way you were talking, that you'd gone off to deal with that."

"It's a bigger issue than we both knew at the time," Bob said. "The guy causing you headaches? He's got a lot of resources, the kind of money that's damned near impossible to compete with. But you can help me deal with him outside of the business arena, as it were."

"And how do you figure that's going to happen?"

"He's got an office on the waterfront, half of a big building, lots of security. But it shares its ventilation system with the other half of the building, which he rents out to a nightclub, a couple of weed dealerships and a cosmetic surgeon on the ground floor. According to a schematic an associate obtained for me, there's ductwork running between the men's room in the club and the third-floor offices' atrium. If I can cross over using it, I can bypass most of his men."

"And in the meantime, we do what?"

"You create a significant distraction. They have a big parking lot, always half-full at least with high-end cars, Porsche, Ferrari, Lotus. If a crew were to roll through it, maybe shoot up a few of those cars, set off a bunch of car alarms, and take their time making their escape..."

Brown was nodding as if he agreed. But then he looked up, scowling. "So you want me to take a chance at one of my men being capped by some powerful dude – about whom you have told me not one sweet fucking thing – or, at best, being spotted at the scene of a drive-by, making us fair game for every cop in town. And in return, you'll... what, exactly?"

"Oh... I'm going to kill the guy," Bob said. "Don't ever doubt that part."

"Because..."

"He's due."

"No," Brown corrected, "I mean why shouldn't I doubt you'll pull it off? A building full of guards, a six-foot-something man with broad shoulders trying to squeeze through vents, an active nightclub adjacent for maximum panic if things go wrong. It sounds ideal. And... who is this guy, exactly?"

"Anderson Rowe."

"The BILLIONAIRE? Fool, you must be crazy! What makes you think you could even get close to a guy like that?"

"Well... let me ask you this," Bob suggested. "When I came here last time, did you doubt I was going to get close to you?"

"Yeah. Okay, I'll concede that. But... Anderson Rowe. Huh." Brown shook his head doubtfully and looked at his phone. "It's ten thirty. This strikes me as just about the equivalent to *Die Hard* cosplay and, therefore, insanely dangerous and unlikely to work. When were you thinking about putting this absolutely crazy plan into action?"

"Club stops serving at 2 a.m., and everyone has to be out by 2:30. If I go in at cut-off time, most people will be leaving already. By the time I get through to Rowe's side of the building, it'll be closer to 2:30, and the civilian risk will be next to nothing. Just make sure that when you open fire out there, you don't actually hit anyone. Aim at the ground; use flat points or soft points. Just make a lot of noise, and I'll do the rest."

"Annnd... you're sure he'll be there. Why? Even if he assumed you were around the corner, would he be there at this time of night, or bunkered in some mansion?"

Shit. He's got a point. Bob rubbed the bridge of his nose with a thumb and forefinger, the fatigue beginning to hit him, the two days of drinking still blurring his thinking a little. "Possible, yeah. For sure he has no reason to be there when the club closes. But I figure he's expecting me, and he knows I know where his office is."

"But what you really need to know is where he actually is

before anyone goes off doing anything stupid. And... remind me again why I should help you, other than abject fear?"

"Always a good motivator," Bob said dryly. Then he added, "And as much as I hate the idea, it'll get rid of your competition in City Heights."

Brown smiled at that, a wry little grin, perhaps a sweet moment of victory after Bob's earlier visit. "Business is business, after all."

Bob looked around the expansive apartment. "Clearly it's been good to you." He fixed Brown with a stare. "Just so long as you're clear on where we stand AFTER this is done."

"And that is?"

"You seem like a chilled-out sort of fella, Pascal. Not at all like your image on the street. The problem I have is that you sell cocaine for a living. I mean, not you personally. You don't sully your hands with street-level traffic. But you make sure addicts get their fix every day."

"I don't turn them into addicts, man, and I don't have to 'sell' them drugs. They buy that shit whether I'm the guy slinging or not. I didn't make them poor or mentally ill."

"Yeah... you just take advantage of their human frailty, the weakness of human biology in the face of addiction, and you bleed them of what little they have to survive, money that often is supposed to pay their rent or feed their kids or pay for insulin or other medication."

Brown leaned back again and crossed his arms once more. "Man... for a guy who needs my help, you sure know how to make friends."

"That's just it, though," Bob said. "I'm not here because I'm your friend. I'm here because you want this guy gone as much as I do, and because you know how easily I can get to you."

Across the room, one of the guards twitched a little, clearly irritated. His jaw clenched, as if grinding teeth, and his gun hand began to lift ever so slightly off his lap. "You going to take that disrespect, boss?" he muttered.

Bob turned his head and looked at the three heavies blankly. "Tell your boy to calm down, or they'll learn really quickly that having their guns drawn isn't enough, not against me."

Brown made a shushing noise and gestured downwards with both hands. "Chill, gentlemen." Then he returned his attention to Bob. "I don't respond well to threats."

"Nobody does. But it's less a threat than a contractual guarantee. Or..."

"Or?"

"You help me get in to deal with Rowe, and I'll disappear in short order and never darken your doorstep again."

"You'll leave town? Just like that?"

"Just like that. Rowe's operation will be done, and he'll be out of your hair." Bob fixed a hard stare on the man. "But if you don't and Eric Williams pays the price, I guarantee you, Pascal Brown, that by the time I'm finished with all of you, you'll pray for death more seriously than you ever wished for money."

Brown studied Bob for a moment before answering. Eventually, he released a slight sigh and looked downcast, an alternative not presenting itself. "If this is going to happen tonight, it'll have to be soon."

Bob figured Renton could find a home address for Rowe in reasonably short order. "Midnight," Bob said. "The club next door will still be open for two hours, so I still have a route in, if he's there, that doesn't involve a prolonged shootout."

"And if he's not? If he's at home or some other location?"

"I'll find out where he is in the next hour and call you. That should still leave you twenty minutes to get to wherever we need to be. Can you handle that?"

Brown's head wobbled from side to side slightly as he weighed it. He glanced over at his men briefly, then back at Bob. The dealer was probably considering whether to just try to take him out, take his chances on superior numbers, there and then, Bob figured.

Instead, Brown sucked on his tongue for a few seconds, the decision affirmative but clearly not to his liking. "Okay. We'll do this your way. And how exactly do you intend to get his home address?"

"I have a helpful contact," Bob said, taking out his phone.

"No doubt someone you've scared half to death."

"Not yet," Bob said. "But who knows what will happen." He tapped the phone's screen to unlock it.

Before he could do so, it began to ring.

The display read "Unlisted number."

Bob answered it. "Go ahead."

"Mr. Davis, I take it you're back in San Diego."

It was Sebastian Krug. "Soon enough. How did you get my number?"

"You left it on your friend Ms. Williams's voicemail. I figure you've been back for hours. But we haven't seen you. If you knew my uncle as you claimed, and as you have no fingerprints on record, I have to assume you worked freelance after the military. As such, you will be accustomed to operational tactical assessments. You'll be planning your next move. So... I figure that's what you're doing right now."

"Astute," Bob said. "And?"

"I'm going to save you the bother. We have your friend."

The line went silent for a moment. Then Jasmine's voice rang through. "Bob! I'm okay; they—"

It faded, and Krug's voice returned. "Midnight at the office. Come alone, bring any evidence you have from Colombia. Men will escort you from the lobby and up the stairs to the third floor. Mr. Rowe has insisted on having another word."

"Up the stairs?"

"If you think I'm putting you in a closed, close-range environment like an elevator with my men, Mr. Davis, you're kidding yourself. No, you'll have three escorts, and one of them will be behind you, out of reach. You so much as twitch the wrong way, and I'll have to explain to Mr. Rowe why we didn't interrogate you for whatever intel you've gathered before killing you. I don't know who you are, but I know where you come from, and you will not be handled lightly. Any divergence and she'll face the consequences."

"Okay. We done?"

The call dropped.

"Who was that?" Brown asked.

"Our target's assistant. He's expecting me there in a little over an hour."

"Uh-huh. So..."

"So we go now."

41

Bob sat on the wide bench back seat of the Humvee. Even in an extra-wide vehicle, the two men sitting to either side of him basically filled the rest of the bench. Both were at least three inches taller than him with refrigerator dimensions.

"Totally meant what I said back at the apartment, there, eh?" Bob said. "No offense to either of you, and apologies for the wounds."

Both men turned their heads slowly and glared at him before returning to their vacant forward gazes.

"Okay then," Bob said quietly. He was lucky Brown was a bright guy; almost every outcome of the evening benefited the drug dealer, no matter whether he killed Rowe or died trying. For that, a little diversion wasn't much to ask.

But the man was smart enough not to accompany them. Instead, the mil-spec vehicle was filled with his four guards and a fifth man, the driver. They'd brought an M16 knockoff, a Chinese-made Norinco chambered with Remington .223s. They'd spray a couple of cars and peel out. The Humvee had been stolen for another job a week earlier, the surliest guard had mentioned, and would be torched once they were done to eliminate any DNA evidence.

Bob was getting dropped off a block early. They'd timed the distance so that the gunfire would start just after he stepped into the club's washroom.

Taking Krug's offer had been out of the question. Men as ruthless as Rowe wouldn't release Jasmine. They'd just wait until they had him, then kill her. And Krug had been helpful enough to detail just how cautious he planned to be. A three-man detail with help nearby would be next to impossible to slip.

So we use what little time we have.

The vent system for a large office complex would be tight but, under local code, couldn't be so narrow as to possibly trap a person. But he'd have to move slowly; the sheet aluminum would creak, moan and wail until his presence was noticed, and the stretch from the back of the club's washroom to the middle of the atrium ran for nearly twenty feet.

He'd lose any element of surprise as soon as he kicked through the vent to get out. The screws would be on the outside, leaving no other choice but to force the issue. He felt the weight of the .40 Glock on his hip. Two extra magazines were in his left pocket, offered up by Brown, incredulous that he'd even had the balls to ask.

The Humvee ground to a halt.

The man on the seat next to him threw the curbside door open. "Out."

Bob pushed past him and jumped down to the pavement. "Nice working—" he began to say, but the door slammed shut. The Humvee lurched forward.

He could see the club up ahead. Even at eleven ten at night, there was a short lineup of five people waiting to get in, a barrel-chested middle-aged doorman with weightlifter muscles manning a red vinyl stool at its head.

About thirty feet past the line, two men stood on the sidewalk outside the front doors to SatMast International. Both were in dark suits, but wearing body armor and openly carrying AR-15-style rifles. Bob saw the Humvee pass them, the parking lot another fifty feet away, down the side of the three-story complex.

Bob stayed close to the building as he walked up to the front of the line, using the bodies to shield him from the two guards. He pulled a twenty-dollar bill from his pocket and scoped out the doorman's name tag. "Evening, Mike," he said, reaching out to shake, the bill palmed.

The doorman looked at the twenty, then at Bob. He considered it for a second, then sighed, resigned to the drudgery of his job, and nodded over his shoulder. Bob walked past him and inside, eliciting a groan from those kept out.

The lobby in the commercial half of the building was mostly occupied by a cannabis dispensary and a plastic surgery, both closed for the night. He walked over to the elevator and pressed the up button. There were club-goers on the stairs, and he wanted to avoid any confrontations.

SEBASTIAN KRUG STOOD in the atrium to SatMast's executive offices, anxious. He checked the antique Rolex Perpetual on his left wrist, wrapped in an olive canvas band for protection. It was nearly ten past the hour, and his hackles were up.

It had been Rowe's idea to have Bob come there. His

loyalty notwithstanding, Krug was beginning to suspect the old man was a sadist. He'd talked about feeding Bob Davis to his shark, and his eyes had fairly lit up at the prospect.

But the man's judgment was poor sometimes, blinded by narcissism. *Why didn't I see that earlier?* He'd told Krug to ignore the buses, but they were now reasonably sure Davis had come back to San Diego by bus. He'd claimed they wouldn't risk the heat from killing a journalist, that Abigail Sanchez would be let go. Then, stoic exterior notwithstanding, he'd lost his cool at the airport and shot her.

It was one thing to work for a man who was ruthless, confident and loyal to his people. Krug felt a certain kinship in that, a familiarity that, if not comforting, certainly didn't alarm him. But it was quite another to work for one who was beginning to see himself as invulnerable. Overconfident people made mistakes.

The drug smuggling seemed to fit the pattern. Though he knew little about it, Rowe had bragged to him that it made $28 million a month. But... the man had been a billionaire for a decade. He made that legally in the average week. Why risk all of that to just try to win control of the cocaine trade nationally? He had to know that eventually his enterprise's growth would draw unwanted attention from criminal cartels, the kind of outfits whose owners were almost as rich as him, but far more anonymous, far harder to reach.

At that point, Krug knew, his loyalty wouldn't mean much of a damn.

What is he missing this time? What has he not considered tonight?

What if Bob shows early?

They had two men on the front doors, eight more in the first-floor atrium, three waiting at the base of the stairs to escort him up, two more on the second floor to make sure they didn't lose him somehow. He glanced over at the two men standing guard outside Rowe's office, then at the man by the glass doors to the elevators.

There were two more on the first level, by the back-door exit, where staff routinely walked to the parking lot.

He's one man. He's not going to get through a team of twenty men.

Somehow, the notion did nothing to buoy his confidence.

He's survived up until now. He's not stupid enough to try, no matter what Rowe thinks. He knows that's suicide. He'll look for another angle, a safe ingress.

Krug had studied the building's blueprints exhaustively when Rowe hired him, three years earlier. He'd gone over them again at the beginning of the year.

So what am I missing?

He turned and glanced at the atrium's massive back wall. Behind it lay the aquarium. It had outside access. *But he's not insane enough to try to swim past a shark.* In any case, the tank access was from a second-floor stairwell that could only be reached, again, by going through their men.

He stared at the elevators, through the glass doors. There was the upper mechanical room access from the roof, but there was also a sensor array that would trip the building's security if he so much as stepped foot on it. Even then, the mechanical room was locked off efficiently from the rest of the shaft.

Krug turned and considered the wall behind him, the

two offices facing the road. The windows were floor to ceiling and couldn't be opened.

No matter how I slice it, he's got nothing to work with. Maybe I'm being paranoid. There's careful and there's paranoia.

Above his head, the air conditioning kicked in, cold air rushing through the large, rectangular vent.

Krug's eyes narrowed. Where did the vent system run? He'd seen it in the blueprints but couldn't recall. He nodded towards the guards by Rowe's office. "Hey, where does that vent run to?"

"Whole building's hooked up to the unit on the roof."

"But… it's all interconnected, right?"

"I guess, yeah."

The building was divided into two halves, but it stood to reason the commercial side was on the same system. That meant…

Krug began to drift toward the glass doors.

Rowe's door opened. He leaned out to ask one of the guards something, then saw Krug walking away. "Sebastian?"

"Just… checking something out," Krug said. "I'll be right back."

THE ELEVATOR DOORS OPENED. The club's front entrance sat at the midway point of a ten-foot-wide square concrete concourse that circled the third floor, overlooking the atrium forty feet below. It was filled with bodies, people who should've been inside the club, based on the number of drinks.

At least half were vaping despite still technically being indoors.

Bob pushed gently through the crowd, odors of orange and bubble gum and grape enveloping him, the temperature rising from body heat and elevation. The thump of club dance music grew louder, a woman's voice aching of soul but paired with a soulless, mechanical beat.

He was taller than most there, peering above the crowd, looking for any sign of security. Near the open entrance another doorman sat on an identical vinyl stool, next to a lectern with a guest book on it, the kind used by invitees at corporate events.

He looked bored. He was likely there in case anyone underage got past the bouncer downstairs, or was making trouble. There was no sign of a weapon, which Bob supposed was probably for legal reasons.

The music swelled to a deafening level as he entered the club. The place was probably big enough for five hundred or so patrons, and they milled between tables and around the central bar.

Ahead of it, a dance floor took up a third of the room, bodies in neon yellow, silver sparkles, emerald green and onyx swaying and swerving under black lights as the bass drum thumped, a pair of go-go dancers on a central stage jerking and gyrating to each beat.

The back wall was familiar, the other side of the giant fish tank that made up one wall of Rowe's office.

"IT'S A SHARK TANK!"

Bob squinted against the shrillness of the high-pitched voice screaming into his left ear and partially turned to look at the source. A blonde girl – resplendent in a miniskirt, sparkly top with shoulder straps, and knee boots – had a drink in each hand and braids in her hair.

She looked all of eighteen or nineteen, Bob figured. He

held up his left thumb as a sign of thanks, rather than engaging. He ignored the urge to yell and ask if she didn't have school in the morning, or whether she valued her hearing.

Jesus H. I got old, I guess. Not that it had ever been his scene, even when young.

She cupped a hand near his ear and yelled again. "DON'T WORRY, I ASKED. REINFORCED GLASS. HE WON'T BITE."

Bob felt his eardrum swell from her astonishing bellow. *Why is she talking to me?* The smell of vodka on her breath was powerful. Bob wandered sideways, towards the bar, pointing at his left ear. "AT MY AGE," he yelled back, "THE HEARING GOES IN HERE PRETTY QUICK."

She nodded but clearly hadn't actually understood him, her face expression stuck somewhere between offended and dazed by booze. He raised a hand in a goodbye wave and headed in the opposite direction.

He checked his watch.

Two minutes.

42

Anderson Rowe stood at his office window and looked out towards the Pacific Ocean. Forty feet below, the parking lot to the adjacent nightclub was nearly full. He smiled at that. The building was turning a solid profit less than a decade after its construction, the financing long since taken care of.

It shouldn't have mattered to him, he knew. He had so many holdings now, so much money. An empire. But the building sat on the former home of the Standard Illumination and Telephonics Company Ltd, one of the first electronics firms founded in the city. It was also the former inheritance of his deceased mentor, and tearing it down had filled him with a sense of utter power.

"You really don't need to do this, Mr. Rowe," Jasmine Williams suggested. She was tied to a chair ahead of his desk, garbed in sweatpants and a San Diego Wave soccer shirt.

Her calm impressed him, but he could tell from her small, jerky movements and constant blinking that she was really terrified. That felt empowering, too. It nearly always did.

But he liked her attempt at stoicism. It felt almost respectful. In that sense, she reminded him of Sebastian. "I do hope this hasn't proven too frightening, my dear." He didn't actually care, of course, but she'd struck him as the kind of person who appreciated manners.

"Mr. Rowe, whatever you think I've done, or whatever you think I know, I can assure you, it's not the case. I know this isn't you, whatever's causing this. You've donated so much—"

"It's not really about you, my dear." She would have to go, of course. Krug would arrange something. Another inner-city charity do-gooder would hardly be missed. But in the meantime, there was nothing to be gained from upsetting her. "We're waiting for your friend Mr. Davis to make an appearance."

"Bob's not my friend. I barely know him."

Lying? Now that would not do, he decided. "Now, my dear... let's not compound your problems when we're getting along so well. We're well aware that he went to Colombia on your brother's behalf, and what he got up to there."

Her expression shifted, the fearful look giving way to moroseness. She was silent again for a few moments, and he watched the light surf lap against the hulls of yachts moored across the road.

"I thought he'd lost his mind, suggesting you were involved in any of this," Jasmine eventually managed. "All those trips. All those volunteers and people working to help the less fortunate. And all so that you can smuggle drugs."

There was no point holding his cards tight. She'd be dead in a matter of minutes. And he longed, on some level, to brag about what he'd accomplished. "Drugs? Not just drugs, my dear. That just pays for it. I can bring in anything I want. Money, museum pieces, priceless works of art looted during the Second World War; I could drop a dirty bomb on Coronado Beach and they couldn't touch me. When you have money, you can get away with almost anything. When you have a customs waiver for thousands of shipments a year and a Presidential Medal of Freedom? Well... they pretty much cover the rest."

Her brow furrowed for a moment, and then her frown turned to a look of profound sadness. "But... why!? You're wealthy beyond belief already. You could use that time helping other people, changing lives, turning things around in neighborhoods across America."

She was a simpleton, he decided in the moment, clearly incapable of recognizing that the same standards did not apply to great minds. "And why would I choose to do that?" he asked. "Because I care about the parasitically weak? Due to my abiding sense of social justice and patriotism? This country has become as parasitic as that" – he waved his hand dismissively as he sought the right term – "poverty-stricken rabble you so value. America needs to be shaken up, with a new order of leadership, men who value strength and perseverance above all. Men who dare to take what they want and do what they want."

"With you leading them, I suppose."

Rowe beamed. Now she was seeing it. "Most men can only dare to dream," he said. "I make my dreams reality."

From somewhere outside, Rowe heard a faint series of pops, like fireworks at a distance. He wandered back over to the picture window in time to see flashes of light streaking across the parking lot.

. . .

On the other side of the vast, circular bar, past the three bartenders and the dancers under lights, Sebastian Krug studied the room, keeping his eyes on the front door.

There were people coming and going, but it was late enough that foot traffic had slowed a little. As he'd suspected, there were ventilation ducts in the club big enough to accommodate a grown man, but the only one easily reachable, in the washroom, still had both screws in place.

Perhaps I overestimated him.

His hand drifted to the back of his leather dress belt for the barest moment, ensuring the speed holster was still safely clipped there. He didn't want to bring the fight to a public area, but he also had no intention of letting Davis get anywhere near Rowe.

And then, maybe, it was time to find a new employer. His duty demanded dealing with the situation at hand. His old man would've been horrified if he'd turned yellow and run.

His earpiece blipped, and Rowe's voice sounded through clearly. "Sebastian? Report."

"I'm next door, sir. Just ensuring a point of ingress is cut off."

"A what? It's very loud there, Sebastian. You'll need to speak up."

"A ROUTE IN, SIR. SECURING THE PERIMETER."

"Fine. Get back here as soon as possible. We've just had some gunfire in the parking lot. One of the men from the front door is investigating."

In the parking lot? That didn't... A thought occurred. "Call him back, sir!"

"Sebastian! Your tone..."

"Apologies, sir. It's a distraction. I'm certain of it. Call them back."

"It's still thirty minutes until he's due to appear."

"Yes sir, understood. But he'll come early. I know this man, or his type, at least. My uncle..."

Rowe sighed audibly. "Yes, yes, he was a national hero. So you're fond of reminding me. Very well. Get back here soon, then, yes?"

The line went quiet. Rowe tapped the earpiece. "Smith, Nowak." The two men were the extra cover in the second-floor atrium, next door.

"Boss," Nowak confirmed.

"Head over to The Deep nightclub and meet me near the dance floor."

"Sir?" He sounded confused.

"Just do it."

It made sense to play the odds, Krug decided. There was no way for Davis to get past the crew next door by coming in hot. That meant infiltration was required. And he'd have clocked Rowe's intentions the moment they shot the reporter. He'd never just give himself up.

But he would do his research. And he'd know about that damn vent. He looked past the bar, watching patiently through the gaps as the bartenders and customers moved back and forth. A six-foot-plus boomer was likely to stand out like a sore thumb, he figured.

Where are you, Mr. Davis?

43

Bob made his way around the bar, his passage interrupted repeatedly by small groups standing and drinking so they could get close enough to each other to hear the occasional word. The place smelled of sweat and perfume.

He looked past the nearest bartender to the dance floor. His disinterest hadn't slowed the friendly young blonde, who had made her way over and was flailing around impressively, laughing with her friends. There was someone standing just to the left of the dance floor, but the bar pillar cut off his view.

He heard the faint shrillness of a distant scream. He turned back towards the entrance. A few other heads turned as well, but it seemed most had been rendered oblivious by the loud music.

But a ripple effect should hit in a few moments. If things went as planned, the patrons nearest the parking lot would run, screaming, past the entrance. Group panic would filter to those just inside, then up the stairs lined with vapers.

Just a few feet to his left, a barman picked up a microphone from its spot by the coffee pot. The music faded out, a new tune taking over. It seemed vaguely familiar, irritating in its repetitiveness.

Where have I heard this before?

"Ladieessss and gentlemen, it's eleven thirty, and you know what time it is! It's time for the Wonders of The Deep! If Roger the blue shark makes an appearance between eleven thirty and eleven thirty-one, drinks are half price for thirty minutes. Are you READDDYY?"

The tune to the children's song "Baby Shark" began to build in volume, bass thumping, the disco balls above the dance flood spinning, light sequences strobing the room with sparkles of color. As the singer belted out the first two words, the crowd answered "doo doo doo doo" in response, and again, and again. They raised drinks while doing it, taking a slug after each refrain. The dance floor rippled in bobbing waves of giddy exaltation, a pair of go-go dancers on its raised central platform spinning in time to the beat.

Bob cringed. *They turned this abomination into a drinking song?* As a former drunk, he wondered if perhaps it dissuaded at least a couple of patrons from that final drink of the night. If so, that was sort of a win, albeit an irritating sort of best-case scenario.

Across the room, Roger glided into the aquarium, smoothly menacing. The crowd cheered.

The song repeated. The crowd bounced in time.

Bob looked back towards the doors. Nobody was fleeing; if the gunshots had occurred, as he'd expected, the nightly ritual had drowned it out.

But perhaps it didn't matter. There were no signs of any additional security, and certainly none of Rowe's men. They were concentrating on the offices next door. If he could get to Rowe quickly, he could avoid anything at street level, where the club-goers might get caught in a crossfire.

He tried to ignore the song and the cheering, electrified club-goers and headed for the rear corner of the room and the washrooms, apologizing as he gently squeezed past small groups. The room was hot, his light jacket adding to his growing sweat.

He checked the room again, turning both ways briefly, searching for any sign of approach, or even just too much attention. But the bulk of the room was watching the aquarium, hoping Roger would hang around for just a few more seconds, the prospect of cheap booze spurring them on.

He reached for the bathroom door but stopped halfway, Krug stepping up behind him.

"Before you get any ideas, Mr. Davis," Krug said, "I have a steel plate in my head. Any attempt to headbutt me would probably fracture your skull. And as nimble as you appeared to be at the airport in San Francisco, I can guarantee you, you won't turn and disarm me before I shoot." He felt the barrel move up, to the base of his skull.

Another hand felt around his waist until it had located his pistol. Krug confiscated and pocketed it. "Turn, please, and we'll head along the back wall, behind the crowd, and towards the entrance."

Bob did as ordered, Krug circling to remain behind him. He looked for potential weapons within reach. On the first table they passed were two empty beer bottles, and he saw the potential, a bludgeon to the side of the head perhaps enough to throw the man's aim off.

But... the odds wouldn't be good. And if he missed, there was every chance Krug would hit an innocent bystander.

The song's pandemonium hit a crescendo, the shark still in the tank at the end of the minute, drinks raised high, the crowd bouncing to the chorus, cheering "doo doo doo doo doo doo" in unison. Ahead, through the gathered partygoers, Bob could see two more men standing by the entrance. He had perhaps twenty feet to act before they slapped wrist restraints on him.

The sea of bodies on the dance floor parted for mere moments, a figure striding out of it and right towards them. Bob clocked the young blonde from minutes earlier in his periphery, before Krug had noticed her. She raised both arms high above her head, her sequined top glittering under the disco lights, a glass in one hand.

"WOOO-HOOO!" she whooped. "HALF-PRICE TEQUILA SUNRISE, BEBE!" She staggered towards them, Krug picking her up too late to redirect them. She leaned forward, her eyes glazed, and tried to drape her left arm around Bob's neck. "Hello, Daddy," she slurred.

He felt the pressure of the barrel disappear as Krug tried to reach around him and dissuade her. Bob dropped low and spun around her, shuffling into the dance-floor crowd at a crouch, below Krug's eye level.

"FUCK!" he heard from ten feet behind him.

Krug would become desperate within moments, he figured. He didn't have much time. He turned sharply left, staying low but heading directly for the two men at the entrance, a dozen bodies now between him and his would-be captor as he squeezed through the crowd.

Five feet from the edge of the throng, he grabbed a glass of clear liquid from a man's hand, gambling it wasn't water. He retrieved his disposable lighter from his jacket pocket and lit it.

He stepped out of the crowd and hurled the drink towards the first of Krug's men, the flaming liquor catching his clothing, his eyebrows, his hair. The guard yelped and began trying to beat the flames out, his colleague turning his way, then shrinking back slightly, reacting to his fear of also being burned, rather than the man stepping towards him.

Bob's fist hammered the second guard across the side of the chin, his legs gone in an instant. He caught the man before he hit the floor even as his friend tried to drop and roll, the flames almost out. Bob lowered the man gently, retrieving the pistol from his shoulder rig before letting him down completely.

Behind him, a pair of gunshots shattered the room's reverie, Krug's arm held high. People ducked low out of instinct, affording him a clear line of sight to the entrance. Bob realized he was completely exposed and ran, sprinting along the edge of the crowd as Krug opened fire, bullets shattering front windows as he passed, glass fragments showering anyone within ten feet.

The crowd flew into full panic, people sprinting to the exit. Bob dove behind an overturned table towards the back of the room, by what remained of the windows. He considered escaping through the frame, but it was half-filled by jagged glass teeth, the concourse beyond it bursting with escapees, some falling in the throng, others trampling over them.

Shit. Exactly what I was trying to avoid. Someone in the panicked throng would call the cops; others would no doubt stand outside and shoot video with their phones. He looked over the top of the table. Krug was near his colleagues, his eyes scanning the surroundings, trying to parse the fleeing bodies and spot Bob.

His eyes locked on the overturned table, and he levelled his pistol that way. Bob ducked down again. The cheap metal-and-plastic table wasn't resilient enough, nine-millimeter bullets cutting through it like tinfoil, holes punched out just wide of Bob's head.

Bob leaned over the table again and sighted Krug, aiming center mass. His finger began to squeeze the trigger, but a pair of fleeing bodies filled the gap, then two more.

They'll chew this table up in no time. Have to move.

44

Bob scuttled around the edge of the last group of stragglers as they tried to squeeze out of the club. He stayed low until he reached the back side of the low-rise stage abandoned by the go-go dancers. Its lip was perhaps two feet above the ground, the center riser a foot above that. It wasn't much, but it was visual cover.

"CIRCLE AROUND!" he heard Krug bark. They couldn't have been more than twenty feet away. The Glock had serious capacity, a seventeen-shot mag. But it wouldn't help him, he knew, if one of the men got behind him.

Bob popped up out of cover. Krug turned side-on, using the frame of the entrance for cover. The man beside him was less cautious, seeing an opportunity to end things. He turned head-on, raising his pistol. Bob's second shot caught him center mass, the third in the throat, making any issue of body armor moot.

The other two men opened fire, triggers yanked furiously, Bob ducking, covering his head with a forearm instinctively as bullets pinged off the concrete floor behind him. One struck the aquarium glass, its exterior showing the slightest of chips but holding firm.

He looked up again in time to see Krug running to his left, the other man to his right, past the broken windows. Krug would think twice about firing into the crowd outside, he knew. Bob rolled to his right, shooting from a prone position, his sudden appearance stopping the second guard short, his shots clustered perfectly in a circle around the center of the man's chest, the man's body crashing face-first to the polished concrete floor.

He didn't wait to see the man drop, throwing himself backwards blindly, feeling the firmness of the edge of the stage against his back as Krug's shots took out what remained of the first window, two of the shots slamming into his already falling comrade.

Bob heard someone work the slide on a pistol. *He's reloading*. He glanced down at the Glock. The magazines in his pocket were for a G19, a different model. That meant he had...

Nine shots left. He glanced over at the window. Traffic had almost emptied on the concourse, people pouring down the stairs and outside to safety. He knew it might be his only way out. If he ran for the doors, Krug would gun him down before he'd made it ten feet.

He heard a scratching sound to his left and instinctively threw himself sideways, Krug's gunshots missing him, slamming into the lower left corner of the aquarium, the surface once again splintering in white splotches of powdery glass, but holding. Bob scrambled around the stage so that his back was to the tank but Krug's line of sight was cut off.

In the tank, the shark was agitated by the noise and light, twisting and turning as if chasing an invisible foe, ramming its nose into the glass, hammering at it, defeated by technology.

Above, giant speakers continued to blare the song, on repeat. "Baaaaybe shark..."

Bob leaned over the stage and squeezed off a round, Krug realizing he was now alone and diving back behind the cover of the doorman's lectern. A figure strode through the doorway, and Bob lined up the new arrival, one of the guards from next door.

Shit. Reinforcements.

The man had a strap around his neck supporting an FN Minimi machine gun, chambered in 5.56mm, its belt-fed ammo looped over his other arm. He sprayed the dance floor with fire, bullets cutting through the stage, the central rider, the tables, high-velocity rounds slamming into the reinforced glass of the aquarium, now dotted with white powdery spiderwebs.

Bob thought he heard the glass cracking, the structural integrity giving, but it was drowned out by another volley of machine-gun fire. A bullet cut through the edge of the stage inches from his face, and he shielded his eyes from splinters of wood.

Can't stay here. He'll chew up this cover in no time. He glanced to his right. The bar was made of solid oak, it appeared, or perhaps walnut. It also wouldn't stop bullets, but with two sides and four surfaces between him and his attackers, it was a better option.

But it was fifteen feet away, at least.

Going to have to chance it. He'd have to create his own cover fire, he knew, then run for the bar while they were pinned down.

But that'll eat most of the remaining ammunition.

There didn't seem to be another option. To save himself and have a chance at reaching Jasmine, he needed to get next door. The only way that was going to happen now was to get past Krug and his cohort. *And they probably have more on the way.*

Bob popped out of cover and fired twice, but the man with the FN didn't flinch, unleashing a second torrent of gunfire, chewing through the ammo loop, empty casings clinking off the floor at his feet. Bob dropped as low as he could and covered his head again, the bullets crashing into the glass tank. The spidery cracks grew, joining one another like river tributaries, whole hunks of glass popping out where the gunshots had initially hit, water beginning to stream out of them as "Baby Shark" continued its booming drone, the DJ booth clearly abandoned.

The glass gave fully, huge sheets crashing to the ground, water pouring out like a slowly collapsing waterfall, the six-foot-long blue shark sliding out with it, thrashing its tail angrily as it tried to find purchase and escape its fate.

Doo doo doo doo doo doo, the club speakers blared.

The water cascaded across the dance floor in a flood, carrying the shark with it, its gigantic maw opening wide and snapping shut as defensive instinct kicked in, over and over again. It slid in a direct line towards Bob, its bone-smooth, almost imperceptible scales not slowing it, the darkness of its open jaw careening ahead. He tried to backpedal, his spine pressed against the stage, the triple rows of triangular, razor-sharp teeth beginning to fill his vision, the snapping sound like bone on bone. He raised the Glock and fired once, twice, three times, the bullets striking its torso, its nose, inside its mouth, the great fish unfazed.

He raised the barrel and looked frantically for a vulnerable spot, the jaws snapping again and again.

The eye.

He leaned back and to the right as the fish flopped over him, its snout inches from his body, its tail flopping. He yanked frantically on the trigger as the teeth drew nearer, bullets penetrating the soft surface of the shark's eye. The jaw opened one last time, so wide it seemed to engulf him... before slamming shut, the beast's head coming to rest on his kneecaps, the eye dead and lifeless.

Bob forgot about the men behind him for a moment and leaned back, exhaling his stress. A bullet pinged off the stage, and he rolled to one side, sliding his legs out from under the shark's motionless head, coming up facing the machine gunner, who'd crept closer. Bob yanked the trigger three more times, his attacker too slow, his body shuddering as he collapsed to the ground, the big gun spilled to the dance floor.

He turned back towards the entrance just as Krug leaned around the corner and fired another shot. Bob ducked back into cover, his trousers soaked through, the club's floor covered in two inches of water and flopping, dying exotic fish. Near the bar, an electrical socket began to spark.

Shit. That could be a problem. He stared at his wet trouser cuffs.

"You're out, aren't you?" Krug called out over the music. "I counted seventeen, and that's your max."

"That's for me to know and you to find out." Bob tried to concentrate, count backwards the number of shots he'd heard that sounded like a Glock. "But if you miss, I figure you're down to your last two."

"You're thinking of making a run for that FN. But you

won't make it. And even if you somehow managed to beat me, there are a dozen more men on the way."

"Will they get here before the cops? Face it, Krug, you're going down tonight, one way or another. People will have filmed you opening fire in a busy club."

"Well, that's—" Before he could finish the sentence, Bob had sprung to his feet, sprinting towards the FN Minimi. Krug fired two more shots, the last cartridge expelled, the slide on his gun kicking back. Bob dropped and rolled, grabbing the big gun smoothly, turning, pulling on the trigger.

The belt-fed ammo jammed immediately, the big gun rendered useless.

Krug heard it cough and fail. He stepped out of cover and reached down towards an ankle holster. Then he looked around the room frantically.

Empty. He had a backup piece, but he's lost it.

Undaunted, Krug reached back to the rear of his waist and drew a long blade from a sheath. Bob spotted a dagger-shaped wedge of glass two inches from his position. He grabbed it and threw it in one motion, the deadly improvised weapon zooming towards Krug's throat.

The stocky, shorter man stepped to one side, the glass shattering harmlessly on the concrete floor somewhere beyond him. He strode towards Bob, the blade extended. Bob whipped off his jacket, slinging it across both fists, then twisting it, rapidly, into a length of cloth.

Krug dove in, the slashing motion starting near his throat but moving downwards on the diagonal, the younger man trying to get under Bob's guard. He intercepted it, using the makeshift guard to slow each thrust, looking for his opportunity as Krug pushed forward with short, stabbing attacks. He held one thrust a moment too long, and Bob was on him, quickly swinging his right hand over his left, tying up Krug's wrist with the jacket, yanking it down, then up, trying to shake the blade loose.

Krug's other fist flashed across his periphery, and Bob turned his head at the last second, knuckles crashing into his temple. He held Krug's immobilized forearm firm, kicking down and away with his instep, trying to strike his opponent's knee joints.

He allowed too much slack, Krug yanking the eight-inch blade back and up, the razor edge cleaving through the thin cotton jacket. Bob didn't pause, timing the punch just as his hands came free from each other, the jacket now makeshift gloves, his fist slamming into Krug's solar plexus.

Krug staggered backwards, his wind gone. Bob charged forward, a straight kick disarming Krug, dropping into a sweep kick that took the other man's legs out from under him. He crashed to the ground, and Bob was on him, trying to lock up his arms, to "ground and pound" his opponent unconscious.

Behind him, from the concourse, a gunshot sounded. Both men froze for an instant.

"OFF HIM, NOW!" the other guard yelled. He had two colleagues with him, both armed.

45

Bob rolled sideways without hesitation, his hand finding the pistol dropped by the entrance guard. He raised it and aimed center mass once, twice, the trigger pull smooth, two of the men going down on the spot.

A foot flew in from his right, knocking the gun from his grasp. Bob threw himself clear as Krug attempted to brain him with another kick. He rolled up onto his feet.

At the entrance, the third guard leaned around the doorframe.

Outnumbered, outgunned. No weapon in reach. Think real quick, Bobby. He stood frozen for a moment, panting, the adrenaline keeping pain from kicking in.

He nodded towards Krug, whose mouth also hung open. Both men were soaked, exhausted. "Your uncle would be real proud: you... you get to battle a guy he hated more than anyone on this earth face-to-face... and you're going to punk out." He nodded towards the gunman. "Shame. He was a hell of a fighter, was ol' Edson; couldn't beat me, but he was a hell of a fighter."

Krug raised his chin in a haughty, reflexive show of contempt. “My uncle never lost a fight,” he said. “Not mixed, not boxing, not judo. Never.”

Bob smirked at him. “Your uncle never beat me. Never. Yeah, nobody could knock his stubborn, sociopathic ass out. But they carried him out of the ring the last two times we fought.”

The man at the door took a half-step forward, raising his gun. Krug held up a palm towards him, warding his man off. “NO. NO, THIS SHIT JUST GOT REAL PERSONAL,” he yelled over the music. He closed to within six feet. The two men began to circle. “You're a real piece of shit, you know that? You're a goddamned liar, too.”

“Your uncle was no hero. He just liked killing people. You want to talk pieces of shit? He was one of the biggest I ever knew.”

Krug thrust out an index finger, clenching his teeth. “You dirty sonuva...” He let the snarl trail out. Then he charged, enraged, dropping low at the last second, sliding towards Bob, his fists a blur as he struck for Bob's groin. Bob blocked downwards with crossed palms, shoving his attacker's blows wide, stepping aside in the same motion, twisting to throw a hard palm strike, driving through his target, Krug's temple.

The younger man turned away at the last second, the blow grazing. He had a young man's speed, coming up standing, spreading his feet wide in a fighting stance, trying to lock up Bob's arm, yanking the taller man towards him.

Bob fought the change in momentum, kicking away with both feet, his soles finding Krug's midsection. Krug stumbled backwards as Bob scrambled back to his feet.

In his periphery, through the glass back wall of the

aquarium, he could make out Rowe peering through the unbroken surface, trying to determine what was going on.

The distraction was badly timed, his momentary look away coming just as Krug ran forward, lashing out with his boot, the heel catching Bob on the button. He fell backwards, slamming to the ground, his legs momentarily numb.

Krug was on him in a second, pinning his arms to open up his face for punishment.

"YOU WANT TO KNOW HOW HE DIED!?" Bob blurted.

Krug froze for a split second. Bob swung his right leg up and around Krug's torso, twisting at the hip so that he could throw the man off him.

They both rolled to their feet, panting. Bob could feel blood trickling from his nostrils. Krug's left eye was already half closed.

"You... you know what's real funny?" Krug panted. He smiled rows of large, white teeth, then chuckled.

"What?"

"If... if you beat me" – he gestured behind him – "he shoots you dead. You... you're a fool, Bob, or whatever your damned name is. You hang around with society's refuse in City Heights. And I get it; you... you want family... neighbors and shit. But people like us? We don't get that. We're only wanted until they know us, and they only want our help until they get it. They only want the monster when he looks like a man."

"So... you want to know what else is true?" Bob demanded. He shuffled slightly to his right. Krug mirrored the move.

"Yeah? What?"

"How your uncle died." Bob shuffled a few more steps,

trying to reposition his opponent between him and the other gunman. "Because I killed the motherfucker. Bet you didn't know that part."

"LIAR!" Krug charged forward, his fists a blur of crosses, hooks, and straight hands. Bob used a cross-arm defense, warding off the force of the punches, protecting his head and chin as bruising blows bounced off his forearms and shoulders. "GOD DAMNED LIAR!"

"He DIED BEGGING, A COWARD!" Bob spat. Krug tried to headbutt him, following up with a high knee that Bob barely deflected.

"I'LL KILL YOU, YOU DIRTY MOTHERFUCKER!" Krug howled. He grabbed at Bob's shirt collar with one hand, trying to steer him into a right hook with his other.

Bob resisted, leaning, then bobbing backwards slightly, his foot coming up hard, his sneaker catching Krug square in the testicles.

Krug's eyes widened, his face flushed, his hands reflexively dropping to cup his damaged balls. He staggered backwards slightly, trying to overcome the pain of testicular torsion, the blood likely already filling his scrotum.

Bob spun on his left heel, the spinning high kick catching Krug's chin flush. He went down hard.

Bob looked up. The man at the entrance crouched slightly for balance, bracing his right wrist with his left hand. Bob dove ahead into a forward roll, coming up with a hand on the hilt of Krug's eight-inch blade, using his spinning momentum to hurl it end over end. The knife slid through the guard's jugular and the back of his neck, pinning him to the doorframe behind him.

The guard dropped his pistol lifelessly.

Bob jogged over and retrieved it, ignoring the pain in his

arms and ribs from Krug's repeated blows. He looked past the entrance to the now-empty concourse. The screaming had subsided, the rest of the commercial side of the building now empty. He heard the whine of police sirens, then gunshots.

The diversion had done its trick, Brown's men occupying most of Rowe's guards. But they'd leave at any moment, he suspected, to avoid dealing with the authorities. The sirens grew louder.

They're close.

Behind him, the FN Minimi scraped on the concrete as Krug, kneeling, retrieved it. Bob turned as the other man yanked at the ammo belt, freeing the jam. Krug pivoted the big machine gun in his direction.

Bob raised the pistol and shot him twice, once center mass, throwing him off balance, the second through the forehead.

Krug dropped the gun and toppled onto his back.

Bob walked over. The younger man's eyes were wide, but instead of shock, it was a look of pure fear.

"Puhp-puh-please..." Krug asked. The bullet had done neurological damage, the former soldier trying to move, but unable to. Bob could see it in his left eye, that fright, the same look that baby deer had had when he was a boy, left to fend in the woods and forced to put it out of its misery. That knowledge that there was no time left. The horror of knowing his life was about to end.

A tear rolled down Krug's face. Bob felt a swell of sadness. *He's a piece of shit, but he's still a person.* He raised the pistol to finish him. *What a fucking waste.*

"My-my... my uncle..." Krug managed, unable to get out what he wanted to say, unable to offer a final moment of devotion to the man whose life he'd tried to mirror, even if most of it was legend.

Bob didn't know why he felt nothing but sympathy for him. *Doesn't deserve it. Not really. Raised up an animal, but thinks he's a knight.* He hadn't shot Abi, that had been his boss; he'd tried to kill Bob, but that had been another man just doing the business, a soldier's duty.

He glanced at the back wall. There was movement in Rowe's office, more than one person, but he couldn't make it out through the warped high-density glass.

He turned his attention back to Krug, his life literally oozing from a hole in his forehead. "My... my uncle..." He tried to get it out once more, but his vocal cords had ceased functioning. His eyes danced nervously around, the fear growing.

Bob leaned down to be sure he was heard. "Your uncle... your uncle was who you think. He died honorably, a hero. He died doing his duty, just like you."

It was there, a slight spark. A sense of recognition in the man's eyes.

Bob stood up, took aim, and shot him twice more in the head.

From somewhere three stories below, a clamor of voices announced the police had arrived.

46

Through the glass of the aquarium, Anderson Rowe peered into the nightclub next door, trying to figure out what was going on. The surface of the transparent wall was just thick enough to deceive, smudging out images that were more than a few feet away.

The gunfire had started several minutes earlier, his prized tank shattering from the other side. He'd called Krug but received no response, although seconds later, his assistant's call for more men had come across their group channel.

He lamented the death of Roger the shark. Saving it hadn't been mercy; it had been a sheer example of his dominance, his power over mortality. He'd taken a creature not supposed to get cancer but had it nonetheless, and he'd saved it when, no matter how powerful or ferocious it could be, it could not save itself.

Not many men could do that.

He looked back, towards his desk and the restrained

Jasmine Williams. Krug had evidently been correct, Bob Davis had arrived early, and a gunfight was underway.

There were still at least a dozen of his men in their side of the building. The prudent decision seemed to be to stay put, bunkered in his office and protected. Sooner or later, they'd take the impertinent son of a bitch down.

"You should just call the police," Jasmine suggested.

He gave her a cold stare. "How droll you are! Your friend is clearly a brave man, but ultimately will meet his reporter associate's fate."

She frowned. Her obvious confusion enlivened the billionaire. "You don't know, do you? That he got his reporter friend from Colombia killed!"

"I don't know who that is," she said. "But if someone died because of all this, I imagine you probably killed her."

He strode back over to the desk, opened the top drawer and withdrew a cherry-stained teak box. He opened it and took out a gleaming chrome Colt .44 Magnum. "Curb your tongue, Ms. Williams, or perhaps I'll kill you next."

"You're going to anyway, ain't you?" Jasmine sneered. "I'm just your leverage if Bob gets to you before your men can get to him."

"And you'd best remember it while you still have value, Ms. Williams." He reached up to his left ear and tapped his earpiece once more. "SEBASTIAN!" he bellowed. "Krug, answer me right now, god damn you!"

Across the room, through the glass, he realized the gunfire had stopped. He could see the figure of a man moving about, his shoes swishing through water. Then he stopped moving.

Is he... looking down?

The man raised an arm, blurred flesh-tone streaks from

more than forty feet away; it looked like he was aiming at the floor. Two orange flashes from a pistol barrel followed.

The man paused for a few seconds before striding towards the broken aquarium. He raised his pistol and fired twice, the bullets unable to penetrate the tank's reinforced back wall, Rowe finding himself hopping backwards with each shot nonetheless.

He could barely make out the figure's lanky six-foot-two frame.

Bob.

From somewhere behind him, towards the parking lot, he heard the sirens, just one at first, then others joining in, a midnight cacophony.

Discretion has become the better part of valor. Rowe marched over to Jasmine Williams, fumbling in his suit pocket until he found the key to her handcuffs. He unshackled her wrist from the chair and grabbed her by the upper arm. "Come, Ms. Williams. Your duties as my shield aren't done yet."

He dragged her towards the office door.

"Where are you taking me?!"

"I have a helicopter pad on the roof. I've just activated the emergency beacon on my phone, which means one of my company's choppers, and pilot, will be there waiting for us when we arrive."

He rushed them through the atrium, towards the elevators. The two guards were nowhere to be seen. Rowe frowned. They'd likely heard the police sirens and run. *Damn them. They'll pay for that.* The building's security lockdown alarm sounded just as they reached the elevators, the lights dimming, emergency lighting kicking in.

The police. They've shut down the power.

They've shut down the damned elevators.

They would be raiding the club, no doubt, perhaps taking care of his Bob Davis problem before the man even got out of the building.

But he still needed to get to the roof.

The emergency fire escape, from the fish tank. There was a second-level rear exit that led to metal stairs running up and around the larger fish storage tank on the back side of the building. It led down to the parking lot, and police would no doubt have that covered. But it also ran straight up the side of the building to the roof.

He dragged her towards the door beside the elevators, shoving her roughly towards it.

"Open it. We take the stairs down to two. Go!"

BOB FIRED two shots in vain at Rowe's smudged figure, the .40-caliber bullets unable to penetrate the thick back wall of the aquarium. He heard footsteps on the stairs; the police would be there in a minute at most.

He scanned the room around him frantically. The FN lay next to Krug's corpse. Bob jogged over and picked it up. Krug had cleared the jam. He hefted it back to the tank, getting as close as he could, the rear wall less than ten feet away.

Beyond it, Rowe's office looked empty.

He's fled. Goddamn it.

Bob braced the machine gun with his left arm and squeezed the trigger, fighting off its unruly kick, trying to group his fire in a narrow band. The reinforced glass was chewed up in seconds, cracking, splintering, shattering in a crescendo chime of falling slivers. Bob stepped up into the tank and used the butt end of the FN to smash away enough glass for him to climb safely through.

Behind him, police had arrived at the entrance. A voice boomed through a megaphone speaker. "THIS IS THE SAN DIEGO POLICE DEPARTMENT! DROP YOUR WEAPON, PUT YOUR HANDS ON YOUR HEAD, AND KNEEL DOWN!"

Bob swung the gun around again as he turned, aiming up, towards the chains holding the two giant disco balls and light standards in place. The machine gun's 5.56-caliber bullets chewed through the black metal links, the lights crashing to the dance floor just as he stepped into the next room, live blue arcs of electrical current flashing across the two inches of water in the room.

The police officers jumped back, scrambling to find dry ground. By the time several had opened fire, destroying the lights from the concourse, Bob was next door, heading for the elevators.

47

Bob dropped the bulky FN as he ran out of the office and across the atrium.

The door to the stairwell had been left slightly ajar. *Jasmine's doing? Perhaps.* In any case, the elevators were locked down, so there was nowhere else they could've gone.

Bob took the stairs two at a time. At the door to the second level, he paused. There were footsteps below, murmured voices. But they didn't sound like they were approaching.

Guards, at the stairwell entrance. He opened the door to the office area and slid inside quietly.

The tube lights were barely lit, the cheap Berber carpet of the corridor and an open-plan thatch of salesmen's cubicles just visible. Bob kept his pistol butt braced with his left hand as he followed the passageway, towards the back wall of the building. There were offices to his left, a fire exit at the end of the hall.

The blueprint had a fire escape on the other side but had

been drawn up before the giant tank was added. Rowe wouldn't make it down to the ground without running into the police, and he couldn't very well play innocent with Jasmine at gunpoint.

So what in the hell is he up to? He slowed as he passed the offices, turning partially, keeping the pistol trained on each doorway in turn. At the fire exit, he leaned on the push-bar mechanism, and it swung open, slowed by a pneumatic piston at its top hinge.

Bob peered out carefully. A crescendo of voices rang true, the parking lot full of people. From somewhere close, the staccato trill of an ambulance klaxon sounded. He could hear something else, too, continual, like the muted whoomph of a metal desk fan.

The fish tank was as expansive as suggested, reaching up another twenty feet, to near the roofline. He looked down, between the slats of the metal grating. As he'd guessed, the police had several cruisers parked in the lot, surrounding the expensive sports cars and SUVS. They were a mix of street patrollers and SWAT, the men in body armor patting down detainees even as the street cops asked questions.

His gaze followed the black iron concourse. It reached a short stairwell adjacent to the giant metal tank. A second landing a few feet higher followed for twenty feet, then turned into another stairwell at the tank's curved corner, wrapping around the storage unit.

Bob looked up, the sound of wind being whipped a little more clear.

That's not a desk fan.

It's a chopper.

He knew he didn't have time to worry about the people

below hearing him. Bob sprinted for the stairs, using his long gait to take them two at a time. On the other side of the tank, a third stairwell led directly to the roof.

Bob glanced over the roof's edge.

Rowe was fighting with Jasmine, who had dropped to the ground. He was trying to drag her towards the chopper, which was tilted back to reduce speed and retain some softening lift as it descended.

The businessman hadn't seen him yet. Bob clambered over the final step, crouching low, trying to get a bead on Rowe with the Glock. The roof was empty aside from a few barrels nearby, a first aid kit and flare gun atop them.

Jasmine was trying gamely to shake the man's grip.

She looked back for the barest second and saw Bob.

"BOB!" she yelled, destroying his element of surprise. Rowe reacted instantly, showing surprising strength for his age and size, pulling her to her feet and placing her ahead of him, his .44 Magnum at her temple.

The chopper hovered forty feet above, the pilot able to see the police far below and the standoff much closer. *He's not sure what to do,* Bob figured. Rowe was taller than Jasmine but not by much, and he was astute enough to hide his head behind hers, offering the merest glimpses of a target.

That might have to be enough. Bob kept the pistol steady, closing one eye as he sighted the pip and groove, drawing in breath for a two-second steady hold.

"You can try, but she'll die!" Rowe called out over the billowing gusts from the chopper blades. "And it will mean NOTHING! You know what will happen when I leave here. The police will arrest you, the crazy man attacking a nightclub! They'll probably call you a terrorist! I'll kill your friend, my pilot will land, and I'll leave! PUT DOWN YOUR GUN! Put it down, and I'll let her live!"

"Not a chance," Bob called out. "I've learned a little about your kind, Rowe. I spent a good few months figuring out who I was, trying to live peacefully. I figure you've helped me close the book on that."

"Yes? And why is that?"

"When we first met, I couldn't figure out what was off about you. But when you murdered Abi, even in her final moments, she still had life in her eyes, a soul that demanded she fight. You don't. Yours are as dull as that dead shark's downstairs. You don't even blink out of turn. Everything is a practiced act. And that's the problem with pacifism, Rowe. It doesn't account for human nature. It doesn't account for the people who are just selfish and bad, and nothing but."

Rowe removed his hand from Jasmine's collar long enough to tap his earpiece channel button. "BRING HER DOWN!" he yelled to the pilot. "I DON'T CARE! BRING HER DOWN, OR YOUR ENTIRE FAMILY WILL PAY THE PRICE!"

The chopper began to descend, wind from its rotor blades whipping up clouds of dust. Its skids bounced once on the concrete surface. Jasmine's eyes widened, and she lowered her forehead slightly while keeping the stare leveled at Bob.

She's trying to tell me something. She's—

Bob's training kicked in, Jasmine dipping slightly at the knees to loosen Rowe's grip, his slight lean forward a mistake. She threw her head back and up, her skull cracking the bridge of Rowe's nose.

He released her, stumbling back.

She ran straight towards Bob, cutting off his line of sight. Rowe recovered, leveling his revolver and firing two shots, Bob grabbing Jasmine as he dove sideways, flattening them both against the ground.

48

The chopper landed. Rowe took another shot, aiming backwards at them as he fled towards it.

One of its skids lifted off the ground slightly, the pilot clearly deciding that whatever was going on, he wasn't sticking around for the man with the gun. Rowe spotted the maneuver, leveling the gun at the pilot through the Perspex bubble, circling it quickly so that he was looking through the open door.

He was screaming something at the pilot, but Bob couldn't hear it over the sound of the blades. Rowe reached into the cabin and grabbed at the man, threatened him with the pistol. The pilot got out, cowering, and backed away as Rowe climbed behind the flight stick and pulled on the man's headset.

Nope. Not happening, Bob told himself.

The chopper began to lift off, the skids clearing the ground, the bird's nose angling upwards and its body drifting backwards as Rowe decreased pitch.

Bob pushed off the ground with both hands and took off

running, tucking the pistol into his belt. The chopper was almost at the front of the roof. He kicked hard off the edge, his hands finding the passenger-side skid, hanging on for dear life. He heard a slight clatter from behind him; something dropped.

His weight was unbalancing Rowe's attempts to control the helicopter, and it began to jerk slightly, the body rolling as much as its cyclic control would allow, increasing lift and elevation even as Rowe attempted to shake him off.

Bob pulled upwards, hard, lifting his legs at the hips, straining against his own weight as he wrapped both legs around the metal skid. The belt portion of the passenger's safety rig was hanging out the door, and he gambled, stretching for it with his left hand, biceps and triceps screaming as he tried to lift himself up towards the cabin.

The chopper tilted towards his side ever so slightly more, and he could see inside. Rowe could see him, too. He grabbed at the .44 Magnum he'd left on the passenger seat, trying to take aim despite his own poor flying technique jerking them around.

Bob reached down, fumbling for the Glock, realizing it was the slight clatter he'd heard when he'd sprinted across the roof to catch the helicopter. It was probably still lying there.

Shit. He closed his eyes for a moment. *Now? After all this. After everything, you drop your fucking gun, Bobby?*

"GOODBYE, MR. DAVIS," Rowe crowed as his finger squeezed the Magnum's tight pull.

The flare seemed to come out of nowhere, a red rocket of smoke and light streaking from Jasmine's position on the roof, through the night sky, slamming into the Perspex bubble. Rowe threw up both arms ahead of him instinctively, expecting an explosion, the Magnum flying from his hand.

It tumbled towards Bob, the chopper nearly horizontal. He reached out to catch it. The gun bounced off the chopper's vinyl dash, its direction suddenly changed, flying past his free hand, tumbling out into the night sky. He let go with his other hand, holding on to the strut with both legs. The gun dropped past him. Bob's left hand reached out for it wildly.

His fingers found the hard black plastic of the pistol grip. He looked up, back towards the chopper, Rowe trying to keep it aloft and paw through the dash compartment at the same time, the helicopter veering dangerously over the beach, towards the water.

Bob fired twice, both shots catching the billionaire in the upper torso.

Rowe shrieked, falling sideways across the seats, clutching at the wounds, his grip on the control stick lost, the stick not recentering itself quickly enough, the helicopter falling into a spin.

Bob looked down at the Pacific Ocean thirty feet below and let go.

The last thing he saw before he hit the water was the chopper, nearly inverted, all control lost as it dove diagonally towards the murky black.

The frigid ocean water felt like concrete when he hit it, his body snapped into two directions at once, all sense of direction lost, dizziness overtaking him, his grip on the revolver lost.

It seemed pitch black, and he strained against bruised ribs to hold his breath.

He turned in the water, tried to find up, a route to the surface, his lung capacity quickly dwindling.

He saw a glint of light. Bob pushed towards it. Through the inky depths, he saw a bulky shadow sinking rapidly about thirty feet away.

The chopper.

If the two gunshots hadn't killed Rowe, the crash certainly would have, he knew. He pushed hard, bubbles beginning to escape his lips, his body demanding he expel the old air and draw in new.

His head cracked the surface, a wave almost catching him off guard, wake from the descending helicopter. He pushed through it and paddled in place, trying to orientate himself and keep himself away from the helicopter's undertow.

In the distance, he could see a searchlight from another chopper. It seemed to be closing but was still some way off.

The shore was at least fifty feet away. He started a slow, steady crawl towards it. He could hear motors and turned his head slightly.

Rescue boats. He pushed off again, quickening his pace. He needed to be out of their spotlight range by the time they arrived.

49

BUENAVENTURA, COLOMBIA

Poni Alvarez stood across from the office building, a rucksack on his back and his hands jammed into his pockets, and watched as the police milled around the front doors. He slouched against the wall along with some men from the neighborhood, just another curious onlooker.

The police had been there for hours but had been stopped from raiding the place by the last-second intervention from Rivas's lawyer. He'd presented a court order reaffirming that no search was permissible without a proper warrant, signed by a judge. As they had not yet obtained such a warrant, they were in limbo.

But they weren't leaving, either, perhaps expecting the drug lord to return.

Poni had already circled the building once, spotted the two men manning the back door. *But they cannot enter, which means I can still do this.*

Rivas had promised him half the money in the safe,

which totaled more than two million US dollars in cash. For Rivas, clearly, it was just a stake, another chance to start over. For Poni, it was enough money to retire to a quiet village somewhere in Thailand or Vietnam, forget the drug wars and the gangs. He would open a nightclub, perhaps, with more than enough cash to pay off local officials. Perhaps he could even carve out his own small corner of the local poppy trade.

But first, I need to get in there. There were two officers at the bottom of the stairs, to its right, chatting in animated fashion. Another stood at the top of the stairs directly in front of the doors. *But how?*

There were windows on the building's east side, about seven feet above the ground. The chances of being spotted and someone tipping the cops seemed high, assuming they could even be opened. At some point during the day, he knew, they would finish compiling a list of Rivas's known associates, obtaining warrants to arrest them as well. His name would likely be on it.

Think! There must be a way.

His eyes drifted to the building next door. It was close to Rivas's property, the alley between them no more than six feet wide. He looked up, to the parallel roof lines.

And perhaps there is.

It took him less than ten minutes to find a board long enough and strong enough to support his weight. He carried it into the building next door under his arm, like a worker, without even looking up at the police.

If they'd taken interest, no one had stopped him. It made a certain degree of sense; people had been coming and going from the second building all day.

Poni carried the board up to the fourth floor and leaned it against a wall. The two nearby offices seemed empty, dust in each suggesting no one had rented them for a while.

He climbed the ladder up to the roof access hatch, secured with a simple hasp and padlock. He removed the half-sized crowbar from his rucksack and easily pried the hasp off. He pushed the hatch open, then climbed back down the ladder, retrieved the six-by-two board and tossed it up through the hatch, onto the roof. Then he stashed the crowbar and slung his pack across his back before climbing the ladder once more.

A few moments later, he'd slung it between the two roofs.

He stood at one end, looking across the gap. Then he looked down.

He diverted his attention back to the other roof instantly, the forty-foot drop looking three times that from above. There was a policeman in the alley, and he knew he had to be careful to not just avoid falling, but also alerting him.

Just do it. One foot in front of the other.

He placed a sneaker on the board cautiously, then slowly lifted his other foot and advanced a step. He kept his arms slightly elevated to help with his balance, the wind just enough to frighten the club owner.

A gust hit, buffeting him with his left foot in midair. Poni swayed left, then right, frantically trying to rebalance himself using his arms, balance shaky, his standing leg tiring.

The wind died. He exhaled deep relief, then continued on.

On the other roof, he left the board in place for his return trip and crossed to the hatch. It was unlocked, unsecured, probably unused for decades, the hinges creaking as he pulled it open.

Poni lowered himself cautiously down to the fourth floor. The place was silently deserted. At the stairwell, he jogged down to the second floor, avoiding the landing window.

Rivas's office was at the end of the hall, next to the conference room. He hurried along it, aware the security cameras would pick him up. It was irrelevant; by the time the police realized there was continual monitoring, both men would be out of the country. Rivas had a plan to get them across the border to Ecuador.

He crouched by the corner floor safe and took the slip of paper with the combination out of his pocket. The tumbler rotated with smooth, tiny clicks at each number.

He opened the safe door and whistled gently. The dollar bills had that new-money smell, bundled in piles, each worth ten grand. It had to be the two million Rivas claimed and then some.

He'd seen piles of money before; it was a side effect of being in the cocaine trade to begin with. But he'd never held it in his hands. He'd never had control over it, what happened to it.

What if...?

What if the money wasn't there when he arrived? At least officially. What if he just took it and disappeared on his own, without Rivas's protection?

Did the man really hold any power anymore? Poni didn't think so. Though he couldn't read, he'd heard about the newspaper story from associates. They'd both been named, both been tied to the coca paste thefts and the explosions at rival gang properties.

Neither had a future in Buenaventura.

But... He is a terrifying man. A psychopath, without a doubt. Poni had always backed himself in a fight, usually because he'd paid others to protect him. But those men were dead or gone, or would be among those trying to claim the contract that would doubtless be on both men's heads within hours.

And that would leave him facing Rivas alone.

Poni knew what he was, and what he was not. And he was not a coward, he told himself. *But I've survived this long by being practical. He has offered half; he has bought me a ticket to Hong Kong.*

I need an ally.

He took off the rucksack and opened it. He began to take out the stacks of US hundred-dollar bills.

Poni felt the cold metal of a gun barrel pressed against the back of his head.

"Please!" he said without turning. "I am just a delivery boy..." He began to swivel, hoping it might distract the man enough for him to reach for the crowbar.

"Do not turn; do not move."

He had never heard the man's voice before.

"I am not the man you want," he said. "You are—"

"I am fully aware of who we want. You are Poni Alvarez, a captain in Daniel Rivas's gang."

Poni felt a chill shudder through his body. The man's accent was not local. There was no point in denying it, he supposed.

"I am. How did you get past the police?"

"They let me in. We have friends everywhere."

"I can give you half the money."

"No. All I needed was a confirmation of your name."

The suppressed pistol fired twice, two .22-caliber bullets benefiting from deceptive muzzle velocity, both shots striking Alvarez in the back of the head. He slumped forward.

A booted foot curled around his torso and turned him over, onto his back. Poni was still conscious, but just barely.

The last thing he saw was a blurry figure hovering above him.

50

SAN DIEGO, CALIFORNIA

Jasmine Williams sat at the circular glass patio table, under a Cinzano Bianco-branded umbrella, and watched a yacht negotiate its way out of the harbor by motor.

The breeze was light, and ant-sized men on the deck tried to tack the sail, swinging the boom arm around, hoping to pick up enough speed that nature would suffice.

She liked the little café, but didn't visit often. It was miles away from City Heights, and she rarely had free time.

Until a few days prior, that had remained the case. Now, the branch of Hope Street that she'd volunteered at for more than a decade was shuttered, its contributing founder dead in a helicopter crash after what the press termed a "bizarre" gun battle between a phalanx of his employees.

Within a day, police sources had leaked that forensic investigators were turning his multinational telecommunications conglomerate inside out, trying to determine what had prompted the explosion of violence. What the press did not know was that they'd interviewed Jasmine for nearly eight hours, collectively, that she'd told them about Rowe's smuggling admission. They would be revisiting her brother's case, at the least.

But that wasn't enough to improve her mood. The man who'd saved her, who'd stepped in when no one else could help, had last been seen dangling from a chopper skid over the Pacific.

She hadn't lied to them about Bob. They'd seemed skeptical, a detective eventually revealing they'd found no sign he existed. The apartment where he was supposed to live was empty, the landlord claiming to have never actually set eyes on the man in person. He'd left no fingerprints that they could tie to anyone in their files.

On her third day visiting police headquarters, a man in a dark suit had interrupted her discussion with the detective. She'd crept over to the ajar door and tried to listen as they chatted but hadn't understood much. But the man in the suit had been holding a photo of Bob; younger, but definitely him.

They'd spent three days following her, she was sure, the same three cars switching back and forth as she moved between the rapidly failing charity, the Catholic archdiocese – where she was already negotiating help for those affected by Hope Street's closure – and the sweat-equity homesite. On the fourth day, it had been down to one car. By five that evening, it had seemingly disappeared.

She couldn't be sure why, but somehow she knew. *They're hunting for him. They don't think he's dead, and for some reason, they want Bob.*

In a sense, it was a comforting notion, that he might have survived the chopper's sudden plunge. But there would've been a sign by now, she was sure. However much of a mystery he'd been, Bob seemed far from heartless and wouldn't leave people wondering.

Not if he could've avoided it. She took a long sip from the glass of iced tea on the glass table.

A figure slid into the chair opposite her, blocking her view of the harbor with his bulk, a sweatshirt hoody pulled up to cover his head.

Jasmine couldn't hide her shock. "BOB!"

He held up a forefinger for a split second. "Shhh. They might still be watching you. I don't think so, and I'm usually pretty good at spotting surveillance, but just in case, eh?"

She tried to bury her happiness, but it wasn't working. Jasmine rocked forward, leaning on the table with both forearms. "I thought I'd never see you again!"

"I've been lying low in a derelict place about a mile from here. I tried to look you up after getting back to shore, but they've had people all over you, so..."

"But... you're in the clear! They're ripping Rowe's company down to the roots trying to figure out what he's been up to. Why not just go to the police..."

He shook his head. "I can't. I told you, I have things in my past. They'll have internal video now from the club, images of me shooting and killing Rowe's men."

"But it was self-defense, I'm sure of it! I can tell them Rowe drew you there to kill you."

"It wouldn't change anything. And I'd never see a courtroom. They'd hand me over to the NSA or the Agency, and that would be the last time anyone hears from me. Look... Jasmine, I have to get going pretty much right away. But I didn't want to go without thanking you for being such a good friend. I... let you down. I had actual evidence of your brother's innocence and lost it. I didn't—"

"It doesn't matter!" she interrupted. "Rowe admitted what he was doing. Police have my statement. They'll find more evidence. Eric will be fine."

He nodded and smiled gamely. "I sure hope so." But she could tell he wasn't sure.

"Bob... Rowe said he killed a friend of yours."

Another small nod.

"You... want to tell me about it?"

A firm shake. "Won't change it. Won't fix it."

"No. But it might help you feel better."

He stared at the table, unable to meet her gaze. She'd seen that look before, too, usually among the inner-city folk she helped. Shame, guilt, sadness all rolled up into one.

"You're beating yourself up, I can see that. But you saved me, Bob. Am I right?"

"I mean... yeah."

She reached across the table and took his left hand in hers. "You have nothing to be ashamed of, Bob. Nothing to be guilty about. Not saving everyone isn't the same thing as condemning some."

He smiled a little at that, but his mouth was a feeble line, weak, unconvincing. "Sure." He rose suddenly, pulling his hand away. "I have to go."

She moved to get up, but he held up a palm.

"When will we see each other again?"

He glanced down again, a tell of sorts, Jasmine figured. "Soon. I'll... I'll come back soon. Goodbye, Jasmine. Take care... okay?"

The urge to have a good cry bubbled up. Instead, Jasmine nodded quickly twice and smiled.

Bob turned and headed across the patio to the stairs and the street beyond.

. . .

Bob headed down the street, towards the bus stop. He'd take city transit to the wrecker's yard, where a thirty-year-old beater that nevertheless ran fine was waiting for him. The car was going to cost a grand, but would be provided no questions asked.

Adam Renton had come through again, and a package would be waiting for him at the mailbox store en route. The driver's license was the latest favor in the long list Renton had provided over the week prior, and Bob now owed him nearly $10,000, as well as a favor.

That would leave him less than a thousand in the bank, with nowhere to go, no prospects.

He knew he should feel at least some sense of justice, of righting things. Rowe and his flunky Sebastian Krug were dead, the Agency thwarted once more, Eric Williams likely to go free in short order. No doubt there would be a settlement of some sort for his wrongful arrest, as well.

But none of that mattered. The one person that he'd failed most was the one who couldn't do anything about it. Helping him had cost Abi Sanchez her life. All she'd wanted to do was make Buenaventura a better, safer place for people to live.

As better off as people in San Diego would be without Rowe's influence, Daniel Rivas was still sitting in a mansion somewhere, while people with little other choice rebuilt his drug lab.

His new burner phone buzzed in his pocket. He turned away from the street as he answered it, in case of passing police. "Go ahead."

"It's me," Renton said. "How are you?"

"Good, Adam. I mean… I think."

"First off: violets."

"Eh?"

"You wanted to know why the lab stank of flowers. They were probably using violet ionones – the scent molecules from violets, when concentrated, defeat drug-sniffing dogs."

"So even if they're double-checked …"

"The ionones built into the suitcases' separators kill the dogs' abilities for an hour or two."

"Clever." That was the last thing Bob figured he needed to hear, that Rivas had gotten away with something else. "Great. Not that it does us any good now. I doubt Daniel Rivas is worried."

"You… still think he got away with something, don't you?"

"Because… he did."

"I'm sending you a JPEG," Renton said. "It's the front page of the English-language edition of today's *El Pais*."

"Adam…"

"No, seriously. Take a look."

Bob waited a few moments. The file popped into his chat, and he opened it. "Former FARC boss sought in cocaine blaze," the headline read in 72-point Times. The underline continued, "Rivas fronted massive gang vying for control of Buenaventura drug trade."

Above the first paragraph was the byline: By Abigail Sanchez and Porfirio Torres.

The pictures next to it were familiar, Bob's photos of the cases being prepared in his lab, the cocaine being processed. Under it, in bold text, they'd broken out chunks of his conversation with Anderson Rowe. A smaller mugshot of Rowe sat amidst the three-quarter-page chunk of text.

"Rowe... Supplied financial support," a cutline underneath announced.

Beneath it, a sidebar story announced that the three biggest gangs in the city were meeting, trying to hammer out a permanent truce.

She filed it. She filed her story before they got to her.

She did it. She took that son of a bitch down.

Bob inhaled sharply, his breath ragged, a sense he might cry again held back, his hand coming up to his mouth involuntarily in shock. The story seemed comprehensive, even outlining his theft from the cartels.

Bob had dealt with them before. If Rivas wasn't dead already, he soon would be.

"Bob...! Bob, you okay, bud?" He could just make out Renton through the tinny speaker. He put the phone back to his ear.

"I'm here."

"You okay?"

No. Not really. But... better. A little better.

It wasn't much. But it was something to cling to. A little hope, maybe, that sometimes, even when bad things happen, good can still win the day. Abi wouldn't see what her work produced, but her cousin would know, her colleagues would know.

Her boy would know.

He felt the tears coming again, and this time didn't fight it, hot streaks rolling down both cheeks. Renton could clearly hear him sniffling. "Bob... are you..."

"Crying? Yeah... but it's okay." He wiped the tears away with his jacket sleeve. "Just... you know... don't advertise it or anything. It's okay for a little while."

The sun was approaching the horizon. The wrecker

would be closing soon, Bob knew. "Look, I have to get going. Running short on time."

"I'm here when you need me. I mean... you owe me a fuck-ton of money... but I know you're good for it."

"Goodbye, Adam. And... thank you."

"It never happened," Renton said. "Okay?"

He ended the call.

Bob put his phone away. He had a mile to walk, and he wanted to get off the main drags, stick to the backstreets, where an enterprising patrolman was less likely to spot him.

It felt like the Agency had given up, at least for a few days. But he had to be careful.

He had to keep moving.

EPILOGUE

DARIEN, COLOMBIA

Daniel Rivas had been sprinting from room to room for twenty minutes, gathering papers, stacks of cash from his office safe, the few art pieces he truly valued. It culminated with him in his office, leaning on a suitcase lid, trying to get it closed.

All of it needed to fit into two oversized Globetrotters, hard-shell suitcases that would withstand damage and protect his money and belongings until he got to Hong Kong. It would not be easy; he was wanted by the police for questioning about the lab fire and the deaths of two of his men.

To the right of the case, on the bed, sat two refundable tickets, one in his name, the other in Poni Alvarez's.

He'd received a call at six thirty in the morning from one of Rowe's men in California. The Silicon Valley tycoon was dead, his assistant Sebastian along with him.

The agreement was over.

Internally, he seethed and cursed Bob Davis's name.

A nobody, a man with no real identity. And he has ruined me.

His partners in Mexico were expecting a shipment imminently. His source expected a four-million-dollar payment for the last batch of coca paste.

Both necessitated disappearing.

He'd have been tempted to stay, to fight to clear his name. There was a real chance of success, given how poorly the justice system in Colombia handled complex cases involving unclear property ownership. He had supporters from his legendary FARC days. He'd have argued that Americans had intervened to frame him, more meddling in a culture and economy that was not their own.

But the cartel was another matter.

The cartel would not care if he offered a deal, or repaid the theft, or even if he offered to make them a handsome profit. There was a matter of principle at hand, a matter of honor and lost reputation.

They will send someone for me, of that there is no doubt.

But the cartel was also an enormous, multi-headed beast, with internal political considerations, other holdings in Colombia that had to be weighted and factored in. That would buy him a day, he supposed, but no more. Possibly less.

It hardly mattered. Soon, Poni would return with the rest of his money. He would kill Alvarez, leave him in the mansion with a suicide note explaining his full culpability. Then he would drive the Land Rover across the border to Qito, in Ecuador, using a smugglers' back road near the town of Ipiales. He would cash in Alvarez's open ticket at the airport before his flight. If all went to plan, he would be in Asia by the following day.

It had been necessary. He needed a proper stake to rebuild his life, and much of his cash was in the safe at his other office, in Buenaventura. He'd assumed Poni might betray him, but it was a risk he had to take, a risk tempered by his knowledge that, deep down, Alvarez was a coward.

He leaned on the suitcase lid with all his might and reached down, managing to clip the fasteners closed. He picked it up, surprised by its weight, and lugged it out to the hallway, then down the double-wide stairs to the ground floor. He pushed it across the marble, leaving it ten feet from the front door.

One more to go. He looked at his watch. Poni would be back soon. Once he was dead, his fingerprints on the "suicide note" pen, Rivas knew he would have a few hours to make it across the border.

He turned towards the stairwell but heard a creak behind him. He turned quickly.

The man who had stepped through the door was over six foot, sturdily built in a jet black suit, cowboy hat and lizard-skin boots. He had a Ruger pistol in his left hand, braced with his right, the barrel down and away.

"Daniel Rivas," he said.

Rivas's hand shot towards his waistband and the Colt 1911 in his speed holster. His fingers had barely grazed the grip when his opponent raised the pistol to eye height. "I would not advise it," the other man said. "Your hands: raise them, if you please. And down on your knees."

Rivas did as commanded. His eyes scanned the lobby, looking for another weapon, the best route to run, anything that might turn the tables. He was a survivor, he knew, and this was not his time to die. It never was.

"I have money," Rivas said. "In the case, there is close to two million. There is another two million on its way here. You can take it. All of it." There was a second pistol in the case, tucked into the lid pocket for emergencies.

"Show me," the man said.

Rivas walked cautiously back to the case, crouched and opened it.

"Turn it around and leave the lid open."

He did as commanded, leaving his right hand on the lid. The pistol was just inches away. *I just need a moment's distraction.*

The man in the suit motioned to Rivas's left. "Move aside. Remain kneeling and turn around."

Is he...? "It would be a mistake to kill me," Rivas said. "I have lots of money and can get more. Cocaine, too. Fine art."

The man threw something down on the floor in front of him. It was that day's front page of *El Pais* newspaper. "There is nothing that can be done about this."

Rivas stared at the headline, horrified.

Abigail Sanchez.

She filed her goddamned story.

God damn her.

The man remained silent. Rivas felt a swell of panic. "I have friends. I was a high-ranking FARC officer. I have powerful friends."

"You had powerful friends," the man said. "They are your friends no longer. And when they are upset, your friends, they call for me. You probably do not know this down here in Colombia, but when the Gravedigger visits, he is the last person any man sees."

Rivas's eyes widened. The Gravedigger was a legend in

narcotics circles, a myth – or perhaps a nightmare – used to keep young soldiers in line. "But... but you are not real," he stammered. "This cannot be real."

"Then I wouldn't let it upset you," the Gravedigger said.

"I..."

Rivas didn't finish the sentence, the suppressed Ruger kicking twice, the former drug lord slumped over on his stomach, a pool of blood forming around his head.

Hector Ramirez used the toe of his cowboy boot to flip Rivas over. His target's eyes were empty, dull and dark, the light already gone. To be certain, he shot the man once more in the head, and twice in the heart.

The cartel's intel had been exhaustive; the mansion, once owned by a lesser Corsario captain, had no cameras or recording equipment, having long been used for illicit activity. It would not do for someone to find an image of the Gravedigger at work; much of his efficacy was bound to his anonymity, the mythology of a man who never died and never left a living target behind.

He took out his phone and speed-dialed a number in Mexico City. The call was delayed for an extra second while being rerouted through encrypted channels. Another man came on the line. "Go ahead."

"It is done." Ramirez ended the call and pocketed his phone.

He walked back to the front door, took out his handkerchief and cleaned off the handle, as well as the numeric punch pad for the deadbolt.

The money in the cases would be a nice additional bonus for his employers. He was well paid and did not need to incur their wrath by trying to take any of it for himself.

Ramirez considered himself an honorable man, and there was no honor in theft.

Rivas had just learned that lesson.

He closed the case and carried it to the front door. A minute later, he was gone.

THE END

ABOUT THE AUTHOR

Did you enjoy *Dark Cargo*? Please consider leaving a review on Amazon to help other readers discover the book.

Ian Loome writes thrillers and mysteries. His books have been downloaded more than a half-million times on Amazon.com and have regularly featured on the Kindle best-seller lists for more than a decade. For 24 years, Ian was a multi-award-winning newspaper reporter, editor and columnist in Canada. When he's not figuring out innovative ways to snuff his characters, he plays blues guitar and occasionally fronts bands. He lives in Sherwood Park, Alberta, with his partner Lori, a confused mostly Great Dane puppy named Ollie, and some cats for good measure.

ALSO BY IAN LOOME

A Rogue Warrior Thriller Series

Code Red

Blood Debt

Dead Drop

Hell Bent

Hard Country

Snake Eyes

Body Count

Dark Cargo

Printed in Great Britain
by Amazon

62423896R00190